WRITTEN IN TEARS

WRITTEN IN TEARS

ARUPA PATANGIA KALITA

Translated from the Assamese by
Ranjita Biswas

HARPERPERENNIAL

HARPERPERENNIAL

First published in India in 2015 by Harper Perennial
An imprint of HarperCollins *Publishers*
A-75, Sector 57, Noida, Uttar Pradesh 201301, India
www.harpercollins.co.in

This edition published in India in 2019 by Harper Perennial

2 4 6 8 10 9 7 5 3 1

P-ISBN: 978-93-5302-498-7
E-ISBN: 978-93-5302-666-0

Typeset in 11/14 Adobe Devanagari
by Jojy Philip, New Delhi

Printed and bound at
Thomson Press (India) Ltd

MIX
Paper
FSC FSC® C010615

This book is produced from independently certified FSC® paper to ensure responsible forest management.

Contents

Arunima's Motherland

The day had dawned; Arunima was still in a daze. Abinash rolled down the car's window. Outside, a gentle breeze blew. The perfume they had sprayed all over her last night still clung to her now-crumpled bridal mekhela chador; the lengths of jasmine and tuberose coiled around her hair seemed to perk up again in the morning breeze. Their fragrances mingled with hints of other smells—the turmeric-and-black-gram scrub of her ritual bath, the sandalwood paste, the spanking new jewellery, the streak of oil in the parting of her hair over which her mother-in-law had applied vermilion during the joran ceremony, and the smoky hom, the wedding fire fuelled by ghee and mango-wood. In a heartbeat, she could breathe it all even now.

Over and above all these stood out a heady new scent. When the handsome man who sat next to her in his dhoti-kurta smoothed his silk chador, a few wilted basil leaves and marigold petals from his wedding garland dropped onto her lap. Awash in its fragrance, like a kandhuli fish rippling in a pond and making liquid motifs of rings and bangles, her head grew giddier and her heart beat faster.

Arunima's eyes were downcast, but she knew Abinash's gaze was on her. From the time she had climbed into the car with him, after throwing three fistfuls of rice-grain behind her to symbolize that all her debts to her parental home had been paid, his big dark eyes hovered over her constantly, like a bumblebee on a ridge-gourd flower. As she looked up into his smiling eyes, she sensed that like the bumblebee which eventually takes on the colour of the yellow ridge-gourd flower, her man too was overwhelmed by her nearness and the fragrant jumble of vermilion, sandalwood, turmeric, black-gram and rustling new clothes.

He moved closer, and the heady scent grew stronger. A few grains of rice fell from his thick mop of hair onto her lap. Her palms, decorated with jetuka, picked up the grains. She looked at them and smiled shyly. Yesterday, her cousins, nephews and nieces were ready with fistfuls of rice collected from the brass bowl of dunori long before the groom was to arrive. Even the umbrella of the groom's best man could not save him from the showers of grain that had ushered him into his bride's home. Now he looked at the grains and laughed, saying, 'Look, all that rice showered at your doorstep yesterday is still clinging to my hair.' He bent closer, and the kandhuli fish in her heart swam in the turbulent water, going up and down; the water bubbled with the patterns it created and she felt like an enamoured mermaid. She retired into a world of dreams; there was nothing else in that world—only the bumblebee's hum in her breast, its body yellow in the tone of the ridge-gourd flowers blooming in the evening, the heady smell of dried basil leaves and marigold, a silk kurta to which the aroma of burnt ghee and mango tree wood clung like a film, a mop of dark hair with a few rice grains, the thick hair of his chest peeping from behind two open buttons of the kurta where the gold chain showed off a little blob of dried turmeric and gram paste … Ah, there was nothing else, only this.

'Munu!'

She woke up with a start. Her *uroni* had slipped from her head, the floral-patterned chador was a little awry, one end of the garland entwined on her bun lay on the seat. The garland was in his hand and now he smiled at her, 'You were asleep, weren't you? We are almost there. Look, that's my school; they celebrated a hundred years last year.' She looked outside; the little town was waking up slowly. Some people were already on the street; a few men were drinking tea on the veranda of a tea-stall. It was slightly chilly on this morning of the month of Ahin. She wrapped the chador round her body. The bus with the groom's bridal party passed by. Some of the cars in the cavalcade had already arrived. From the windows of the bus, several smiling faces peeped out and shouted out, waving, 'Bou, Mami, Khuri ...' addressing her, the new bride, according to their relationship with her husband. She giggled; it was as if the bus had left behind a shower of coloured holi powder in the air, it clung to her cheeks, her clothes. He also laughed aloud.

'Munu, do you want tea?' She did not answer immediately. He called her again, 'Munu!' It was so common a name, her parents, uncles, aunts often called her with this nickname. But now the word from this special person made it sound so meaningful, the two letters hid so many expressions of endearment, she mused. Caught in the web of the hidden meaning in those letters, she felt lost in an unknown jungle.

'Munu!' Hearing his voice, the hair on her skin stood up. 'We have still some time before we reach. I feel like having a cup of tea. Munu, are you still sleepy?' The faint smell of basil and marigold assailed her.

'Yes,' she said. She dropped the *uroni* from her head. She felt her body warm up.

'There is a good tea stall close by. They make good samosas, the tea is good too. But there is no place to sit down. We usually have it standing up, but I'll bring the tea for you in the car,' he said.

'Where's the tea?' her aunt who had been fast asleep in the front seat woke up and asked.

'Here we are.' He told the driver to stop. Her aunt got down from the car and came to her and asked 'Are you okay? Why don't you get down from the car as well; you can stretch your limbs a bit.' Her aunt went across to the rear end of the stall looking for a toilet.

'Munu, do you want to get down?' he asked. The shadows of dawn had disappeared by now. Soft mist clung to the trees and grass like pearls. Her husband was telling the shopkeeper to make some tea. She walked to that place gingerly. The stall owner became busy instantly. The big chula was bright with the simmering coal; the gas stove had a pan of milk boiling. As she sipped the tea brewed with cardamom and bay leaf, she exclaimed in appreciation, 'Excellent tea!' The stall keeper offered them hot jalebis on a sal leaf. Despite herself, she took two jalebis.

'Quite good, aren't they, Munu?' he asked. She nodded her head. She felt like teasing, 'Ah, you behave as if you yourself have made it!' She did not say it of course, but smiled and went to sit in the car. Now her aunt came to sit with her in the back seat next to her following social protocol before reaching the in-laws' house. He took his handkerchief to wipe the smudged vermilion on her forehead and arranged the locks of her dishevelled hair.

Outside, the world had woken up to a new day. 'We'll reach soon, just after passing that turning,' he said. Then he asked her aunt, 'After her *ghar-gochoka*, she will stay at your place, isn't it?'

'Yes, she will stay in our house tonight after her ritual entry to the house is over. Now I'll help Munu to do the *man-dhora*; she has brought clothes to present to the elders in your family,' her aunt said as she fixed the veil with a hairclip on her hair so that it would not slip. Then she said, 'You know, Munu, your in-laws' house is known as the "house of flowers" around here. There are so many plants in their garden!'

'Who does all the gardening?' Her question was to her husband.

He smiled and replied, 'You know, Munu, our house is rather ordinary, a traditional Assamese house that my father has built. We have just changed it a bit here and there and painted it.'

But she wanted to hear about the flowers and asked softly, 'My aunt was talking about the flowers in your compound.'

'Oh, flowers! It's an obsession with my father. If he hears about some plant or cut branch of a rare plant available somewhere which is not there in our garden, he brings out the bicycle and sets out in search; he doesn't bother even if he is not well.'

He laughed aloud. She noticed that he lifted his face and closed his eyes when he laughed like this. She hid her smile of amusement with her handkerchief.

He was saying, 'My sisters too have inherited his love of flowers. They are mad about it, actually. As soon as winter arrives, even if I have to take a day's leave from office, I have to accompany them to collect cuttings of dahlia, black and yellow marigold seedlings etcetera. They won't mind foregoing new clothes if they can buy plants instead.'

He seemed to remember something and smiled. He told them about how they were cheated once by a garrulous vendor; they spent their savings collected meticulously in piggy banks made of hollow pumpkins. The plants turned out to be jungle plants without any use. Munu felt sorry thinking about their money wasted, but felt amused too by the story.

He tried to arrange his dhoti and kurta and addressed her aunt, 'You know, mahi, this time in anticipation of the Na-bou, the new bride, they started planting in advance; I think some of them are already flowering.'

Soon the car stopped in front of the house. Her aunt led her to the chalpira, a big wooden stool on stands. Wedding songs welcomed her. There were giggles and laughter, kisses on her cheeks from her mother-in-law, earthen lamp in a basket, laddoos of ground rice thrown in four directions indicating four corners of the earth—amidst all this, she was led to her new house through the red brick path lined by brindabon plants. Without lifting her head, she could make out that the compound was full of flowering plants. From behind her veil, she saw yellow and chocolate-coloured marigolds peeping out between the brindabon plant rows. Lifting her head a little, she saw the grass speckled with a carpet of sewali flowers in their white and orange glory; the aroma of white jasmine and kamini-kanchan flowers assailed her nose, in her chador rested a madhoi-malati flower, its petals now closed in the morning light. She was surrounded by young girls and women from the neighbourhood and family. A group of women who were following her were singing a *biyanaam*:

Sewali flowers will bloom, and falling, will decorate the grass below
Our bride will first go to the shrine to pray
Sewali flowers will bloom, and falling, will decorate the grass
She will first touch the feet of her father-in-law
The sewali will bloom, falling, will decorate the grass below.

As soon as she entered the courtyard, she was led to the shrine in the corner. She walked over the carpet of sewali flowers and kneeled down on the courtyard swabbed neatly with red earth in front of the shrine of wood and bamboo.

Now the song had a strain of sadness, memories of the house left behind by the bride interwoven into it:

O Sita shanti!
I have left behind my mother, my father
And my beloved brother
O Sita shanti!
I have left behind my home where I grew up.

She was now led to the house. While going there, she saw that the veranda was hung with a creeper of beautiful red flowers.

The strains of the *biyanaam* '*O Sita shanti*' followed her too, and now she could feel her eyes filling with tears. Scenes of her mother crying her heart out as her daughter was leaving, the house she decorated lovingly with her own embroidered linen, the flowering plants she collected from different sources—all these scenes floated in her mind. She wanted to run there, but she was not able to; her chador's end was tied to the chador wrapped around the shoulders of this new man in her life. A storm blew over her heart. So she had really left behind her house forever!

She started weeping uncontrollably. Instantly, she was surrounded and consoled—unknown faces, unknown voices, saying, 'Khuri, please don't cry,' 'Bou! We are all here, don't worry,' 'Mami! If you cry we'll feel bad,' and so on.

After sometime, another *biyanaam* was sung softly, '*I rested at your house ... temporarily ... my beloved parents*'.

Within three months, Arunima was already an old member of the family. The day she completed the third month of her marriage, they all heard a hullabaloo early in the morning. It was her younger sister-in-law, Baby, who was shouting. It was her habit to go out to the garden with a pair of shears first thing in the morning to chop off the stems of the flowers after they had wilted.

Everybody came out of the house. They found a beehive hanging in the fork of the ou tree, and Baby was jumping up and down, calling everybody: 'Come, come, Bou, Petai! See, we have a beehive again in our tree; the bees have come back!'

Her mother-in-law smiled. 'The bees will now build their home,' she said.

Her father-in-law, whom Baby called 'Petai', smiled too and

said, 'The bees are building a hive. It's a very auspicious sign,' he said. Looking at Arunima, he said 'Our house is blessed with a Lakshmi now, we are fortunate.'

The turmoil in the house even woke up their neighbours. Behind their house was a small stream. In front was the main road. To its east was government officer Jayanta Saikia's shining modern house; on its west was the wood and bamboo cottage with a thatched roof. Ever since she had arrived as a bride she had observed that the relations between these two neighbours and their household were not cordial. In fact, the house in the west was isolated because nobody liked its owners. She had heard from her sister-in-law that the householder was known as a seasoned burglar. These days he was associated with a gang of dacoits. His father had been a good man. She had heard from Baby that their grandfather had himself set him up here by giving him land to build the house because formerly he used to work as a farmer in their paddy fields. He had given the man responsibility to look after the house when he was absent from home on work. The grandfather died, the man too expired. Somehow the son became involved in nefarious activities. But his fortune was turning these days. The rumour was that he was cutting down on his activities as a dacoit and was involved in the some black marketeering activities. Arunima sometimes saw him; that fair-skinned, thin man was said to have murdered quite a few men. However, her in-laws' family disliked the government official even more than the dacoit. Her father-in-law especially made no bones about his displeasure over mixing with that family. He had been the head master of a school. He thought that the real-time dacoit was the officer. She remembered the officer's wife's comment when she came to meet the new bride: 'Ah! How could you put her in this room? Couldn't you build at least one additional room?' In reply, her sister-in-law said something, but she could not hear it in the noise around.

Arunima's new abode was like the beehive in the ou tree—tidy, orderly, with everything in place. The people in the house who rose with the birds were soon busy with their own work, much like the bees in a hive. Her mother-in-law who entered the kitchen after a bath early in the morning looked meek, but there was a streak of steel behind the timid façade; her father-in-law who did not mind cycling miles to get hold of a rare plant was well-regarded in the community; the two fresh-faced sisters-in-law; the ever joking young brother-in-law Rupam. And her man? The one who lifted his head and closed his eyes when laughing? In her heart the beehive was collecting honey in every nook—precise, neat, without any aberration. This was her beloved new family.

The only person who did not seem to belong to this neat little beehive was her elder brother-in-law. Looking at him, she felt as if a black crow had bitten off a part of the precisely constructed beehive. Without doubt he was intelligent; she understood that immediately after a few exchanges. She noticed that he was in this house, but his mind was somewhere else. He had not noticed the new beehive at all; to him perhaps the bright flowers in the compound were like everyday stars in the sky; what was the big deal after all? The day the newborn kittens in the house died, nobody had the desire to have a proper dinner; he was the only one who had a hearty meal. He was not even aware that the house cat had given birth to two milk-white kittens. He was not aware of anything around the house. The officer's wife employed a daily labourer to cut a canal to let the dirty water flow into their kitchen garden; early in the morning old and young from Subhas Pally tried to invade their garden wielding sticks with pegs to steal flowers; his mother was suffering from a swollen vein in her left leg; his father had only one year left for retirement and then the whole household would have to depend on the elder son's income; the elder sister's marriage had to be arranged within the next two years. But he seemed least concerned about these. It was as if he was a guest in the house. He had passed the Previous exam of the post-graduation course with quite good marks, but he did not appear for the final exam. His father was banking on his becoming a professor. He still regretted making his elder son, her husband, take up a job early as a rain check against the future. Sometimes when the brother-in-law disappeared for two to three days, he locked the door of his room. When his name came up in a discussion everybody seemed to stop talking. One day her mother-in-law had told her while cooking in the kitchen: 'My dear! I am very worried about him, you know!'

She was going to cut the fish and had rubbed ash on the fish to make it easier to hold, but putting it aside, she cried silently. Looking as restless like the kawoi fish rubbed with salt and kept on the bamboo sieve, she gripped Arunima's hands even though her palms were full of fish scales and told her, 'He is chasing a *dhanguloi*, a will-o'-the wisp. One day that elusive flame will consume him, I tell you.' Her mother-in-law's voice had trembled with an unknown fear as she continued, 'You know, my dear, the day he was born an ominous horned black owl was sitting on the roof. We will have to leave our old home of three generations, his horoscope says …' Just then he entered his room passing by the veranda of the kitchen. He had returned home after a week. Both of them noticed that one side of his jacket was bulging unusually. Her mother-in-law looked like the fish lying still, dead, and wept silently, saying, 'Boari, his horoscope says he could be the cause of his mother's and father's death.' As she fried the fish, she said sotto voce, 'I have done whatever I could. I have offered a gold flower at the naamghar; to the temple I have offered a trident. I always fast on the day of the week of his birth; I always light a lamp in his name at the shrine at home. What else can I do?'

While passing her the ground mustard for the fish curry, Arunima asked, 'Ma, didn't anyone try to make him understand?'

'When the hills call a man, when the water beckons him, or when the magical power of fire dances in the distance, a man loses his reason, my dear! Who will be able to make him understand?'

'Ma, shall I try?'

'His father and siblings couldn't do that. How can you?'

'Let me ask him what he wants, what he is looking for.'

'What will you ask? He is enamoured of a fire guarding the treasure buried by Yama, the god of death,' she said. Streams of tears flowed down her shrunken cheeks, 'I'm afraid for you. Let not that fire engulf you as well.'

'Please don't talk like that, Ma.'

He stormed out of the house again. This time it was not the jacket but the airbag slung on his shoulder that bulged at the seams.

She felt the hair on her skin stand on end. Some unknown fear made her body go cold.

Yes, sometimes the hills beckon, the water calls, and in the dark night a magical fire beckons. People die in that fire, like moths drawn inevitably to the flame.

The second son of the house went away with the fat airbag, and it seemed to be for good. At first when the family laid the table, one plate was always kept ready for him, but after sometime, two bowls of curry, fried vegetable and a container with rice and dal were kept so that they could be warmed quickly. After sometime they stopped that too. The blood pressures of both the parents went up; the mother could hardly sleep at night. Whenever there was a sound at night she got up to check; her regular fasts thinned her down.

Her mother-in-law did not want pregnant Arunima to cook, but her health was not permitting her to do all the cooking. Often when the young sisters-in-law were in college and she tried to finish the chores, her head reeled. After putting a little oil and cold water on her head, she would call Arunima, breathing heavily, 'My dear, only the fish curry is left. Can you ...?'

That day was 6th or 7th of August. Only Arunima and her mother-in-law were at home. It was cloudy but not raining. For the last two days, it had been like this, sultry without a leaf stirring. The clothes were clammy with sweat and clung to the body. As her mother-in-law was frying the banana flower for the vegetable curry, she felt her head reel. Arunima heard her calling out faintly and put her in bed. Just then a truck full of army men stopped by their gate. She went out to find what it was about. By that time, the soldiers were in the backyard. The men rudely asked the whereabouts of the son who had left home—where was he? Did he come home? and so on. Then they entered the house and swooped into his room like eagles plunging on a prey. They searched the room and threw out everything out—the clothes, papers, notebooks and then, collecting some papers and tying them into a bundle, went away. Now Arunima too put oil and water on her head which she had prepared for her mother-in-law. Her head seemed to reel as well; it felt as if her innards were ready to spill out. She left the curry uncooked and lay down beside her mother-in-law.

The household had suddenly become very restive and filled with a sense of foreboding. The house had always been organized and disciplined. Now there seemed to be a certain listlessness. The members of the family did not seem to notice how things were lying about or the work remained half done. A sense of dread pervaded the atmosphere in the house. Not only their house, the whole town seemed to be overtaken by fear. The people were sure something was going to happen before the Independence Day on 15th of August. Some people had seen a few of them near the reserve forest; some said they saw a few near the oil pipeline. In front of the army camp, trucks and jeeps were assembling in droves. People also talked about an unusual vehicle; they heard that it was a bullet-proof, anti-mine vehicle. The atmosphere was like a dry grassland—just a little spark, and it would burst into flames. In this dryland, a whispered rumour was passing from mouth to mouth—that the son of this house was seen somewhere around; that he looked quite formidable with a luxurious growth of beard now.

At home, Arunima's mother-in-law now had taken to bed permanently with a constant headache and weakness. There was only one month left for her father-in-law's retirement. The man who had considered the school his life's main inspiration now ceased going there. He did not dare leave the house. People had seen his son around. If he visited the house, or those who invaded the house from time to time came, what would people at home do—his sick wife, his pregnant daughter-in-law? His eldest son had to go to office, the girls had to go to school and college, the younger son had been sent away to his maternal uncle's house. So he stayed put, but at home, too, the old man could not find any peace; he went to check the front gate from time to time. Suppose his son returned suddenly from the jungle? So at night, too, he walked up and down the veranda. No, nothing was certain, they could not depend on anything. Who knew if the calm water on the surface hid some unknown sharp thorns underneath? A grinding fear, an oppressive sense of dread, hung over them all.

Her father-in-law had gone to sleep towards dawn after walking around the veranda almost the whole night. The members of the household fell asleep too. They were also awake all night through; who could sleep if the old man kept pacing up and down, restless like a kawoi fish cut into pieces but still jumping and waiting for life to drain out?

At first the men could not wake them up even after banging on the door. Arunima woke up first. Newly pregnant, she slept fitfully. She shook her husband awake. When all of them went to the door and saw the four men who were their second son's friends, they almost croaked with fear. The mud stuck on their heavy boots soiled the floor. They had guns on their shoulders and all of them carried heavy bags in their hands. They wanted to have some rice and curry. By that time, the mother-in-law with her sharp rabbit-like ears woke up and came to see what was happening.

She almost screamed, 'Is he all right?'

'He's fine. He has returned from Kachin twice by now. His rank is much higher than ours.'

'His aim with the gun is admired even by the commander,'

'Once he had contracted malaria.'

'Now we have to take permission to meet him.'

They seemed to answer the query altogether.

'Ma, we haven't eaten for the last two days.'

'Now if you give us some food we'll eat and go to the hills before the day breaks.'

'I am very hungry, Shalini!' one of them said, looking at Baby. She left the room in a huff.

'Does he go hungry too?' her mother-in-law asked as if she were speaking from a sick bed.

'It's common to go hungry; so what?'

'Sometimes we have to go on empty stomachs, but sometimes we eat very well too.'

Her mother-in-law went to the kitchen to cook. Arunima and Baby followed too.

They left after having a full meal before daylight broke. As they walked out of the house, Arunima's family stared at their departing figures disappearing beyond the shaddock tree.

Her father-in-law commented softly, 'All of them grew up together.'

'They have all been beckoned by a terrible fate,' her mother-in-law said, wiping her eyes.

'Oh, that guy asks me for rice! He hasn't forgotten the name he had given me—Shalini or Falini, I don't care. Am I his wife that he calls me like that?'

Watching her younger sister-in-law let off steam, Arunima was about to smile but stopped as her husband's desolate voice warned, 'Baby! Never ever utter their names, never discuss them with anybody.' Looking at his pale face, Arunima felt her heart swell with sadness. How long it had been since she had last seen him smile? Not only him, the whole household seemed to have forgotten how to smile from the time the second son left the house.

She looked at the ou tree. Was the beehive still there? Yes, it was there, and it was getting bigger and hanging from the branches. It seemed to sway a little in the breeze.

Following her eyes, everybody else looked at the beehive silently.

'It looks like honey is forming,' the elder sister-in-law commented.

'Let it be; they go away when we try to collect the honey?' said her mother-in-law, looking intently at the hive.

'Forget it, let's not smoke away the bees; so what if we don't have the honey?' said Baby. A few minutes ago, her soft face was contorted with anger, hatred and fear, but now it was back to her usual calmness.

The day was 13th of August. These days the people in the house were not sticking to their usual habit of retiring to bed at ten in the night and getting up at dawn with the crows. In fact, they hardly slept at night; who knew who could visit at night? The feared, unwelcome one? Or his friends? Or those 'others'? Only towards the dawn they could shut their eyes.

That day, too, the family had retired after dinner after switching on all the 100 watt lights on the veranda, just like others in the town. The eldest daughter in the family sat with some embroidery work. Her marriage negotiation was almost in the final stage. The boy was a librarian in the college she studied in. He was quite good-looking and his family was well-known too. He had known her for four years and sent the proposal himself. It was Arunima who suggested that she buy the material and start readying the embroidered linen for her trousseau. She loved observing her rather quiet sister-in-law as she played with the skeins of coloured threads; in those many-coloured skeins many of her dreams were woven perhaps! Baby was busy with her books. After sometime she took out the book on flowers. Arunima looked at her. How intently she was reading the book! It was an illustrated book with pictures of many varieties of flowers. The day she got it for Baby, she was so happy that she jumped around like a goat's kid. Was she reading the book or was she in a dream flying about like a butterfly in her garden? It was already August and soon it would be time to plant seasonal flowers for the winter; she had already marked out the patches—here would be the dahlia flowers, here would be the poppy flowers, there, in that corner, she would plant the marigolds, and then the sweet pea beds and over there the chrysanthemums. Baby consulted the book from time to time.

Today it was the turn of Arunima's husband to be on guard duty of the locality. The whole town was under army surveillance.

Anything could happen any time. Already in three places in Assam, trains had been derailed by bombs; the radio news and the TV were reporting cases of unrest at different locations. As Abinash was not there at home, both her sisters-in-law came to sleep in her bedroom to give her company. Bandhs had been called by the rebels on both days preceding and following the Independence Day.

Arunima got up at midnight to go to the toilet. Both the girls woke up instantly.

'What happened, Bou? Are you feeling unwell?' Baby asked her.

'Bou, do you want to go to the toilet?' Omi, the elder girl, asked and brought out an umbrella. The bathroom was outside in the courtyard and it was drizzling.

The sharp ears of the mother-in-law caught the strain of the conversation from the other room and now she called out, 'Omi, do you hear me? Take your Bou to the bathroom, no use taking her to the toilet outside. If she stumbles in the slippery courtyard it'll be disastrous.'

She was grumbling to herself: 'I've told him so many times to build a toilet attached to the bathroom so that my Boari can use it at night, but he says he doesn't have money. He has money for everything but this! It's pure laziness; you can't expect men to understand women's problems.'

'Don't worry, Ma, I'm going to the bathroom here,' Arunima assured her. She felt a bit shy with all the attention to her condition.

Baby brought a bucket of water to the bathroom. 'Bou, don't worry, I'll pour the water afterwards. Please don't lift the bucket; Ma will scold me.'

She heard her father-in-law telling his wife in the next room, 'You don't have to tell him. I'll do it. How much money it will cost anyway? He is a young man, how will he understand these things?' He cleared his throat and continued, 'Listen, tomorrow ask Moneswar to sprinkle some sand and stone chips on the courtyard. It's really slippery now.'

The rain gathered momentum and the tin roof resounded with its force. She could not hear her in-laws any more. The electricity went off and the room was filled with a thick darkness. Omi got down from the bed immediately and lit the hurricane lamp kept on the right side of the room for such emergencies. A soft yellow light washed over the room, which still bore the fragrance of a new bride. Omi and Baby slept on both sides of her as if protecting her. Outside, rain was lashing and thunderbolts streaked down from time to time; they seemed to enter the room through the glass windows.

'Bou, Dada and others with him must be taking shelter in somebody's veranda,' Omi wondered aloud.

'Runjun's father is also on guard duty today, they must be in their house,' Baby rejoined, her voice betraying fear.

'Runjun's mother must be making tea for them,' Arunima said smiling a little. She felt lonely without him by her side in the bed. He never went anywhere without her, these days more so. He often said he wanted a pretty little girl. Oh, the things he did sometimes! He put his ears on her belly and exclaimed, 'I seem to hear a sound.'

She fell into a light sleep. She dreamt of a garden full of flowers, and there were skeins of many colours too, hanging like spider webs in the air. They shone as if dewdrops had fallen on them. A little girl with red ribbon in her hair was running through the flower beds, disturbing them. The colourful threads touched her cheeks—Arunima extended her hands to hold the girl in her arms …

Suddenly there was a huge sound tearing at their ear drums. She sat up, shocked. Omi and Baby screamed. An unfamiliar red light streamed into the room through the windows and the ventilators. Her in-laws ran to her room; her husband came in too. They watched dumbstruck from the veranda a huge fire to the east. The fire was going up and up. They coughed as the burnt smell invaded the air; a blanket of smoke spread over the town.

'Go, take the torch and unfasten the cows in the shed,' she heard her mother-in-law's instruction to her husband without a tremor in her voice. 'Omi,' she continued, 'Go unlatch the bird coop; don't forget to open the gate of the goats' shed too.'

Arunima ran to the room and tried to catch hold of a suitcase. 'Boari, don't worry about your possessions now, think about the child in your womb,' her mother-in-law said as she looked up and joined her palms together in prayer. 'What are you looking at?' she said urgently to the family, 'Let's go! Can't you see the fire is coming this way? We'll be burnt to death.'

They left the house hurriedly. The street was full of panic-stricken people. Someone shouted, 'They have bombed the pipeline.' Someone else screamed, 'They haven't been able to put out the fire; we'll all die.' The air was thick with the sound of people shouting, cows mooing in fear and cawing of crows. Arunima was only conscious of Baby holding her one hand and her husband the other.

She was yet to come out from her dream world of the flower garden, the coloured threads and the little girl with a red bow in her hair. Her eyes smarted with the smoke and the feeling of unreality. A herd of cows joined the scared people aimlessly running around on the road. Freed from the sheds by their owners, they merged into the crowd of people. Arunima could feel the hair on her skin pricking up in fear. What would happen now? Would her dreams end up like these roaming cows losing their homestead? What about Baby's dream? And Omi's? And her husband's? And the little dreams of her parents-in-law? The cows mooed. People were screaming—everywhere dreams were scattering like the cows disoriented without their familiar ropes.

'Where shall we go, Dada?' Baby's voice was a whisper in fear.

'Where the fire won't get us,' she said in a voice as if coming out in circles from a deep well.

'What a big fire!' Omi sounded as if her voice was slowly getting buried deep somewhere.

'Where shall I go with my children?' her father-in-law's voice was cracking as if he were weeping. He was looking back behind him every few minutes.

'Deuta! Please hurry up. The other people have gone much ahead,' her husband's voice crumbled.

'Dada, where will we go?' Baby cried out.

'Baby, however big a fire, it can never burn down the whole world,' Arunima said almost in soliloquy.

Her eyes were again hypnotized by the images of coloured threads spread in a spider web, vibrant flowers and a little girl with a red ribbon in her hair.

She almost shouted, 'Ma, please walk faster!'

Birds fly out in the morning but return to their nests in the evening; animals too do not forget their own sheds and habitat. Eventually, the people too started returning to their abandoned houses.

Her father-in-law stood stunned, holding on to the gate.

'What's happened, Deuta?' Baby asked, smiling.

'My house, my compound, they are still here ...' he uttered the words slowly, his voice trembling.

'Come, Deuta!' Arunima said as she led him to the house.

She made a cup of tea, asked him to lie down and then with her mother-in-law, Omi and Baby went to the kitchen garden at the back to check its state. The cows had returned too and now they were munching on the grass in the shed. The new-born calf was suckling forcefully on the mother's udders. Everything seemed to be the same; the only difference was that black particles floating in the air from burning objects covered everything. The green of the grass and leaves in the trees were lost. They all went to the bank of the pond. She screamed loudly and hearing her, the others ran to see what had frightened her. Now Baby, Omi, even her elderly mother-in-law screamed. The pond was white with the underbellies of dead fish. Hearing them, her father-in-law and husband came out running. They were silenced by the sight of the white, dead fish. Even Rupam who had come from the hostel that day came running, the suitcase still in hand. Looking at the floating fish, he sat down in shock on the ground. He had collected the Rohu fishlings from the fishery himself. The fish were getting big, weighing one to two kilograms by now.

Suddenly there was commotion as ten to twelve army personnel entered the compound. They had already rampaged through the house. One of them now took hold of Rupam's arms. Another snatched his suitcase and broke it open; two sets of clothes, packets of pitha and pickles, a few branches of a flower tree spilled out to the ground. They questioned the members of the family about the son who had left the house and then dragged Rupam away. His brother, her husband, did not eat anything and, putting on a shirt, went out. Again, that routine would follow, he knew. Police, court, etcetera. No, Rupam could not be kept in the house any more. He was in the third year now. It was planned that after graduation he would go to the university. He was good in studies, majoring in history. The exam marks were good too. The family had given up on the second son, now their hopes lay with this younger son. He was quite mature too. He managed to finance his own studies, giving private tuition to students or sometimes through some small business ventures. He had invested in the fishlings thinking about the tuition fees in the university. He already had a coop with thirty chickens. It not only supplied the eggs required for the household, but he sold the extra ones in the market. He also looked after the betel leaf creepers, the betel nut trees and the cows and goats in the shed. For sometime now, he had been talking about bringing a few ducks too. Thinking of his hardworking brother, his elder brother's heart felt like it were filled with the white bellies of dead fish. He had been harassed by the police and the military since his elder brother left home. He walked faster. Something had to be done. Who knew what they were going to do to Rupam? Everybody seemed to be on edge.

The surroundings around the house seemed to be full of dead fish too. On both sides of the house, the 'dacoit' families were employing labourers to clean up the place. They exchanged words in between the work, but the jibes were aimed at them—as if they were the ones who had deliberately done it though they themselves seemed to be half-dead. They had to bury the dead fish, had to feed the cows and chickens, they had to organize some food. But they just stood around, unable to push themselves to do these tasks.

Arunima's mother-in-law quietly tried to milk the cows. The calf had suckled through the night. Still she could extract some milk. She heated it, washed some flat rice, mixed it with the milk and brought it to Arunima telling her, 'My dear, don't forget the baby in your womb.' Slowly the people in the house started getting busy with the pending chores.

In the afternoon, her husband returned with Rupam. He had signed a bond promising that as soon as the rebel son visited home, he would inform them and, on that condition, Rupam was allowed to go home. Everybody insisted that Rupam go and stay with his maternal uncle; he could study there and if necessary, also appear for the exam. But Rupam refused. How could he leave everything to his elder brother who worked in the bank and old father, he argued. If he decided on something, nobody could force him to abandon it.

In a short time, the twenty-one year old young man became like a guardian of the house. He even petitioned and obtained compensation for the households which had been affected by the fire and also brought fresh fishlings for the pond. With broken pieces of brick, he segregated sections in the garden for Baby to plant different varieties of flower. One day Rupam went to the big town to collect flower plants and seeds. When he brought a plant with flowers like balls of fire, Baby jumped with joy. He also told her he had placed an order for fifty cuttings of dahlia. Baby was already imagining how people would stop by and admire her dahlia flowers in full bloom, the petals in different sizes, different colours. With care, each could become as big as lotuses. Hearing the descriptions, Baby's eyes widened with anticipation. Soon, the people in the family also became enamoured of dreams again, dreams like the many-hued dahlias. The courtyard was filled with stones and sand and a toilet was built next to Arunima's room.

Her body was now quite heavy. Even on the now hardened courtyard, she walked very carefully.

One day Rupam called a few men to collect honey from the ripened comb hanging from the ou branch. On the full moon night, when a fire was lit under the ou tree to smoke out the bees, Arunima along with Omi and Baby created a hue and cry, worrying that the bees would leave forever. Rupam scolded them: 'What a fuss you are making! Once the bees make a comb they don't abandon it so easily. They build it with so much effort; it's not easy to go away.'

Arunima looked at Rupam. In a short time, he seemed to have grown up to be a man of the world. The honey filled up a big bucket. He told his sister-in-law affectionately, 'Won't we need honey soon? Where will we get pure honey then? I have seen my younger uncle looking everywhere for good honey for the child.'

That night she could not sleep well. She dreamt of honey bees in fitful sleep. She dreamt that they flew away from the honeycomb again and again; once she tried to hold them with the end of her chador. Or she saw a bare branch of the tree trembling in the wind, or the base of the tree filled with dead bees. She cried as she was about to stamp on them; the bees flew away and she tried to run after them. Unable to catch up, she shouted Ru—pa—m! She moaned, waking up the entire household. With round eyes bulging with fear, she held onto her younger brother-in-law's wrists and, as if in a trance, started uttering, 'Rupam, the honeycomb full of honey! The dead bees!'

Her mother-in-law made a glass of Glucose and, giving it to her, uttered in distress, 'Why on a Saturday, that too on a full moon night, did she have to stand out there under the ou tree?'

She scolded her younger son, 'See the consequence of your hankering for the honey. I am sure a bad spirit has taken over her. Before you were born, I also had a similar experience walking under this ou tree while going to the toilet.'

She called out to the older son, 'Go to the bej; he will sanctify some water for her to drink.'

She leaned her heavy body on Rupam and said, as if unaware of the surroundings, 'So many dead bees! Is the comb still there? The honeycomb ...?'

Omi wiped her face with a wet gamocha. Her husband hurriedly put on a trouser and shirt and said, 'Let me get the doctor; she hasn't slept a wink through the night.'

Rupam told Omi, 'Omi-ba! Please open the windows towards the kitchen garden!'

Omi opened all the windows. Outside, the sky was getting lighter; a pink cloud hung in the ashen sky.

'Look, Bou! There, the honeycomb is still there. Look carefully. See?'

Rupam helped her drink the glucose water.

Slowly she sat up. Rupam urged her again, 'Please look, Bou! The bees are again busy collecting honey for the comb.'

She looked through the window opening out into the kitchen garden. Yes, the comb was shining in the morning light; only this time it was not long in shape but round.

In the morning, all of them were enjoying freshly fried luchis with honey. Omi was planning to knit a white sweater for her betrothed, and now was taking help of Arunima to wind the skeins of wool into balls. As she tried to put the required stitches on the knitting needles, she exclaimed without thinking, 'Oh! So many stitches! What a wide back!' Instantly shyness took over the quiet woman. Arunima whispered in her ears, 'You're getting a handsome husband; you have to take this much trouble.' Omi's face reddened. The white wool seemed to take on the colour of her pink cheeks.

Baby asked her elder brother, 'Dada, are you going out?'

'What does our young princess want now? I have already brought the flowering plants,' Rupam made a face at her.

'Oh, keep quiet now,' Baby stopped him and addressed Abinash, 'Dada! Yesterday I trimmed the rose plants; can you please bring some manure? The other flowers will bloom beautifully, and now if the roses don't do well I'll feel so bad.'

'Don't worry, I'll do it. What's the name of the manure?'

'Rose mix, Dada,' Baby said promptly.

'Our lady will write the names of flowers in her exam papers on physics and chemistry, I'm sure,' Rupam teased her, taking a luchi from her plate.

'Oh, you don't know, this time in the First Year exam, I was the only one to get an A. The principal had sent for me and said if I tried, I could even get a position.'

'Okay, okay. You study well. I'll see to it that you can go for a medical degree,' Rupam ran his fingers on Baby's curly hair.

'Will we be lucky enough to be treated by home-grown doctor?' her father-in-law wondered aloud as he came to join the breakfast table coming out from the puja room.

'Why not, Deuta! Of course, it will happen!' Arunima said as she placed the plate of luchi in front of him and went to the kitchen to make tea for him. These days he took tea without sugar.

After milking the cow, her mother-in-law handed the milk to her, saying, 'Boari! Please heat the milk.'

Omi kept aside the wool and knitting needles and came over. She asked her mother, 'Ma, why are you telling Bou to heat the milk? What if it boils over? She may get burnt, we should be careful.'

She saw that after a long time, her husband was smiling the way he used to, his eyes half-closed as the face tilted upwards.

'What's there to laugh? I have been asking you all to bring a milk-cooker for a long time,' Arunima said irritably.

'Well, I've been looking for your milk-cooker all over but haven't been successful. Actually, consumers like you are rare these days; the company can't make profits and so they have stopped manufacturing it altogether,' he teased.

'Oh, don't you have anything else to say?' she was getting slightly angry; her nose was covered in a film of perspiration.

'Bou! You can show me the old one. I'll try to see if it can be repaired. Only the whistle is malfunctioning,' Rupam said. He asked Baby to make another cup of tea.

Suddenly the calling bell rang. Tommy started barking. He was of an ordinary breed and had been in the house for long time. Now he was getting old, his eyes were bad and he walked around on guess-work. These days he was not interested in barking either. After eating rice, he just lay down on the veranda outside. Even if cows or goats made a feast of flowers in the garden outside, he did not bother. Baby scolded him constantly. But now his barking disturbed the calmness of the morning. They jumped up. Rupam ordered Baby rather roughly, 'Go inside the house!'

Her husband looked at Rupam and told him, 'You stay inside as well,' and went out to check. An army officer stood there. But he did not come inside, just waited on the veranda. The handsome officer shook his hand. The genteel, senior officer was looking for his father.

Nobody was interested in going to the kitchen to cook lunch now. All other work came to a standstill. They all sat in the drawing room. The next day there was going to be a function to mark surrender by some militants. Senior army officers, the chief minister himself, a central minister, media persons from television, radio and newspapers would be present at the solemn occasion. Arunima's father-in-law was invited to attend the function.

'But why me?' the old man's mouth fell open in surprise.

'Why not? You are the father of a famous terrorist!'

Her mother-in-law started feeling unwell; when her head reeled like this, a mixture of oil and water had to be put on her head. As she went to do that, she asked croaking, 'He too …?' Arunima saw that her eyes were moist. She held her hand and led her to the bedroom. As she put the oil and water on her head, she heard the neighbour's wife, who was pretending to wash clothes at the water tap outside but actually speaking loudly for their benefit, 'Don't know why these people don't go away from here … for them we also suffer … police, military come and go all the time.' She was beating a towel forcefully on the floor of the newly-built red enclosure meant for washing clothes in the backyard. Arunima shut the window. After putting her mother-in-law in the bed to rest, she stepped into the veranda to go to the drawing room. Seeing her, the dacoit's wife came out.

'What's happened? Have they arrested Rupam?' she was smiling.

'No, it's about something else,' she replied.

'Something else? What happened, has the other one died?'

'I don't know,' her face reddened as she retorted.

The woman seemed to sympathize with her. 'Ah!' she said, 'Seeing your face makes me sad. What bad luck that you have to live with this family of criminals!' Anger and insult made Arunima's eyes fill with tears. 'Oh, Oh! Why are you crying? What can you do, it's in your fate after all,' the woman said. Now she came nearer and confided, 'You know, yesterday they sent a demand notice for money. Some jealous person must have informed them; you know how much my husband toiled to build this house.' Her voice was a whisper now as she said, 'Can't you tell them to reduce the amount? It depends on you people ...'

Arunima jumped away from her, as if she had seen a venomous snake. This woman, who on other days shut the door of the house when she saw policemen or army men entering their house and went on hurling unspeakable abuses from inside the house, was greatly sympathetic to her today; now she understood why.

The woman smiled meaningfully and asked, 'Have you built a new bathroom yet? Have you used tiles or marble in the latrine? My husband has spent seventeen thousand rupees on the commodes alone. When do you plan to build a bathroom? You people, however, don't have to build a house like us.'

Streams of tears washed Arunima's cheeks. The woman went away.

In the meantime, it was decided that Arunima's father-in-law would attend the event to welcome the surrender. How could one fight with the crocodile when you lived in the water?

One day Baby told the family that on her way back from maths tuition, the man who called her Shalini offered to give her a lift home. Stunned with fear, the people in the house realized that the girl who was mad about flowers was herself turning into a beauty, a dahlia of many colours. Rupam now had another duty added; he could not allow her to go alone anywhere. He also decided that when he would join the university in Guwahati, he would take Baby along, too, and admit her in a college there. His father meanwhile went to visit the prospective groom's house and fixed Omi's wedding date in January. The groom was building two additional rooms for the house, so they had to wait these few months.

Forget about the sudden pause in Baby's tuition class, the whole town now seemed to stop in its track. Militants blew up a minister and his car on the main road by a remote controlled bomb. News in dailies and on TV named the perpetrators who took responsibility for the blasts. The second son of the house was also among them. He had taken a new name; these days it came up often in the media reports.

Even before the crater made by the bomb on the road was filled up, people in the town got another shock. Three of the surrendered militants who had now started living in Guwahati were shot dead while on their way home here.

It was as if the crater created by the bomb in the trunk road had entered their house, making it sink. The whole family seemed to be thrown into that huge hole; they were submerged amidst the dead bodies and blood. Those three bodies in the isolated field, their blood dried over their corpses, it seemed as if someone had dragged them and placed in their room. The flesh was rotting, the odour made their stomachs churn. They could not breathe, they could not eat, they could not sleep.

In the morning, Arunima's father-in-law took Baby and Omi along with him to his brother's place in Tezpur. He wanted the girls to stay out of the town for the time being. But he returned by the afternoon bus with them. His brother said he was having his walls painted; it would be inconvenient to accommodate guests in the house.

The tuition teacher told Baby that she did not have to come any more, he was planning to keep the class suspended for sometime. The officer Saikia put up a huge wall between their compounds. A few days later, they celebrated their little baby's annaprasan, the first rice-eating ceremony, with lots of invitees. From this end, they could hear the noise of laughter and giggles of guests congregating for the feast, but they were not invited. Even the dacoit put up a bamboo fence on the border of the compound to shut them off. These days you could not hear clothes being washed noisily or abuses being hurled from that side. An ominous quietude hung over the place.

One night, the blood pressure of Arunima's father-in-law shot up and his face pulled down on one side. Not a single doctor agreed to come to their house to examine him. In the morning, somehow they managed to take him to the civil hospital. By God's grace, this time, at least, he could return home without any permanent damage. But no one from the neighbourhood visited the house to enquire after his health.

Winter was almost at the doorstep. There were so many things waiting to be done. The kitchen garden needed ploughing to loosen the soil, the bamboo scaffolding for the gourd needed repairing. If the gourd seeds were not planted now they would not grow in time. They had to make the fence for the urohi beans too. And Baby's flower garden? The garden divided into sections with bricks painted with lime. The fifty dahlia cuttings where flowers bloomed in seven colours, getting as big as lotuses—who was going to plant them?

Rupam noticed that of late he came across some unknown faces on the road. He smelt a conspiracy. Somebody was following him as if to catch him in a net, he felt. A few nights ago, when he was returning home, a Maruti van stopped near the big tank and a few men with black handkerchiefs tied over their faces got down and blocked his path. Luckily two trucks came that way lighting up the road with their headlights, so they left quickly in the van.

A few days later, Abinash called him and took him out on the pretext of a stroll. There he told Rupam about twice meeting men with faces covered with black clothes. Putting his arm around the shoulder of his brother seven years his junior, he broke down, crying, he said, 'Rupam! I feel scared now.' Rupam's eyes widened in fear and he uttered, 'Dada! I have also met them. One day ...' His voice choked. A Maruti van with tinted windows suddenly sped past them. Both of them left the road and returned home by the dirt road through the paddy fields. In their hearts, they carried a hole which the torn limbs of human bodies and blood filled in.

That night after dinner, Omi and Baby were washing the utensils in the corner of the courtyard. In the banana grove, something moved. Baby threw a stone towards the sound. Suddenly they saw two men with guns, their faces covered with black clothes. Leaving everything behind, they ran inside the house. Once inside, they could not say anything and sat trembling like leaves. After a long time, Omi uttered, 'Men with black clothes on their faces ...' Abinash brought the torch to check but Rupam caught him tightly from behind and almost screamed, 'No, Dada, don't go!' He buried his face in his elder brother's chest and cried.

'Don't cry, Rupam. People go through hard times,' his elder brother tried to calm him.

'I am not afraid of hard times, Dada! But this is something else,' Rupam replied, sounding like a small child.

'What have we done? What's our fault, Dada?' he rallied.

Seeing Arunima coming in, he wiped his face. These days she slept quite heavily. She did not know what was going on. Her eyes were wide with fear as she said 'Rupam! Some people were talking outside the window of my bedroom. They were whispering.'

Her husband tried to allay her fears. 'Oh, you are really something. You wake up and see bees flying away from the honeycomb!'

Rupam seemed very agitated. He told his brother, 'Dada! Please take Bou to her parents' place tomorrow itself.'

'Why, Rupam, I was supposed to go after one month!' she was a surprised, and a little hurt too.

'No, Bou. Please leave tomorrow itself.' Hearing Rupam's changed voice, she realized that something was amiss. When did so much fear gather in the boy who gave courage to everybody in the family?

'Rupam is right. I'll take you to your parents' tomorrow. Over here you are depressed and not keeping well.' Her husband's voice seemed to be coming out of a well of tears.

'I'll go but not tomorrow. After a week perhaps. I have to organize the things, you know,' she said. She tried to smile but failed. Then she said, 'I'll take along Omi and Baby too.'

All this time, her father-in-law was sitting quietly. Now he said, 'No Boari, you don't have to take along my daughters.'

'But why, Deuta?' she cried out.

'They too have been touched by the ominous shadow. My own brother, whose study I financed, arranged his marriage and settled him down, could not bear their presence. I have fallen into a deep canal, Boari.'

Outside, Tommy was whining, making a peculiar sound. They went out to see what was wrong. The old dog was foaming at his mouth and circling round and round in agony.

'He has been poisoned,' her father-in-law said, trembling.

'Don't think it's only Tommy, they are going to poison us too,' Rupam said, his face going deathly pale.

'Who will do that, Dada? Why poison us? What have we done?' Baby asked, sounding helpless.

'Baby, don't ask who, why and for what reason,' Rupam said.

Abinash took hold of Rupam's hand and led him to his room. 'Come, sleep in my room today,' he said.

As soon as he lay down on the bed, Rupam jumped up, almost screaming 'Listen, there they are!'

Arunima, Rupam and Abinash heard the sound of heavy boots receding from near the wall of their house. The three of them stood frozen where they were.

'No, I'll take you to your parents' tomorrow itself,' Abinash said with a finality after a long pause.

'Go, Bou. If you stay here ...' Rupam said, his voice cracking with fear.

She was getting ready to go to her parents' place for three to four months. Rupam and her mother-in-law would go with her. They would leave around 10 o' clock in the morning. They had thought of hiring a car, but Rupam suggested that a public bus would be better. At least there would be other passengers around.

In the morning, when she got up, she saw that Baby was already at work in the garden with a hoe, wearing an old skirt and tee shirt of her brother's. This attire of hers was familiar to the family; they called it kamjari dress referring to workers in a tea garden. She was intently breaking down the mounds of earth separated by brick lines. Two of the beds were already flat like fish eggs.

'Baby! What are you doing?' Arunima approached the girl.

'Bou! Should I allow my nephew to enter the house with a garden bare of flowers? By the time he comes, all the flowers will be in full bloom,' Baby said as she looked at Arunima's protruding belly.

Hearing a sound from the gate, both of them jumped up. These days the household seemed to get worked up even at the rustle of a leaf. Omi's future husband was entering the compound.

Baby and Arunima led him to the drawing room.

'Omi-ba!' Baby called out happily. She had not told anyone, but she had seen her sister crying silently at night quite a few times. She knew for whom she was shedding those tears.

Omi entered the room holding a cup of tea and snacks. Her sombre face was lit by a joy she could not suppress.

'Our Omi was like a moonless night all these days, perhaps the noon will show up tonight,' Arunima teased, hinting at his arrival; his name was Chandramohan Barua.

But he did not take the cup of tea Omi had brought and said rather abruptly, 'Bou, it seems the truth lies in a moonless night.'

Stunned, Arunima and Omi looked at him. She saw that Omi's eyes were welling up. By that time, the other members of the family also came into the drawing room.

The father asked eagerly, 'My dear! Have you finished building the rooms?' He was anxious to see his daughter married.

The man did not partake of anything offered with the tea. 'We've stopped the work for the time being,' he said.

'But why?' Arunima could not help asking.

'So you are not going through with the wedding now?' Rupam asked sternly.

'I didn't say that but let better days come,' he said.

Omi left the room.

'Why don't you say frankly that you don't want to marry into our family?' Rupam asked, his voice rising.

Abinash asked him to keep quiet. He knew if Rupam continued he would lose his temper and become hysterical. For sometime now Rupam had become a volatile man.

'You had sent the proposal yourself; we had in fact received quite a few proposals,' Abinash tried to speak level-headedly but could not.

'These things hadn't happened then.'

'Like?' Baby asked without beating about the bush.

Chandramohan kept his eyes down as he said, 'One of your sons has become a terrorist.'

'The country has laws to deal with that. We are not involved! My elder brother, my younger brother—none of them has become a terrorist, neither has my father or mother. So why are you treating us like this?'

'Baby, keep quiet!' the mother scolded her younger daughter.

'Let me speak, Ma!' Baby's lips were trembling. 'How can everybody in the house be the same? Your younger brother is a known drunkard; he's often found in a canal. But did we say because of that we won't allow my sister to go to your house as a bride?'

Baby's voice was getting sharper, more accusing: 'Your elder sister's husband has been under suspension for corruption. Does it mean that you too have been jailed? Or your job has gone?'

The entire household stood as if turned into stone. Who knew that there was a fire inside the girl who had been passionate only about flowers? Who had lit that fire?

'You may not marry my sister, but you can't treat us as culprits,' Baby was ready to leave the room, her eyes blazing and tearful in indignation.

'Baby hasn't said anything wrong. Tell me Chandra-da, you are an educated man; tell me aren't we living in a civilized society?' Rupam intervened.

'Of course, we are. Afghanistan hijacked an Indian plane, the whole world criticized,' Chandramohan's voice was dry as he added, 'Yes, we are living in a civilized society.'

'A son of this house has chosen his own path. This is his way. Time will judge whether he is right or wrong. But why do we have to live like this?' Rupam asked as he gathered up his pajama. His leg had a bandage over a raw wound.

'Look, Chandra-da. Somebody took a shot at me last night.'

The people in the room started with shock.

'I don't know who shot me. Luckily it hit the leg. On the road some shadowy figures follow us, Baby and Omi see them while going to wash utensils in the backyard, my sister-in-law hears them whispering near the window of the bedroom. Someone may kill us at any moment. We don't know who.' Rupam covered his wound now.

'Yes, Chandra, we are living in fear. You somehow organize a simple wedding and take her away,' the elder brother sounded somehow like his father.

Chandramohan got up to go and said, 'Let times improve.'

'Not the times, but it's the mindset that has to improve,' Omi's sombre voice penetrated the room.

Without saying anything, Chandramohan left the house.

Arunima's husband and mother-in-law were ready to go with her to the bus stand. Rupam had decided not to go at the last minute. Her mother-in-law and husband would stay the night at her parents' place and return the next morning. She would stay for a few months. Baby kissed her cheeks and said, 'Bou, you will see how many flowers I'll plant. You'll be surprised when you come back.' Omi also came to stand near her. Looking at her smile, she felt her heart break. Omi said, 'Bou! Keep your mind happy. We'll visit you in between.'

As she got into the cycle rickshaw she looked at the particular branch of the ou tree. The honeycomb was again getting elongated; it would be full of honey in a few days.

When the rickshaw started, she asked it to stop and called out to Baby, 'Listen! I'll send a branch of parijat flower with Ma from my home. Plant it under the ou tree; I've heard that honey from parijat flower is very sweet.'

'Okay, don't worry, Bou!' her sisters-in-law said together; their eyes were wet with tears, missing her already. Rupam's face reddened with emotion. She looked back at the house full of plants and vines.

A question churned inside her, questions Baby and Rupam asked: What had these people done? Whom had they harmed?

The rickshaw gathered speed. Slowly the house disappeared from her sight. Only the aroma of many flowers stuck to her nose for quite a distance.

She gave birth to a healthy boy. All those who came to see the baby as per custom, commented that he had taken after his father's side.

On the day the baby completed one month, all of the in-laws' family came in the morning bus. They hovered around the baby. Baby and Omi had brought tiny dresses with hand embroidery. The grandparents presented a gold chain, Rupam brought a rattle. And her husband? He bought everything from the bazaar that he thought was right for the son. Some of them were redundant, of course, and she felt like smiling at his simplicity. She looked at the baby who was moving his hands and feet as babies do and thought, how many people were lucky enough to receive so much love?

Her in-laws were ready to leave after tea.

She came back to the room and asked Rupam, 'Anything new happening there?'

'It's been quiet for sometime now,' Rupam said, but his voice betrayed suspicion.

'Do you see them?'

'For the last month or so, we haven't seen them.'

'The cars with tinted glass?'

'Haven't seen them either.'

'Hope the trouble is over.'

'I don't think so, Bou. They must be planning something diabolic. Did you read yesterday's newspaper?'

'I did,' she said, her voice almost a whisper.

'After reading the news, my father shuts the doors and windows by early evening. That night two died, that day at midday five in the family ...' Rupam's face was flushed.

'When do you plan to fetch me from here?' she asked, trying to change the subject.

'You know, Bou, in that house the old woman was ninety years old and the child four years,' Rupam continued. He got up to go and said, 'Bou, you stay here for some more time.'

The people were ready to leave. In the room she, the baby and her man, were alone. She went near him ... two eager arms encircled her ... a little warmth ... she seemed to get a familiar aroma of dried marigold and basil leaves ... a little dry paste of turmeric and black gram ... ah, there was nothing else in the world beyond that, nothing.

She took the baby in her arms and went out to the veranda to bid goodbye to her in-laws. She asked rather loudly, 'When are you coming to fetch me?'

The answer came from her elder brother, 'My new car will be delivered in the first week of next month. You don't have to come, I'll bring her myself.'

'Bring along sweets also to celebrate the new car,' Baby said, laughing. After a long time, Arunima heard her laugh like this.

They all stood watching until the people disappeared from view. Before going back to his room, her elder brother looked at her and said, 'I wonder how a son of this cultured family could go astray.'

'Like it happened with our elder brother,' she said without hesitation. The members of the family looked at her aghast. In this house, uttering the eldest son's name was taboo. He did not finish his studies, took to drinking as soon as he entered college, then married a girl from an ill-reputed family who could not adjust in his household. He had also a brood of children and they heard that he dealt with smuggled goods from Siliguri and stayed in a rented house on the fringe of the town. Yet, in this family, one was a doctor, one a lawyer, two educated daughters-in-law; of the three sons-in-law one was a professor, one an engineer and another a banker. So in their houses, the name of the drunkard eldest brother was never to be mentioned at all.

She broke the silence herself, saying, 'Whether he is right or wrong, my brother-in-law has gone away seeking something. But our eldest brother? Why has he gone astray? Wasn't he brought up in a cultured family?'

A few women entered through the gate. They were invitees to today's ceremony. The people got busy quickly looking after them as if relieved.

'Come, auntie!'

'When will uncle come?'

'Oh, look at Monty, how big he has become!'

'What about Anju's result?'

As the guests kept coming, the uneasy air cleared.

She stopped short at hearing the news. Again, some elusive killer put an end to four persons in a family. The villagers lit four pyres. All those unknown, mysterious killers seemed to play a prolonged game of tennis or badminton. If you have one point,

I have three points; if you have three, I have five points. The newspapers, TV channels gave out news as a matter of fact, one of this side was killed today; the next day two from the other side, and so on. Arunima felt restless. What was happening in her in-laws' house? How were they keeping?

One day she packed her baby's clothes and her own too. Her brother's car had arrived almost a month back. She noticed that recently her sisters-in-law had also stopped insisting that she should stay a few more days. Her mother did not say anything either. She seemed to hear the strains of a *biyanaam* … *'I rested in your house for some time.'* She was desperate to leave for the house with flowers. Her mother kept busy with her kirtan at the naamghar these days. The household was run by her two sisters-in-law. Of late, if she wanted to have biscuits with tea in the morning and afternoon, she had to approach them for the keys to the meat-safe. But she gave a good amount to them from the money her husband left with her. When he came, he bought more than enough baby food. Most of it was finished off by the children of her sisters-in-law; her own was too small to need much. Now her son was two months old. She sent word that she would reach home after three days. Her father-in-law told her that she should leave after four days as the day was auspicious according to the almanac.

There were only four days in between. After that, this baby, who was among many in this house, would be honoured like a prince in that house. She told stories to her baby about that house:

'There are two aunts waiting for you in that house. If you fly away—turned into a swan under the spell of a witch, your aunts will wait for you taking a vow of silence, and knit clothes with wild vines and make you human again.

'You have an uncle. If a wicked wizard steals you and keeps you prisoner in a place on top of the mountains, your uncle will cross seven seas and thirteen rivers to free you.

'You have a grandmother. If a witch turns you dumb by casting a spell, she will go round your bed for seven days and seven nights with a lighted earthen lamp in her palm without eating, without sleeping. She will bring back your voice though her palms will be burnt, her face will be blackened, but she will bring back your voice.

'You know, you have a grandfather. If a demon infects you with a deadly virus, he will fly out of the land, bring the whole Gandhamadan hill as in Ramayana and cure you with its medicine.

'And you know, you have a father. For his prince, he will do anything. If you want a bird singing from the branches of a silver and gold tree, or if you want the bird made of diamond shining in the sun, he will sail in his peacock-tailed boat to go beyond the seven seas looking for it. In your hands will dance the bird made of diamonds, its eyes made of pearls; its wings will shimmer with precious stones.

'They will all hover around my prince; you will dance to the beat of *ta-dhin-dhin-na, ta-dhin-dhin-na*; your black hair will be adorned by a peacock feather. Your waist will have jewelled belt. The anklets will resound musically with your every step: *rinjin … rinjin …* you will be our little Krishna, our chubby Gopal. All will pray to you, you will be like an angel among all those flowers.'

And what will the mother of Gopal do? Even if some evil wizard transformed her into a duck and tied her to a tree, her man would demand that the duck be brought to him, that a piece of wood from that tree be cut for him; he would go hungry for days until his demand was met. He was silently calling her all the time—she could feel it with all her body and mind. She would be the queen in the palace of golden fruits, silver leaves, diamond flowers and precious stones.

Telling the story of her beloved house, she would often fall asleep. In her dream, too, she would be dazzled by the bejewelled palace.

On the day she was ready to leave, her brother got an urgent call for a meeting in the office. By then the luggage was already loaded; she had only to change her dress. Her brother suggested that they could go the next day. But she was impatient to leave; she did not want to waste a single minute. So she told her brother, 'Dada, since we are ready, let me go anyway. There won't be any problem, the car is new and the driver is there too.'

She had thought that others in the house would object to her going alone with the baby. She waited with bated breath. No, nobody objected. In the other house, they never let her go out alone. Even when she had to go to the bathroom, it seemed that all of them woke up. The little murmur of protest from her brother and sisters-in-law made it obvious to her that it was just for civility's sake. Perhaps the resting honeybee took too long a rest?

She got into the car without waiting.

The car entered the small town in the afternoon. In the golden light of the setting sun, she had really become the queen with the little prince in her lap. The car was a heavenly cart drawn by white horses. Her people were waiting for her. Her brother had called them to inform of her arrival. What was her husband doing? They must be waiting outside on the veranda—Baby, Omi, Rupam, her parents-in-law. Baby must be checking her flower garden, chopping off the dead flowers. She must welcome her nephew with fresh flowers. Omi perhaps was putting the last stitch to the baby's new dress and pressing it with the iron. Had Rupam bottled the honey? He had seen that his uncle was always searching for pure honey for his child. She giggled. Her mother-in-law must be throwing mustard seeds in the four corners of the compound to drive away evil spirits who might harm her grandchild. Her father-in-law must be insisting on milking the cow though there was enough at home, while others in the family must be smiling at his obvious restlessness.

'Oh, look at his concern!' Her mother-in-law must have smiled hiding it with the end of her chador. A smile that was so endearing.

'Oh, it's me alone, is it?' her father-in-law must have teased his wife. 'We have seen the granny in the kitchen from the morning cooking something or the other, as if the two month old would eat it all like young man!' her father-in-law was laughing aloud.

Was her man laughing too? Looking up as he did, his eyes closed?

The car entered the town, passed a good portion of it; then it passed the school where he studied that had celebrated hundred years. But why did it feel that she was not entering the town? Something had happened. Where was the shop that sold samosas? And where was the stall selling tea mixed with bay leaf and cardamom and hot jalebis in sal leaves? It used to be here, she was sure. She saw only rows of wooden doors, all shut. All the shops were shut. Why? There was no car or rickshaw on the road. There was no one on the street to ask too. There, she saw a few soldiers crossing the road, and then went four vans full of police. The house was just after the next turning.

They crossed by the turning. The air was full of a rancid smell of burning. The house was just a few minutes from there. The car could not go forward; the road was full of people. Why were so many people here, leaving the town behind like a cremation ground? Police, military, an overwhelming burning smell. What happened? Who? Her house? She could feel her heart jumping up. Did her absconding brother-in-law come? She pushed through the throng of people and went forward. In front of her beloved house, there was a chain of policemen and soldiers. And the house? What had happened to it? Three fourth of it was blown up. There was no tin roof, walls or pillars. What was left of the house were only burnt cinders, a few flickers of fire showed up here and there. The wooden splinters had been thrown upto the ou tree, the tin roof was still burning. Everything around—the bamboo trees, the betel-nut trees were burnt to their roots. She stood frozen with the baby in her arms.

'The people …?' the words tumbled out of her trembling lips. She followed the eyes of the crowd and saw, lying on the road, three cloth bundles of burnt flesh. Now two soldiers brought out a cloth bag with a burnt dismembered leg. They threw it near the three bundles and went inside again. Two policemen were searching something in the burnt cinders.

Around her the weeping increased. Someone was saying, 'The sound of the bomb could be heard from two miles away; the sound even broke the glasses of the next house.'

Someone went up to retrieve a hand stuck on the ou tree. The honeycomb was exactly there. She threw herself on the half-burnt hand of a man. She was crying soundlessly. A woman picked up the baby wrapped in a towel and placed it carelessly near the cloth bundles with the burnt flesh.

Some people brought a newly made bamboo bier near the cloth bundles, which they were trying to lift and place on it. Somebody lighted an earthen lamp near the bundles. Somebody else brought a piece of banana stuck with joss sticks; one in the crowd brought a new earthen bowl with handle to light up aromatic incense powder. Arunima stopped crying and looked around. Suddenly like a mother holding a baby, she wrapped her hands around the mangled bodies. There was no sound as she cried; only her back was heaving up and down.

Nobody dared take away the burnt bundles from her.

The baby started crying. Arunima now went to the unknown woman who was holding her baby and, taking him from her, she lay him beside the cloth bundles. She wanted to say, 'Your … your …', but could not. She wept, her body racked by silent sobs.

The Cursed Fields of Golden Rice

A smile lit up the shy boy's face as he emerged from the crowded room, holding on to Father Jonathan. Father Jonathan's face, the colour of the dark thereju berry, had taken on a purple hue now. He wiped his perspiring face on the sleeve of his large white gown. His white teeth gleamed all the more against his dark skin. The boy looked again at that smiling face. Both of them now stepped into the street.

'You have done it, Alfred! You've done it!' Father Jonathan seemed quite excited. He ran his eyes over the mark-sheet again. In all the subjects he had obtained marks above seventy; in English, Social Studies and in Maths it crossed eighty. The priest repeated in his South Indian-accented English, 'Alfred! You've done it!' He stood on the footpath and prayed there itself, his eyes closed, 'Almighty Father! Bless this innocent soul …'

The boy followed the priest to cross over to the other side. Suddenly the strap of his half-worn flip-flops gave way. He stopped. He bent down to pick up the sandal and saw that Father was already on the other side of the road. The cars on the road braked with a screeching sound. Motorcycles, scooters, a few small cars passed him by. Father came over quickly to rescue the young boy standing helplessly with the pair of sandals in his hand. Holding his ward's hand, he led him to safety and almost scolded him: 'Be careful … you must be careful! This is not our Botabari village, this is Guwahati city, do you understand?'

The young boy's mouth opened into an O. He painstakingly pushed the strap into the hole of his rubber flip-flop. But it was of no use. The hole was too big to hold the strap and so it came out again after walking a few steps. Father took him to a shoe shop nearby and bought him a pair of rubber sandals. Alfred put his blue and white coloured sandals, now paper-thin after long use, in the new box. Father looked at his watch; it was quarter to twelve. They must walk fast to catch the bus. Otherwise it would be too dark by the time they reached the village. It was around a hundred kilometres to their place from here and normally should not have taken more than two hours, but that depended on the condition of the road. From Guwahati they had to go to the district headquarter town, from there a road broke away from the highway to lead to a small town; the road here was full of craters, big and small. Leaving behind the town, you would approach a stream sans a bridge which led to Botabari Chowk. From there if you could not catch the mini bus named Jilmil to reach Alfred's village where Father Jonathan had his church, you would have to walk in the dark through a half-broken road.

What Father had anticipated, happened; they could not reach there in time to catch Jilmil. So both of them started walking on the apology of a road in the dark. After sometime, the light from the torch Father carried dimmed and went off. It needed charging. It was a foreign-make torch; properly charged, it gave out a very bright light indeed. Father had not fully charged the torch for the last few days. Where was there electricity enough to charge anyway? The existing few connections were only there for name's sake. Only the church had electricity, but half the time it went off.

It was a very dark night. Father Jonathan's voluptuous white gown looked like a walking ghost without a head. He had been here for ages; he had come as a young man but now his hair showed a lot of salt. Even then he could feel the hair on his skin stand up as he walked against the impenetrable darkness. As on other days, he felt a sadness overcoming him. This place was only a hundred kilometres away, at most a hundred and twenty, from the capital, but look at the way it was mired in darkness of every kind. But the nineteen-year-old young man's body was in full bloom of youth. His skin was fair and had a head full of stiff dark hair. His dark eyes were small and bright; they disappeared when he smiled. His body was without flab; even in the darkness, he shone like a white cat. As soon as he reached Botabari Chowk, he took off his shirt and trouser and the new pair of sandals and changed into a gamocha he had left behind at the cycle repair shop. At many places from there to his home, the streams did not have bridges at all nor had ramshackle ones at best. So they had to wade through the water at most places. He held onto Father's hand. Like leading a child, he guided him through the makeshift bridge of betel-nut wood, through the banks eroded by the rivers, broken bridges now hanging on somehow and a bigger one with flat iron pieces.

The sky was full of stars now. He looked at them. Mainao often said that when people died they turned into stars. Which of them was his mother? He could not remember his mother; she died when he was about four years old while trying to give birth to his sister. His father had married again; now he had six step brothers and sisters.

At last, Father and Alfred stood near the river. He folded his hands paying obeisance to the river. Mainao always did that. When they had left in the morning it was a thin stream, but now it was bulging with water.

'Father, let's go to the right side. The river is too full,' he said and pointed to a small hillock. Father Jonathan did not say anything.

'Are you afraid? I have come here quite a few times. Once you cross here you will reach your church, don't worry,' he assured him and held his hand even more tightly.

Father looked at his face in the light of the pale moon now appearing in the sky. This young simple boy had done so well in the Matric exam from a village 'venture' school which was yet to be recognized by the government! If he got opportunities, he would do even better. His father was least bothered and his stepmother did not even feel like giving him some rice with salt. Till about seven years of his life, the boy had spent playing and doing nothing in particular. It was Father Jonathan who almost forced him to come to the school along with a few friends who were happy spending time playing and catching fish. And look today, how that simple village boy had got this fabulous mark-sheet! Father placed his hands on Alfred's shoulder and said, 'My boy … my son. You must go to college … you must.' He was breathing heavily as he said it.

The boy asked, 'Father! Do you feel tired? Do you want to sit down for a little while?'

They sat under a tree. Father looked at the watch. It was eight o' clock, but it seemed as if it was midnight. Alfred sat leaning against the tree. He could feel his stomach churn with hunger. Mainao must be waiting with a plate of rice for him. She would be so happy when she would hear how well he did in the exam. His stepmother would be sullen, for whatever reason; his father did not care anyway. Suddenly he felt a great urge to meet Mainao. At dawn she had swept the courtyard because she did not want to send him so far away walking over it sullied by the *sua* of the night; she had also cooked rice for him.

A few days ago, his stepmother had said something against him; his father, drunk most of the time, had chased him around with a machete, his eyes bulging and red. Mainao had smuggled him out and brought him to this hillock. She had made him sit down under this same tree. He had cried silently that day. She had put her hand on his back; her silky hair had spread on his bare back. He had looked at her. Her twenty-two-year-old young body was adorned by a green mekhela knotted around her breasts in methoni style. Her fair body shone under the moonlight. He could not take his eyes off her. He had remembered the story of Phulmuthi Mainao had told him. Now she seemed to be Phulmuthi's replica.

Phulmuthi had become a young woman. Her face was like the wide leaf of tora grass, her waist was slim like the middle of the big red ant, her nose was like the sharp thorn of a ghora kagzi lemon tree, the calves of her legs were like the bamboo shoot stalk, the neck was like that of a deer, the eyes were like the brown eyes of a pigeon. With her voluptuous breasts, slender fingers and long straight hair, she looked like the heroine of the folktale.

When he said, 'You are young Phulmuthi yourself', she had laughed and said, 'And do you know who you are? You are Alari Dambra—Alari of unparalleled qualities. You were found by your mother inside the betel-leaf and betel-nut of heaven. The maidens Asagi and Baisagi cried begging in front of Baobuli, god of wind, saying they wanted to marry you.' She had covered him with her long hair so that Asagi-Baisagi would not see him.

'Who were Asagi Baisagi?' he had asked.

She sang:

A little stream with crabs and snails
A tokou tree, a striped cheng fish
A bamboo grove

Old man Ahem came from heaven with twenty pairs of young men and women. By the stream's side, the old man set fire to the bota trees, to the tora plants. That day, Mainao really turned into a Phulmuthi on earth. Her green mekhela pushed up and her calves, strong and toned like unsheathed bamboo shoot lay exposed, her long hair covered her face like the wide leaves of the tora plant; on eyes brown like eyes of doves, teardrops shone in the moonlight and she sang softly:

Riu, riu, riu
Aha, god of wind has won
The god of fire lost
Riu, riu, riu ...

The forest of bota trees were burnt down, your mother swept the floor of ash. There she found betel leaf and betel nut from heavenly abode. She thought of sharing it with her husband, but forgot about it and they remained in the bag. And you were born there. Your mother hid you. She offered betel nut and leaf to the young men and women from heaven, and on their red spit, she sat and told the villagers that she had given birth to a boy. The young women of the village took him in their lap and asked, singing:

Little child, what name would you take?
Bohagu?
The baby shook his head
Would you take the name of Batha Burha?
The baby shook his head
Would you like to be named Alari Dumbra?
The baby nodded 'yes'.

'That's why I call you Alari. Alari, please don't look at Asagi-Baisagi. You'll be chased by God Baobuli,' she had said.

She wanted to hide him by fanning her hair over his body—from Asagi-Baisagi, from his stepmother, from his father who often chased him with a dao in hand.

Father Jonathan got up to go. Both walked down by the hillock's side.

'Alfred!' Father wanted to say something.

He said softly 'Father, you have given me the name of Alfred. Let it remain on the school register. You call me Alari.'

'Alari?' Father pronounced the name with his distinct accent.

'Mainao has given me this name,' he said.

'Mainao? Who is this Mainao?'

'The girl who works at our house.'

'The housemaid?'

'Yes, she doesn't have any family to call her own. My father has brought her to work in our house.'

The light in the church was on. Father walked that way.

He ran towards his house. He observed that there was no light inside the house. His stepmother was not keeping well; she must have retired early. His father was as usual slumped in front of the fireplace, dead drunk. Nobody noticed his entrance. He washed his face; the inner courtyard was circled by small cottages made of thatch and bamboo. He now walked slowly towards the last one. Mainao was waiting there with rice and vegetable curry.

She had kept the rice hot; with it was served banana tree pith stuffed in a hollow of bamboo stalk and then roasted over a charcoal fire, mashed dry fish and a fish curry with chopped gourd and tempered with ginger juice. He started gulping down the delicious meal. After finishing, he looked at Mainao. She was really a Lakshmi as the name indicated. Since he could remember, this was the first time that he had stayed away from her for the whole day, yet he could not say anything to her. She arranged the bedsheets and told him, 'Now you go to sleep.'

'Listen!'

At this Mainao looked at him from the doorway.

'Father has said that I should go to college.'

She did not say anything; her brown eyes like a pigeon's stayed on his face for sometime and then closed. He smiled and told her, 'Now you too go and sleep.'

He would leave for the town the next morning. Father Jonathan had arranged for him to stay in a shed behind a house belonging to one of his known families. Alfred could cook his own food and also attend classes from there. Father had also arranged for two private tuitions for him to earn some extra money. He would go with Father to the town. Today when his own father sold one of the goats in the house to give him some pocket money, his stepmother quarrelled with him the whole day. A few days ago, he went to the town with Father to check out his future living quarters. Father had also introduced him to the families whose children he was going to teach. He packed his minimal things in the old bag Father had given him. When he also put four ten rupee notes his eyes filled with tears. For these few notes, his stepmother had created a ruckus. Instantly the smiling face of Father Jonathan floated into his mind. How kind and loving he was to him! Who would love him like this? Outside, a pani-pia bird flew by calling 'piu piu'. He remembered Mainao's sweet voice singing:

The pani pia cries
Looking at the sky
Why are you crying?
O little bird?

The bird cries, her wings flapping
It looks up to the sky
Even if it rains and floods the land
Why do you still remain thirsty?

What a girl Mainao was! When she heard a bird singing, saw the moon or a butterfly, her voice trembled like the whistling wind passing through tora grass shrubs. She knew so many songs, so many stories. If you asked her where she learnt them, she would only laugh, her body shaking with laughter like jhow grass swaying in the wind. The pani-pia bird looking for water from the sky was still calling out. If Mainao heard it, she would have told him: 'You know Alari, she is the younger wife who was killed by the elder wife. She killed her by setting a snake in the tree. The murdered wife has become this bird. She cries out looking for her children.' As she told the story, streams of tears would flow down her cheeks, which were like the skin of the sour ou fruit with its thick smooth layers. Yes, Mainao was a girl like that. He felt his chest contracting; he was going to leave her behind. Many people were interested in her, he knew; his stepmother made her work constantly without giving her any rest. She did not have anyone to go to. Tomorrow he would go; today she did not once come to him to talk; she was busy serving tea and betel-nut to visitors who had come to bid him farewell. She must be sleeping already; her pigeon-like eyes closed as soon as evening set in. He retired to his bed. The bird was still calling.

'Alari, Alari!' It was Mainao. He jumped up from the bed.

'Mainao!' he called out and came out of the room.

She put her finger on her lips silently asking him to keep quiet. He held on to her extended hand. He led her beyond the compound. He felt as if in his palms he held a soft, warm sparrow. Under the light of the pale moon, they walked and at last reached their private spot under the peepul tree on the hillock. The pani-pia's call 'pani piu-piu' rang through the air.

She was wearing an orange dokhana, knotted over the breasts. Now she took out from its folds a small packet, a couple of hand-woven handkerchiefs, a woollen shawl, two gamochas.

'If my stepmother sees you, she will teach you a lesson,' he said.

'The money for buying the thread and wool comes from my own pocket; I sold two of my pigs,' Mainao said and now took out something wrapped in a paper; it contained three one hundred rupee notes.

'So much money? Where did you get it?'

'Do you know how much money I got for the two pigs?' Mainao was smiling happily.

He felt the warmth of the sparrow in his palms now travelling to his body.

'Tomorrow, I'll go away. How would you …'

He wanted to ask her how she would feel. Her lips trembled like the whistling wind crossing through the tora grass shrubs:

When you go to the Bao Khungi hills
When you go to the Bou Kumari hills
To cut wood
Be careful, don't let the axe fall on your feet …

When she sat like this and sang, her voice softly rippling, her hair flying in the wind, Mainao seemed like a stranger to him. She was not the Mainao he saw during the day, picking up the cow dung, sweeping the courtyard, collecting ash from the wooden stove to throw outside. Now she seemed to be transformed into the heroine of the story she told him—Phulmuthi with her long hair … a honey-like voice that calmed the soul … a nose sharp like the thorn of a ghora kagzi lemon tree. The round moon seemed to hang from the branches of the tree. The moonlight filtering through the dark leaves of the huge tree wove patterns on Mainao's dokhana. He could only look on.

He opened his palm to show her the chain; he had bought it for five rupees at the bus stand on way to Guwahati. The thin white chain sparkled in the moonlight. He tried to show it to her, but Mainao was looking at the moon hanging from the branches of the tree. He saw that the moonbeams created white beads of a precious chain he could not afford to buy on her cheeks and now fell one by one on her lap. She leaned against his arms and now the beads fell on his lap too. Her lips, her slim body, were trembling like the leaves of a tora plant:

The dove is cooing
O' dear, I too shall go with you
The crow is cawing
O' darling, I too shall fly with you
The horse neighs
O handsome young man
Untie the knot of your gamocha

The chain was still lying in his palm. He was looking at her as if mesmerized. She bowed her head. As he tried to put the chain around her neck the loose knot of her dokhana came undone. Moonlight was now painting designs not on her clothes but on her body like a bamboo shoot without the skin.

He felt a strange sense of lightness within him. There was no apprehension or excitement of going to the town the next day any more; he was not angry with his stepmother's behaviour; he was not feeling silent resentment at his father's callousness; neither an overwhelming love for Father, not even Mainao was in his mind. His heart was singing like the ciphun flute made of hollow bamboo:

My dear
Untie the knot of your gamocha
My darling, release my hair from the bun
My love, I won't release your hair
So darling, I won't untie your gamocha either
But why not, why shouldn't we?
We will, and drink in the beauty of each other

His heart was getting overrun by the whistling wind in the tora grass shrubs. The sky in the east was getting light. But he was unable to get up with the weight of that ringing sound in his chest. His eyes closed slowly. He lay down under the tree with the new shawl Mainao had given him wrapped around his body.

Mainao's ears filled with the screeching sound of mice in old woman Ahem's clothes bag; she had kept the betel-nut and leaf from heaven to eat with her man. Her dokhana was stained by the red spit from the betel nut and betel leaf that old man Ahem had given to dozens of young man and women.

The courtyard was full of people from the village. Though looking displeased, his stepmother offered them betel nut with leaf to welcome them. Mainao had swabbed the earthen courtyard with cow dung and water early in the morning. The earthen lamp near the basil plant at the pedestal of Bathou was also lighted up as on other days. The people were sitting looking towards the north-east corner. Now they sent for Mainao to appear. She appeared in a blood-red dokhana woven with yellow and green flowers. She knelt down in front of the crowd. She bit into the white chain he had given her and pronounced his name—not her secret name but the one all others knew him by: Hari. He too came and knelt down beside her. Old Boloram Narjari stroked his straggly white stubble. The people were waiting. He would pronounce his judgement soon. Old man Boloram was the one who had brought Mainao to the house of Hari's father. He lived in a cottage behind their kitchen garden. He lived alone; he had a son who had died. Mainao did the household chores in his house after finishing the work here. Afterwards, she would often sit at his feet handing him the cerja. The mournful tune from the instrument sang a lullaby to the two sad souls, spread warmth and wrapped them with musical notes. Sometimes the old man did not take help of the cerja to sing words of comfort to Mainao.

Now old man Boloram ran his fingers through the sparse hair on his chin and laughed aloud, his toothless mouth wide open. The people were familiar with this laughter, his voice strong and unwavering and yet so sweet. For many years now, villagers of Botabari had been mesmerized by this voice which was like a thorkha made of bamboo. He sang:

Aham Mahadeo maha phorbu
Arou chir bauoi

Hail O great Mahadev!
Hail to others too!
The way they have sinned
We have punished them likewise …

Elephants cry at the base of Odal tree
Man cries at Mahadev's feet …

When he goes to fish, when he goes to hunt
Do not frighten him with your maya
Thinking that he has sinned …

Mainao could feel her skin crawl. Then hair on her skin stood up on end. She had committed a sin. Alari would go away to another land. Her ears filled with old man Boloram's deep voice. Her tears washed over the pedestal of Bathou sanctified with cow dung water. When she knelt down to take blessings from the elders in the village she clung to Boloram's feet repeating, 'Abou … grandpa!' She wanted to say it was her fault, not his, please do not let any harm come to him. But she could not say anything; she only cried her heart out.

But the people were happy; they were more relaxed now. Old man Boloram had spent from his own pocket to organize the feast. The earthen pitchers had zumai, the liquor prepared by Mainao herself. The liquor made Boloram's voice even more cheerful:

The virgin hen, alone in the room
We have captured her

The people clapped matching the beat. Boloram sang on:

Come, come, let's make merry
Let's celebrate to our heart's content

Ponds of zumai, mounds of meat, unending supply of rice. The people were happy indeed.

By now, the women were intoxicated drinking the zumai too. Old man Boloram was singing:

Women, enjoy! Enjoy to the full
Today is a day of festivities
Birds stay in pairs
God created man and woman to stay in pairs too
So enjoy, dance, bless the young couple

The courtyard, smooth with Mainao's expert swabbing, was now getting dusty. It was bound to be. Because Boloram was singing:

Dance, dance, you women
Let your hands and feet move
Swaying as if in the wind

Mainao's Alari was under the spell of zumai too. He went to her and looked at her soft lips; they were heavy with suppressed tears. She did not even look at him.

Someone from among the group of women sang:

Do not weep, dear, do not weep
You are not getting married to a Nepali
Nor to a plains man of the valley
You are going home with a young Boro man

Old man Boloram was well aware of the mood of Hari's stepmother. So he announced, then and there, that from now on Mainao and Hari would stay with him. Whatever he had would be inherited by them too.

So Mainao got married. She was not a bird or a pig to be confined indoors forever. Like the breeze, like the flowers falling from branches, a girl who was not a bird, or a pig, could not be confined forever within a cage.

Boloram took both Hari and Mainao into his house. A new cottage had already been built for them. He told Hari to bring out another pitcher of zumai. Mainao in her red dokhana entered the new house. The old man was intoxicated well and good now and started singing in his strong voice:

The wind makes leaves of kacholi shrub go jrob jrob
The peepul leaves rustle khrob khrob
The girl in the red dokhana enters the house
Oi, she has entered the house

Hari found Mainao sitting with her head between her knees and weeping. He put his hand on her back. She got up instantly. Her eyes were angry and irritated. He was surprised. She ran out and went to Boloram's cottage and shook him, calling again and again, 'Abou … grandpa!' The old man was just slipping into a light slumber. He jumped up, shocked. He saw that her face was pale with fear. She pointed to the bamboo grove in the east. A few crows were cawing; the night's festivities, the singing, the sound of *cerenja* had frightened them into waking up even before daybreak. 'Abou, Asagi–Baisagi got caught while trying to steal flowers from Chandrabao's garden. Chandrabao freed them from the trap, but his hands brushed against them. Nobody knew about it, except the stars and the moon in the sky. In the morning, the big crow started cawing ominously, "Somebody in the village had done *badunga zabai*, the sin was committed'".

'Abou, Abou!' Mainao pleaded with him. She knew he would now go on telling the story. He was too drunk to answer her questions. She wanted to ask him about the cawing crows, of her Alari who had committed the taboo of *badunga zabai*, about those who put him into danger disguising themselves when he went to hunt or fish, of wise old Moun Ching-Ching who came down from the heavens to pass judgement on mere mortals and also to punish, the story of Chandrabao and Asagi-Baisagi and how they were rescued. But she could ask nothing; under the spell of zumai, the old man lay slumped on a mat on the floor itself.

She got up and went to the corner with Bathou and prayed. She then returned to the new house. Her Alari was asleep on the bamboo cot. She took out a sack, spread it on the floor and went to sleep.

She was dreaming. She was entering a garden full of many fruits. At the hand's reach was a tree of kordoi from where the sweet fruit was hanging. But as soon as she tried to pluck one, she got into the trap. A handsome young man, the garden's owner, came and freed her. He had a white chain in his hand. As he tried to put it around her neck, the moon in the sky broke into many pieces and drowned her. Next morning, the dhora crows were hopping across the village, cawing. She and Alari were kneeling down in front of wise man Moun Ching Ching who had come down from heaven and was sitting on a golden stool. Both of them did not have a shred of cloth on their bodies; they were condemned to the life of animals. They were in a cottage near the river with a door made of banana leaves. A fire broke out in the cottage and both of them jumped into the water. Then they came out and put on some clothes; they then drank the water mixed with human waste, pig shit and cow dung to purify themselves. The crows stopped cawing; those in disguise disappeared. Boloram burha was singing in his strong voice:

Aham Mahadeo maha phorbu
The way they had sinned
We have punished them likewise
We purified them with fire ...

Mainao woke up. In the east, the sun was up. A few crows were cawing in their usual way. She listened carefully; no it was the usual cawing. She felt that those in disguise had run away. She looked at Alari; he was still sleeping. She smiled. Outside, she found that the courtyard was in a shambles, with young bamboo sticks lying about, a hillock of thatch brought to build their new house. She had hardly any time to clean this side after doing all the chores Hari's stepmother had ordered her to do. She just collected the water, washed the utensils and cooked a simple meal for the old man. Now as she stepped onto the courtyard a bamboo stick pierced her pink sole. She pulled it out. Alari would get up after some time; he would have a book or paper in his hand. He never looked down when walking. She observed the surrounding. Oh, what a state it was in! The house looked like an orphan child, crying for attention. There was no one to ask for anything, no one to order anything to be done. Feeling like a mother, she sat down to tie together the loose sticks for a bamboo broom.

She packed his things neatly. She cooked rice and chicken curry early in the morning so that he could eat before going. The all-important Jilmil bus was about to arrive at the chowk. But he sat on the veranda, brooding, and it did not look like he was going to stir. He now declared that he would not go to the town, and that he would cultivate the land of old Boloram. Mainao was extremely angry. First, she went to his father. She found him lying drunk in front of the granary. What advice would this man give? His stepmother went on grumbling in the courtyard, 'He has done the right thing. Who's going to arrange his college fees?' She was still angry that her husband had given Hari the forty rupees. Mainao now went to Boloram. He also said, well, if he wanted to stay at home, let him; let him till the land and be happy. Money was another problem. He once had with him a japkhring earring his wife wore till her death, but he sold it to arrange the wedding feast. Now he was penniless. Mainao remembered Father Jonathan again and again who had left for his native state sometime ago. To whom she would turn now?

She called Hari to come inside. He did so; his face was downcast.

'Alari, why are you behaving like this?' she asked.

'I have decided not to go. If I go, who will look after you and Abou? What will you eat? And...' he stopped.

'Say, there's a lot of money required for college education; where will I get that from?'

She ran her fingers through his stiff hair and asked, 'Tell me truthfully, do you want to study in the college or not?'

He was silent; his eyes were full of unshed tears.

'Don't worry, I'm there. Abou will stay with me. There are so many people in the village, don't worry. Don't worry about money either.' She opened the box. It held a few hundred rupee notes.

'Where did you get it?'

'Who else can weave warm shawls like me in the village? Do you think I am a lazy useless woman?'

He kept quiet.

'What now?' she held his hands.

'What about the food?'

'Oh, as if we'll eat rice and chicken curry every day!' she laughed.

More serious now, she said, 'Don't worry. We'll till Abou's land and will have the chicken coop and pigsty to sustain ourselves.'

He couldn't help smiling.

'Who will plough the land? You? Or Abou?'

Mainao's face was sober as she replied, 'My dear Alari! You don't have to plough the land to feed us. Yesterday I spoke to some of the young men in the village, Abou has also talked to them. They have agreed to work as saori, helping as per the village custom. If it's a short stint we don't even have to pay them, giving them zumai will do; not even lunch has to be served to them. People say in my hand the zumai becomes like honey.'

She again burst into laughter.

He wanted to say, you yourself are like a honeycomb but did not utter the words and kept on looking at her face.

She got up to the bamboo cot and brought out some notes from under the pillow and said, 'Look even after giving you the money I have some left. I'll buy a few chickens and ducks, and this time I will also buy a white pig in the weekly bazaar.'

She held his hands and begged, 'Alari, you concentrate on the studies in college, that's all. You must do even better than in the school final.'

'Okay …' He drew a long breath.

'You'll go, Alari?'

'I will but …'

'Don't worry, Abou is here with me.'

'Mainao! Mainao!' A few women had come called out to her.

She looked at Hari and told him, 'They have come to help me. The house has to be organized properly.'

The women were already busy with the work assigned to them. Abou had kept ready walls with woven green bamboo strips. The women now put them up to make enclosures for the chickens and the pigs. They swabbed with wet earth the stove in the kitchen and the walls of the new cottage. One of the women sang while working:

We used to share the betel nut
We used to sleep on the same bed
We had fun together
From today we have parted ways
Your father married you off
Look after the family well, enjoy your new life.

He looked on fascinated at his wife as she moved in and out among the women in the courtyard, clean like a table top to serve food, with tea and sugar He heard her sing in a voice like wind in the tora shrubs

Oh, how time flies by the hour
Even before we have begun, the day seems to gallop away

When she saw him she ran to him and asked, 'Why are you so late?'

He smiled, 'I went to enquire if Jilmil will be coming tomorrow. I also tried to find out if the military is conducting extra checking.'

'Anything wrong anywhere?'

'Nothing much. There was some crossfiring near the reserve forest.'

By now black tea had been made, the cane basket was filled with tekeli pitha steamed cake. The women sat down near Abou, stretching their legs.

Hari went inside the cottage and packed his books and papers. Mainao was illiterate but she arranged his books neatly. She was rather nervous about touching his papers; suppose anything got lost? He looked outside and saw that the women were teasing Mainao. She looked shy. Her face was perspiring with all the labour and became crimson. He felt through his whole being a wind whistling as in the tora shrub.

She wanted to take to bed after lunch, but decided not to. Nowadays her body felt quite heavy; not many days were left before her arms would be heavy with a new arrival. She had lots of things to do now. Yesterday was Mai Bidang ceremony so the first sprig of paddy had already been collected from the field. Abou had kept the paddy stalk with the first rice grain in the huge basket for grains. Today was the day for harvesting. They did not have much land so two part-time workers would do. Her eyes almost closed, heavy with sleep, but she did not go to bed giving in to the age-old belief that doing so immediately after lunch would spoil the harvest. Fortunately the crop was good. There was no man in the family to do the farming; they had to depend on others. Abou had advised, 'Go for bao rice; it's a saviour in hard times, a rice for the poor.'

Who could defy Boloram's advice as he sang in praise of the kekoa bao rice:

The crab in the water
Where do you go?
You'll have enough to eat
I'll manage it at one go

At least there would be no dearth of rice through the year, even if it was a coarse variety. Hari's exam was four months away; by that time she could sell the piglets from the white pig to manage the exam fee. The eggs from the coop paid for the salt and oil. She would have to start weaving the warm shawls earlier this time. She must keep some money for herself too; there were only few months left for the delivery. These days she found it difficult to sleep on one side. She was a heavy sleeper though. He often teased her that if a burglar lifted the whole bamboo cot along with her she would not wake up. Half asleep she would go to the bed, then would be like a piece of wood instantly, and only in the morning when the sky whitened she would wake up. When he was home he studied deep into the night. She never knew when he came to bed. Often he tried to frighten her by saying that a thief might come in and sleep by her side and she would never know. She would only shrug, irritated. She worked untiringly the whole day and so when she retired, her body ached. The veins in her legs contracted with pain.

Like on other days, she got up as soon as dawn broke. She finished cleaning up the night-sullied house and courtyard, then she had a bath and steamed a basket of tekeli pitha and took out the pitcher of zumai. Half-day workers would be happy with zumai. She organized the tea and snacks. Had the young men from the village not helped her, how could she and Abou manage to bring in the harvest?

She had let the shuttle fly a few times on her loom when the young men arrived with their dangoris, sheafs of paddy tied together, on their shoulders. The duli she had covered with earth smoothly was now filled with the ripe rice stalks. She saw a dangori of superior quality sali rice along with the coarse bao grains and looked at the men. They were sitting near Abou. One of them played on a flute made of nara grass. The sunlight danced with the tune of the flute. She brought tea and on a banana leaf the tekeli pitha. But they refused to eat. Mainao was yet to sing to welcome Goddess Lakshmi, deity of the harvest. Was she too proud now that she had got an educated husband? Then she began, keeping with the tune of many flutes made of nara grass:

Ashu mainao, Sali mainao …
Ahu lakhimi, Sali lakhimi
Lakhimi, you are with us
O my heart
O part of my flesh
You are our life …
Ashu mainao, Sali mainao …

As soon as Hari stepped into the courtyard, he smelt the freshly harvested paddy, zumai and the pitha. He took a long breath. Now he smelt her too. Everybody looked at him. He had brought all his books. The college was closed for two months. He had also stopped the private tuitions for the time being. He would prepare for the exam studying at home. The men who had worked for her got up to leave. She ran to point to the dangori of sali rice. A young man smiled and said, 'Our boy lives and studies in the city, how can he eat coarse bao rice?' Mainao felt embarrassed. But they had already reached the front gate, playing on their grass flutes.

When his exam results were announced, Mainao gave birth to her son. He looked like her, fair, rounded, bright eyed. Whoever saw him wanted to take him in their arms. His father gave him the name Siddhartha. She did not like this kind of name; she could not even pronounce it. She was always on alert. Would her adorable son be harmed by so much attention? So she named him Daokhi, which meant chicken shit. She wanted to protect her dear son from the demons in the air by giving him an awful name.

Mainao became obsessed with her child's well-being. She always placed him under a mosquito net when he fell asleep. The demoness Than-Thin could not enter through a net. She was the one whose head shone like a comet when she went around the earth at night; if she touched a dead body, it turned black like ash, if her mouth touched cooked rice and curry, they turned black too.

She never let the baby sleep naked. Her husband said, 'Good, he won't suffer from malaria.' She hung the scaly skin of the pangolin on the baby's plump neck; she never stepped on places where people threw leftover food in case the baby got affected by the *sua* of the unclean. If her son suffered from even a small infection, to shoo away the bad omen she would collect milk from a black cow and, putting it in a banana-leaf cup, chant a mantra like she had learnt from Abou:

Isi najar bisi najar
I touched the untouchable
With this I drive away the bad omen

This way she also drove away her own fear for her child. If Daokhi vomited sometimes or had loose motion, she would go even farther with her rituals. As soon as the evening set in, she would bring a half-broken wok, put mustard seeds, dry chillies and with a stick from a bamboo broom chant, *Isi khuga bisi khuga jo kham* … with this I burn all,' believing that the ill omen about to fall on her son was burnt in the wok. Sometimes when Hari looked at his plump son suckling his mother's breast hungrily even he became a little superstitious. What would happen if Abou was not there? Mainao's world revolved around the baby, pigs, chickens, her loom, her house and Abou. If somehow three years could be passed, he would be a graduate. He was not sure what was happening around him and to his people. They were like the characters from a Greek mythology where the courageous young man looking for the golden fleece threw a stone among the dragons to start a war among themselves. They did not bother to find out who had thrown the stone, and from where. Brothers fought like snakes and mongooses. He often balked with apprehension. He had decided to take English major after passing the Higher Secondary exam. The books for English honours were quite expensive. Could he manage with his earning as a private tutor? How much pressure Mainao could take? He felt his chest contract when he thought of her.

Suddenly he saw that a group of boys had entered their compound. They were not like the boys who came in the morning to help Mainao and played on pipes of nara grass, their bodies undulating with the rhythm of carrying the heavy baskets of paddy.

He asked Mainao to go inside and went to meet them at the gate. They wore boots, uniforms like military fatigues and on their shoulders were slung the latest model of guns. He felt his legs tremble at their sight.

'What do you want?' he asked, his voice hardly audible.

'We have come to eat. Rice with chicken curry. Bring out zumai too,' they ordered and sat in the courtyard.

Mainao cooked the rice. She wept when she had to kill the hen, which had just started laying eggs. But they did not drink the zumai though they had ordered Hari to bring it. They drank from bottles of foreign liquor they had brought with them. While gulping down the rice and curry, they threatened him that he should not be selfish thinking of his own studies and keep living in the town; they had got together to fight for their own state; he must also join in.

That night Mainao could not sleep. Hugging her knees, she wept through the night. If they took Alari away what would happen to her? She said repeatedly, 'You go away to the town, don't worry, they won't do anything to us, only you…' Her voice became smaller and smaller.

The next morning boys of the other party visited them and warned him that he was a student and should remain so. 'Don't get involved with them, the army is going to target you,' they said, 'Tonight itself the soldiers are going to come to the village and go searching from house to house; he should make himself scarce' etc.

The young men of the village hid themselves in the reserve forest. The news that the soldiers were coming had spread by now. The group which ate at Mainao's place had placed a bomb under a bridge and an army truck had fallen victim; two of the injured soldiers had died. Mainao sent Alari away too to join the fleeing men.

True to the rumour, the soldiers arrived at night and scoured through the village. All the members of the group who had blown up the bridge were not able to flee to the hills; three of them had died in the army firing. The villagers understood that the two parties would be on the warpath next. Unless somebody in the know pointed out the dilapidated house on the edge of the cremation ground where the militants hid it was not possible for the army to know.

In the morning when Hari returned he found that Abou was taken away by the army to the town for questioning. People came to know that the group of militants had had lunch at their place. In the morning, he got ready to leave for the town. A few elderly men, including his father, had also been taken away by the soldiers. He went to see his stepmother. The usually quarrelsome woman was crying quietly. He felt uneasy. Somehow the woman who was ready to quarrel at the drop of a hat was more familiar, more acceptable, to him now. Not only his stepmother, everything seemed to have changed around him.

Accompanied by some other young men from the village, he made rounds of the police thana and military base to get a release order. When he arrived at the bus stand with Abou and the other elderly men, he saw his English teacher coming towards him. The teacher thumped on his back enthusiastically and exclaimed, 'Well done! Well done!' He was surprised. Seeing his uncomprehending look, the professor clarified, 'You have obtained the highest mark in English in the university. Just six more marks and you'd have got a rank.'

'When did the results come out, Sir?' he asked.

'Yesterday. You didn't know?'

'No.'

'Now where do you plan to take admission? In our college?'

'I won't study any more, Sir!'

'What do you mean, Alfred?'

The bus, Jilmil, was ready to leave. He jumped into it. He saw that the professor with a bag on his shoulders was looking at him astounded. He waved to him from the bus.

Hari decided to work in the school attached to the church. He would get five hundred rupees a month. Mainao did not say anything to that. The ever-laughing woman seemed afraid all the time. Not only her, but the whole village seemed to live in constant fear. This year nobody tilled the paddy fields and so they remained bare. Hemmed in by the military presence, frequent fights between the two rival groups, hurling of bombs and gunfights, who would dare to go to the fields to plough? Nowadays nobody came to ask for advice or judgement from Abou either; whoever had a gun or bomb in hand passed a ruling. Abou's deep voice like the kharga now got buried in the thut thut thut of guns. In his ninety-year-old life, Boloram had never seen so many young men die. These deaths made his old heart tremble with sorrow. In the backyard of his house, there was a bamboo grove; nobody used the bamboos from here except for making biers for the dead. For a long time, no one from the village had come to cut bamboo from this grove. Nobody had approached him to lead the departed soul to the cremation ground with a bamboo stalk wrapped with ewa thread nine times around it. The bodies of the young unmarried men lay without the customary banana trees planted towards their heads indicating a companion on way to the nether world. At the place where the bodies of the two women were left, raped and killed, nobody planted a peepul tree branch chanting a mantra—*dun thaorai, badi khanai phiphor*—wishing for them to have enough thick hair to make buns like the wheels in the next life. Nobody placed near a dead body a *saratia*, a coin to give to the boatman, for the soul to cross the river, a dao to cut wood, a pot to cook rice. People who were used to following the rituals to lead the soul after death to the life beyond were now afraid all the time. Nowadays old man Boloram sat in the courtyard with his eyes closed. Sometimes it felt as if he were a dead body ready to be taken to the cremation ground. After burning the bodies, the villagers would return wearing wet gamochas; they would then chew sukuta greens and spit and say, *thu thu alai balai*—we have left you forever.

The school at the church had been closed indefinitely. The bao rice in the duli was finished; only the bag of sali rice that Mainao had kept aside was left. The coop held a single chicken. Those men with guns on their shoulders were greedy like the witch Than-Thin. At any odd hour, they demanded a curry to be cooked with whatever they could find—goat, pig, chicken, duck, pigeon. If they had not devoured so much, the supply of rice would not have finished so quickly.

After spending two days and two nights on boiled yams, Mainao borrowed some rice grains from a neighbour's house. She ground it and made Hari pluck two coconuts and scraped the meat. She then packed the pitcher for steaming pitha, a few pieces of clean clothes, a bundle of firewood, wrapped Daokhi around her back like a rucksack and joined a group of women who sold zumai and pitha at the chawk.

In the evening when she returned she brought with her some rice, salt and small packets of tea and sugar; Alari loved to drink tea when he studied late into the night.

He was lying on the bamboo cot with a book of English words. His English professor had given him this expensive, beautiful book; he had hesitated to accept the present. Suddenly he remembered his college. The new session must have started by now. He felt deeply sad. Mainao entered the room. At first she kissed Daokhi on both his cheeks. After a long time, she had been able to bring a glass of tea for him. He could not drink the tea and sat with his head bowed. Her long hair escaped from her bun. Her voice rang like whistling wind in tarabon shrubs:

On the thatched roof climb white pumpkin creepers
O my dear, you are a man of letters ...
Take this peacock offered to you
Look at its pretty tail
O my dear, you are a man of letters
My slim waist
Hides in your palm ...

He took her hand; it was not so soft any more. As he welcomed the peacock in her she offered him eagerly, he found the bird's feathers had many colours, many patterns.

Most of the men in the village were engaged in breaking stones for road construction now. Huge chunks of stones from the turbulent river arrived everyday by trucks. Hari too joined the workers. As he sat on his haunches breaking the stones, he saw them often, moving on red-coloured motorcycles with guns slung on their shoulders. Sometimes he saw them whisking away some terrified person from the town or somewhere nearby to their camp beyond the river. He had heard from others like him that those men were hoarding lakhs of rupees.

Mainao avoided looking at his palms full of boils, some ready to burst. She had woven three woollen shawls and kept them aside. Those were the last ones on her loom. Where would she get the thread? Where was the money to buy wool now? Even selling the woollen shawls was getting difficult. Nowadays traders did not come this way. Mainao was used to working all her life; she came to Abou's dilapidated house and turned it into a neat cottage with a courtyard so clean anyone could sit there and have lunch; when winter came she wove woollen shawls; she tended to the coop and pigsty for the extra income; if her dokhana was torn she wove a new one herself; if there was shortage of rice she made pitha and sold in the bazaar for money to buy some. But now she felt helpless; what could she do when all these male versions of the demoness Than Thin roamed the land?

That day as she got ready to go to the bazaar with her paraphernalia for making pitha she heard that the military had blocked off the road to the chawk. Hari had gone out early in the morning to the road construction site. There was not a grain of rice at home. She felt like cursing someone. Was there a curse on her from a former life? The haitha bird carried a curse from a former life, and so today if it landed on earth, it could not fly again and stayed rooted. The water leech that could not be pierced by any hard object could be pierced by stalks of jute; it was due to a curse. She wondered if there was a curse on her, her Alari, her Daokhi—on the whole village. What was their fault that they suffered like this? She felt a pain in a corner of her breast. No, no, in her dream Bathou told her that she had been purified.

She could not hang around doing nothing; she had to keep busy. So now she lit a fire with the firewood she was going to carry to the bazaar. On top of it she placed the broken wok. She put some mustard seeds and dry chillies in it and, with five sticks from the bamboo broom used to sweep the dirt, stirred them. The mustard seeds started spluttering. All her anger, resentment and helplessness burst out as she chanted: *Noungkhow aobai aang* … I've fried you. Don't you feel your body burning like these mustard seeds …'

After many days, she heard Abou's voice. His voice trembled as he chanted too.

'Like the mustard seeds, let your body break out in hot boils.'

She gnashed her teeth as she continued her curse: 'You have done this to us, you'll suffer like this too.'

She did not know to whom she directed this terrible curse—to the military? To those in the jungle? Someone else? But at last, she felt at peace. Then she wrapped Daokhi on her back and stepped out on to the road. Oh, if she could sell even one of her woven shawls, even if at half the price!

Hari was sitting in the courtyard. He could not go to work today; the boils in his palms had burst. Mainao had ground some raw turmeric and applied it on his hands. Daokhi was learning to walk now, moving his plump body on tiny feet to explore the world around him.

'Alfred!' he jumped up. This is how people outside knew him. He saw a familiar looking scooter, blue in colour, and then saw that his English professor was coming towards his house. With him was Asim who had once come to his house. Bordoloi 'Sir' and Asim's eyebrows were full of dust, their hair seemed white; the black trousers and white shirt his professor wore had turned an unrecognizable colour; even the scooter looked more brown than blue. Seeing the unfamiliar people at her doorstep, Mainao came running. As soon as she saw him, she knew that it was the professor Alari was always talking about. She recognized Asim too. Looking at their appearance, she felt her chest heaving with sadness. She went inside to bring a gamocha and a pitcher of water to help them wash up and stood at a little distance. There were four eggs in the house; she put them in a pan on the fire to boil them.

Professor Bordoloi looked at Hari's hands and asked, 'What happened?'

He did not want to say anything and asked instead, 'Sir, how did you manage to come through this horrendous road?'

'Actually I didn't drive; after we left the town, Asim was the one who drove.'

'Did you have anything particular to do this side?' He asked, genuinely surprised.

'Why, we've come to meet you.'

'Me? Why?' he was even more surprised.

'We came to find out why you've decided not to study any more.'

Hari could not say anything, only his eyes became wet with unshed tears. Mainao offered them a plate with the boiled eggs. She was not sure if these townsfolk would eat them. She felt ashamed that she could not offer them a cup of tea. But when she saw them devouring the eggs, she felt happy.

The professor placed his hand affectionately on the shoulder of his favourite student and said, 'I've spoken to the principal; he has agreed to write off your fees. You'll also be able to borrow books from the library. Asim has a room in the courtyard; you can stay there.'

'And Alfred, you'll eat at our place. I have also taken English major. We will study together. If you hadn't helped I would not have been able to get a first division,' Asim said.

'Every month you'll get two hundred rupees from me,' the professor smiled, 'I'm not writing it off. When you get a job afterwards you can return the money.'

Hari stood up and said, 'Sir, you don't understand; it won't be possible.'

'Alfred! Winners never quit, quitters never win,' the professor said.

Mainao called him inside. She handed him the warm shawl she had kept to sell even if at half the price, and asked him to give it to his teacher.

Professor Bordoloi was all praise for the beautiful gift. He wanted to tell the shy woman about women like Jonali Barua of Sivasagar, how they had brought women like her together to start cooperatives, how these poor women earned money enough to have two meals a day. He wanted to tell her how these products travelled beyond to Delhi and Kolkata, how Jonali put her son at the rear of her bicycle and visited villages to seek out expert weavers like Mainao. She could help Mainao too. The next time when she came to Guwahati he would bring Jonali here and Mainao could show her work to her. Professor Bordoloi also said that the threads and other necessary things would be supplied by the cooperative, she would only have to weave this kind of design and they would also buy the finished items at the right price. If she wanted Mainao could also open a branch of the cooperative here. Jonali would come willingly if she was invited by the village women. But Mainao was too shy to come out of the house so the professor told all this to Alfred.

He asked, 'Are you sure they'll come here?'

Professor Bordoloi wanted to tell him about Jonali's political ideology, her struggle, but he did not say anything now. It would not be appropriate. He said instead, 'Please come along with Alfred one day. My wife would be very happy to receive this pretty shawl.'

He debated whether he should leave behind some money as a cost for the shawl at least. But with his experience of working in this area for twenty years, he knew that it would be insulting to them. On many instances, he had come across their strong sense of self-respect.

So while leaving, he just put his hands on Hari's shoulder and said, 'I've already organized your admission.'

Asim started the scooter. Bordoloi looked back as he got into the pillion seat. Mainao was stepping into the courtyard, the baby wrapped on her back; she was smiling shyly.

Professor Bordoloi had come to the college a little earlier than usual today. But even then he found that almost all the teachers had arrived, and the principal was there too. There was no air of levity in the teachers' common room today. All of them sat solemnly. There was going to be an emergency meeting soon, but there would not be any agenda and there would not be any record of the meeting either. They had received a communication from the militants; they had fixed rupees fifty thousand per head for the eighty teachers, altogether forty lakh, which had to be paid within the next week. From where would they get so much money? After deduction and all, they got at most six to seven thousand rupees. By the end of the month, they kept looking out for the date of next month's salary. When the principal and a few senior teachers had gone to meet the leaders at the camp in the jungle they had AK 47 rifles aimed at their heads. The teachers used bicycles to enter interior parts. High tension hung in the air. The police and the military had come to warn them against giving the extortion money. On the other hand, the letters kept coming in during the last month; as a first instalment they had decided to give five thousand rupees per person, but who would be the carrier? How to go about it? The police and military had told them that if there was an encounter the terrorists could escape but they would die instead in the crossfire. So they were overwhelmed with dread and fear. The students were coming regularly though, classes were not cancelled either, at least not yet. Whenever there was a meeting, somehow the law keepers came to know; even the walls had ears.

Suddenly sparks of fire filled the newly built well-appointed professors' common room. It became full of smoke; something was burning. They scrambled out of the room. Many saw a few men with their faces hidden behind strips of clothes and guns on their shoulders running away through the orange grove. Nobody was injured; the aim was not to bomb the place but frighten them. The students ran helter-skelter. It was as if the sparks were ready to ignite a bunch of dry grass. It would burn and turn into a big fire in no time. The girls started running here and there. As they looked on, Alfred ran to shut the big gate and also the two small ones. Then he climbed up on the stones piled up there. The fair complexioned boy turned crimson under the strain. Then he lifted his hands to the sky and shouted, 'We condemn this heinous crime, we won't side with any terrorist …' He spoke of hope, 'Things won't remain the same.'

Then he recited Shelley: '*If winter comes. Can spring be far behind?*'

He was speaking of Prometheus and his fire, of humanity, of struggle.

Suddenly Professor Bordoloi forgot his worry, fear and apprehension. He listened to Alfred spellbound. He realized that he did not have to hold this boy's hands any more; he had learnt to walk.

Mainao did not have to carry around Daokhi these days, he liked to run around on his own. Abou had fashioned a spinning wheel out of jackfruit leaves. He loved to run with it in hand making a sound like *bhu-bhu*. He also had left breast milk. When she had some time, she lifted him and, hugging him kissed resoundingly, and sang:

O' hetuluka bird, O' parrot on the tree
You cry but there's no one to take you in the lap
You jump, you dance around but there's no one to look after you

Often Daokhi would cry out as his mother pressed him hard to her breasts. He too had so much to do! Abou had made this spin, his father had brought him a ball from the town, and there was the dhakua—a sledge made of betel leaves, also the wooden car his father had made last time when he had come home. Mainao would smile but somewhere she felt a pain, she missed the child in her lap. At these moments, she yearned for Alari the most. Earlier he would come home on Sundays or any holiday. Since he had shifted to Guwahati it had not been possible. It was difficult, she knew. Her lonely heart expressed itself as she wove a cloth on the loom:

I miss you when I wash the utensils
I miss you when I have my bath
O my darling, you live beyond the river, you're a man of letters
O my darling, you're a man of letters

Of late she had been suffering from pain in her elbows; when she wove cloth on the loom or swept the courtyard, she could feel this nagging pain, especially when she let the shuttle-cock fly. She had to rest from time to time. Today the air was not misty. The hills were silhouetted clearly against the blue sky. Sometimes clouds scattered over the sky like simolu cotton flowers in the spring wind. In the mango tree near her loom, two yellow sokhioti birds were quarrelling; a yellow feather fell on her loom and got lost in the mustard yellow cloth. She could feel her mind stray as she hummed, '*O my dear one beyond the river.*'

She jumped up at a sudden sound. It was Abou playing his cerza. Now she sang aloud:

The wide leaves of the akchi tree
Wish I could hear his voice free
The akchi leaves are about to fall
My mind on the run to my darling, that's all
O the leaves of the akchi tree…'

He had not come home for quite a few months now. She wondered if he was finding it difficult to survive in the big city, whether he was having money trouble. She had now been able to save some money; she would give it him when he came next. After one faction of the insurgents had surrendered to the government, the villagers had been able to plough the fields and could also keep pigs and chickens at home. She had worked as a *saori* this time helping in the field and there was rice at home too. Though not everyday, she often went to the chawk to sell pitha. She had heard that there was some big project going on at the place where Alari lived now because she saw truckloads of stones taken from here everyday. In this remote place with few stalls, the snacks Mainao and the village women made were finished within no time. So she could buy salt and oil with that money. A boy who stayed near her house worked in the bus that plied between the village and the town. A few boys who had surrendered had taken lease of the bus; it left in the morning and returned in the evening. Professor Bordoloi arranged for the wool and thread supplied by the women from the cooperative in Sivasagar to be sent to Mainao through this boy; she on her part sent through him the finished products and earned some money and kept it aside for Alari.

Sometimes she thought of those girls who had visited her village from so far away. How they had praised the 'daothu godu' dokhana she had woven. She was so shy that she could hardly answer them when they asked how she had woven it. She could only point to the dove which was cooing in the courtyard. The girls had smiled and asked again. She had explained, her voice almost inaudible, *daothu*—dove, *godu*—neck. The girls understood immediately, the dokhana was designed like the neck of the bird. When they inspected her woven *farou megon* dokhana, she did not wait for them to ask her and had pointed to the pigeon; she wanted to tell them that the flowers on the dokhana were like the eyes of the pigeon. The girls had laughed and said, so *farou*—pigeon, *megon*—eyes, so 'farou megon'—pigeon's eyes? By now she had lost some of her shyness. When they were ready to leave she had felt her eyes well up with tears. She had decided that when Alari finished his studies and got a job she would go to the girls' village and have a look at their looms. Even for the plain *chala-matha* dokhanas she wove without any flowers, they paid twice the amount the middlemen gave for the embellished dokhanas. She planned that when Alari got a job she would weave a warm shawl with *farou megon* for that woman in the distant Sivasagar. Sometimes she remembered Alari's professor who had come to visit them, his face and eyes buried in dust. He not only gave Alari two hundred rupees a month but also quite a big sum of money when he went to Guwahati. Alari must return the money when he got a job, she thought.

Mainao started cutting the finished dokhana from the loom. She was yet to start cooking. As she did not go to the chawk today, she had time to think of this and that. She had started to weave a plain *chala-matha* dokhana for herself and handkerchiefs for Alari. She must weave her husband's handkerchiefs along with her own. She was forbidden to give these handkerchiefs to any other man; if she did, in the afterlife, she would have to live with that man like his wife. She folded the handkerchiefs one by one. Tears flowed down her cheeks. The chain he had given her was now discoloured. A teardrop fell down where the chain touched her body and she shivered. She hummed:

The dove is cooing
O' dear, I too shall go with you.

Mainao was sweeping the courtyard. Daokhi had this habit of driving his wooden car over the garbage to make the place dirty again and again. She got angry; knotting her mekhela on her breast, she chased him with a stick. Daokhi ran and found himself in the embrace of his father who had just entered the compound. Instantly her anger turned into a wide smile.

After hearing the news, the villagers crowded into her courtyard. He had got a prestigious job in Delhi. In the competitive exam, he was the only one from the tribal community of Assam to achieve the honour. He would have to join the new posting next week. Mainao was exhausted offering betel nut and leaf to the guests; they were coming in an unending stream to congratulate him. She had also exhausted the tea leaves and sugar in the little containers, even the betel nuts and leaves were finished. Mainao's women friends came too. All of them had tea, betel nut and leaf, and blessed her. Mainao did not know who brought the tea leaves, who brought sugar or betel nuts, and who distributed the food. She did not even have time to look at his face. Hari's father and stepmother treated them with rice and chicken curry. Now his father and Abou sat together sharing a pitcher of zumai. The stepmother too offered betel nut and leaf to the people. To be part of the community and work together in a gatha, to help each other in need she must go to the house even if it belonged to her vilest enemy. She cooked a delicious fish curry with dried sol fish and tomatoes. Hari spent some time with his father and Abou and then came to her.

'I'll get a lot of money as salary. You won't have to toil so much from now on. Tell me what you want,' he said.

She covered Daokhi with a sheet and sat, her head bowed. Then she said, 'A girl.'

He laughed aloud and then looked at her. Truly, even after so much hard work, she had remained a pretty young woman, her face like the leaf of a tara plant, her waist slender as an ant's.

He left for Delhi. These days Mainao did not go to sell pitha in the chawk; she did not sell clothes either. He sent money every month from Delhi. From it, she saved some money. She had plans to buy some land. She could employ a man to plough the land; she could not expect people to help her working as *saoris*. Now she was the wife of a salaried person. Things were different before; now how could she ask for free assistance from others? These days her body felt quite heavy too. When she was expecting Daokhi she somehow did not feel so redolent. This time she also had fever quite often. Abou gave her some traditional medicine but it did not help much. Abou himself was not keeping well these days. One day when she went to serve him lunch she found him lying immobile, his body stiff.

Hari could not see him in his last moments. Seeing Mainao, he understood immediately that she was suffering from malaria. The villagers advised him to take her along with him. Times were not good; how could she live alone with the little son? Mainao did not say yes or no to the proposal; she just sat in the veranda with her head resting on her knees. He got irritated and one day he said, he would take Daokhi with him; she could choose whether wanted to go with him or not. Mainao looked at him—in these few months, he had changed; his clothes were different, he spoke differently; he even looked different. She felt like laughing; these days he even scolded her—her Alari!

The house which had newly installed tin sheets, the chickens, the spotted goat, the fat pigs, the rice grains in the duli—all these they gave to Hari's father to look after and got ready to go to Delhi. Her stomach was now protruding from behind the dokhana. He decided to take her to Guwahati by car instead of the bus. They crossed the broken bridges, the potholed roads, drove through water where the streams did not have bridges, and at last got into the train to Delhi. He had booked tickets in an air-conditioned coach. He was not going to let her travel in discomfort.

Mainao slept all through the journey. The pills given by village compounder Ratan to keep the fever under check were not effective any more. While approaching Delhi, he wanted to tell her about the peacocks he saw roaming like common sparrows, of Lal Qila, Qutub Minar, of Agra with its Taj Mahal, of apple orchards of Kashmir, but could not. She slept all the time, her fever rising.

Alfred had brought medicine for her fever from Guwahati. In Delhi, everybody knew him by this name and so he stuck to it. Towards the morning, she felt a little better. She could hear cocks crowing; the white birds were so beautiful. She was throwing rice grains and they were surrounding her. She opened the pigsty; now the two fat pigs ran towards the kitchen garden. On the tin roof, a pair of doves was teasing each other. She dragged the white and black spotted goat with a rope and tied it to a bamboo pole. The paddy had been harvested halfway, the other part of the field still lying with ripe grains. A flock of tuni birds flew in and disappeared among the stubs of the naked paddy field. She threw a clod of earth towards them; they flew away, scared. What had she done? She drove away a flock of birds that had come for food? Suddenly she felt very guilty. The rays of the sun travelled like birds through the mist and fell on the paddy field. After some time, she went to the newly built toilet. She had a new house now with tin roofs, modern toilet, wooden bedstead with cotton-wool mattress and warm quilt instead of bamboo *chang*. Her mind brightened up like the malati flowers blooming in the corner of the veranda. She was so happy; after a few days her little girl would happily play here with Alari. The train was going over a bridge; it was making a crunching sound. She jumped up. Where was she? She saw passengers sleeping on bunks on both sides. A man was passing the corridor with kettles of tea. She felt like going to the toilet. She looked at Alari. He was in deep sleep with Daokhi by his side. She hesitated. How could she wake him up to take her to the toilet?

Alighting at the station in Delhi, she gave up her shyness and holding his hand uttered, 'So many people!' If she got lost here, what would she do? Alfred took her to a place which he called home; they went up in a lift. She was scared of this box going up with a *gharr gharr* sound and held his hand fearfully. He opened the door to the flat. Two small rooms, a smaller corner for a kitchenette, a small bathroom with a commode and bathing space. She felt like laughing out loud. Even her chicken's coop and the goat cage were bigger than this house! She was scared of lighting the gas stove; she would try and then withdraw the lighter. She could not believe that on this small little circle of fire one could cook rice. Hari made the tea himself. She refused to have the milk brought in a packet and had black tea instead. She felt like laughing at everything—the way he made tea, the sets of churidar-kameez he had bought for her, the flush in the toilet, the lift. Looking at her bewildered face, he also broke into laughter. And seeing them like this, Daokhi also laughed.

Mainao clutched her stomach in pain. The doctor feared she would lose her baby. The blood test showed that she had contracted malaria. The doctor asked again and again—what had she done to cause this trauma to the unborn baby; did she ride a horse? The doctor did not understand, but Hari guessed that though she had travelled by car to Guwahati, the one hundred and thirty kilometre road with potholes and broken bridges had done that to her. After all, he could not build a bridge for his Mainao, neither could he build a metal road. His own aunt died on that road while being taken to the hospital; the same fate took his mother. Who knew how many pregnant women died on this tortuous road on way to the hospital? He was scared and begged the doctor; he asked him to keep faith in god. Looking at him, Mainao understood that something had happened to the baby in her womb, or something was wrong with her.

Alfred left for office in the morning. He took Daokhi with him to drop at the school and a parent with a child in the same school brought him back. Mainao could not go to fetch him like other mothers. When she stepped out from the small flat the cars on the wide road seemed to chase her. She could not speak the language to hail transport to go to the school. Once she finished cooking, there was nothing much left to do. In the huge building they lived in, so many people lived, but nobody enquired after her; she did not know anyone either. Even the people living just opposite her flat were not familiar to her. At first she was very surprised but these days she had got used to it. Here nobody seemed to know anyone. They were like the cars on the street, running in parallel lines all the time.

She often lay in the big bed in the small room for hours. She moved in and out of light spells of sleep. For the past few days, she also suffered from a nagging cough; her throat felt constricted. Whenever she coughed her lower abdomen felt the pain. She trembled with fear when it happened. She remembered Janki's mother; when she had returned from the town she suffered from excruciating bouts of pain like this.

Janki's mother had been afflicted by *baghnisar*, the spirit of the tigress. She used to roar like a tiger and then fall unconscious. Abou had treated her with the juice of the bhedeli creeper, which Mainao had ground and squeezed out of the leaves herself. Then she had packed a duck's egg in banana leaf and hung it as offering to the unknown and had also offered aroi rice, a brown-coloured coin and sprigs of basil leaf. Janki's mother had recovered and given birth to a healthy son.

In her drowsy state, she often dreamt of Abou, how he had daubed the bhedeli juice on her forehead. She could smell the strong odour of the creeper's leaves . Then she would find herself in a jungle; the trees behaved like the cars, running forward, and she found herself lost in that maze of trees. Waking up with a start, she would sit on the bed; she was quite fat now—the result of lying in bed almost always; her ankles and feet had swollen a lot. Getting bored with walking around in the small rooms, she sometimes stepped out into the tiny balcony that could just about hold three people. She found everything the same every day; there was no change. The same air with an acrid smell, an ash-grey sky that hid the sun and the moon, the wide road with its rows of cars. So she went back to the room to lie down. She fell into a light sleep again. For the last couple of days, she dreamt the same dream. She was getting lost in a forest of running trees; nobody could find her. She could only shout, 'Abou! Abou!' She was sure that she was overtaken by *khetra*, the evil spirit that lived in the fields. If the *khetra* took hold of the body, a pregnant woman's feet swelled. Alari's stepmother too had suffered the same way once when she was in the family way. She dreamt that she was flying around in the sky or got lost in a forest. She was chased by tigers and bears. Her feet swelled, becoming as big as a banana plant. Mainao remembered how Abou had drawn the image of a man with ash on a banana leaf; on both sides of it, nine spots were drawn with vermillion, then a fire was lit with a bunch of dry grass, the stalks from era and dimoru plants. She could feel the man drawn with ash looking at her intently, and the red spots of vermillion seemed to move round and round circling her. She screamed in fear, but in the small room, the scream went around like a whirlwind. She fell asleep again, to be lost again in the forest of the running trees.

These days she tried to resist lying down on the bed all the time. Though she could not relax at first, after sometime her eyes drooped and then she would dream of that forest where she got lost, of that black man drawn with ash chasing her and red vermilion spots encircling her. No, it was better to go out into the balcony; from there she could see the street below. Sometimes it felt that the veranda was hanging over the road. Below, she could see a neem tree; a flock of parrots often came there to eat the neem seeds. Sometimes a squirrel too would come and look at her with rotating eyes. This squirrel was not like the ones in Mainao's village, grey in colour; this one was a mix of muga and yellow colour with ash-coloured stripes, and it had a tail with spots. She felt like catching one to keep it as a pet. When the parrots came, the squirrels came too, and temporarily she forgot about the forest and the black man. She also forgot her swelling feet, the irritating cough, the pain in her lower abdomen, even Alari and Daokhi.

She was organizing breakfast for her son and husband. These days they did not eat rice in the morning, they had bread and butter instead. So she had even less work. The sliced bread came from the market, and also that thing that looked like flat rice; it did not even need washing, just pouring milk over it was enough. Alari did not drink tea at this time but a spoonful of coffee with milk.

That was all. There were hardly any utensils to wash. There was tap water too. She took just five minutes to sweep the small rooms. The floor was white and clean. Alfred usually brought something or the other as snacks on his way back from office. So she did not have to make anything for afternoon tea either. For dinner, Alfred cooked the rice and vegetable curry himself, cheerfully whistling all the time. Idle time sat heavy over her, choking her day and night. Sometimes she got up even in the night to look at the neem tree.

Now it had been four months since she came here. She was two months pregnant then. Soon she would hold a baby in her lap. A tune hummed in her mind:

O moon, o moon, give me a banana
Well, not one, give me two
But I don't have any bananas, what shall I give?
A crow ate up the whole bunch
My father-in-law came but he didn't find any
My mother-in-law came too wearing a woven mekhela

The tune came to her lips and hung there, trembling. The nagging cough swept it away like wind does etchings drawn on sand. She kept looking at the road with empty eyes.

Suddenly she saw that a big red car hit a man with white hair and beard sitting under the neem tree and sped away. The man's white beard was full of blood now. He must have had been about Abou's age. Who had let this old man roam around in this crowd of speeding cars? She could clearly hear the man shouting for water. She felt sad. So many cars were going by, why didn't a single one stop? So many people were walking by, why didn't anyone offer him a drop of water? She felt very agitated. She could hear the injured man's agonized cry. She went down the stairs with a bottle of water. She felt stunned and helpless. What could she do? The man's head had split and blood was oozing out nonstop. She poured a little water in his mouth; the man whispered *'beti, beti'* and then his head lolled to one side. Tears streamed down her cheeks and fell on the man. Suddenly a police van screeched to a halt. They asked her questions in a language she could not understand. She wanted to go home, but the policemen would not allow her to. They took her along to the police station with the dead body. She wept uncontrollably. Even outside of sleep and her dream, she got lost in a forest.

One morning Mainao noticed that policemen had entered the high-rise building opposite her own. They went into the flat which she faced while observing the squirrels busy at work. Often she saw an old couple sitting on that veranda; the old woman sometimes tried to smile when their eyes met. She saw the police carrying out two dead bodies from the house. Later she came to know that the servant had bludgeoned them to death and ran away with the money. For two days and two nights, the old couple lay there, rotting. These days she felt scared to sit on the veranda, fearing the old man with the head injury would call out to her for water; or what if the rotting smell from the opposite flat reached her nose? A day after the old couple was found dead, a wedding was celebrated in the hall at the entrance of the building. Music, aroma of food from the feast, glittering dresses and flowers changed the atmosphere. She felt sad. Only a day had passed since the death of the couple was discovered. She again took to the bed. Closing her eyes, she imagined hugging a little girl. She was afraid, very afraid. A little coughing and she could feel the pain in her lower stomach; her feet were still swelling. Alfred had taken her to the doctor many times. The table in their room was now full of medicine bottles and tablet files. But she still felt unwell. How could she make Alari understand that she could not recover this way; she had been overtaken by the evil spirit of *khetra*. One of her aunt's daughters who was also afflicted by *khetra* had died after giving birth to a daughter. She decided that she would perform a puja to appease the spirit.

After her husband and son left in the morning, she started collecting the things necessary for the puja. She needed a small knife—she had that; joss sticks and an earthen lamp—she had the joss sticks, but for the lamp she had to make do with the cover of a bottle. She filled it with mustard oil and used cotton wool for the wick. In place of betel nut and leaf, she decided to use the betel leaf he had brought for her to chew. For the straw to make a *jumuthi* to light up a fire, she used the straw which had come as packing material for an instrument that apparently could instantly clean the dirt. She had vermilion with her. She took a coin and took out red, white and black threads from her own clothes. But where would she get the things so easily available in her village—a charcoal, branches of era tree, dimoru fruit, bamboo and banana leaf? Where would she find a frog or a bat? The most important thing was a banana leaf where she had to draw the man's image with charcoal surrounded by nine vermilion spots. Where would she get a clod of earth cleansed by cowdung and water?

Mainao was losing her mind. How could a woman possessed by the *khetra* give birth to a daughter? Her cough was getting worse, and with it, the abdominal pain. Alfred brought the doctor home on visit. She looked on; the table top was getting filled with new medicines. How could she explain to him what was happening to her? A blue and dead girl that came out of the stomach of Alari's aunt floated in and out of her memory. Which shaman would come here, cross over her body three times and, carrying a big pig, sing '*Baro hira amabunda, ram phareo hogar nangou*'? In her sleep in the forest of moving trees, she kept looking for a frog or a bat to offer to *khetra*. As soon as she closed her eyes, she saw again the little girl, dead and blue, emerging from the body of the woman possessed by the ghost. She did not even touch the medicines Alfred instructed her to take. What was the use?

The doctor had warned earlier that the baby was in breech position. Her cough was unrelenting. The doctor said it was due to pollution. Lots of people suffered from it in the city, especially if they came from the unspoilt hills. So Alfred did not take her out much except for a few times to the park next to their building.

On one such occasion, as they were getting ready to go out, when she put on the orange dokhana, he scolded her. He asked her to wear a salwar-kameez set; at least that would hide some part of her bulging body. She did not say anything and, taking off the dokhana, she put on the salwar suit as he had instructed. Alfred looked at her. How she had changed within these few months! Her fair skin was now patchy, there were dark circles around her eyes. And the body shining like a bamboo shoot stalk without the skin on which moonlight drew flowers—where was it? He looked at her and bowed his head. She saw that look and wanted to take off these clothes too. Alfred went out of the room and sent his son to call her. She came out nonetheless. After a long time, he was taking her out to the park.

As she came out, she looked at flat No 22 next to theirs. A young man and girl lived there. She kept her eyes downcast when she crossed this flat to avoid looking at the girl. Oh, the kind of clothes she wore! Forget about when there was someone with her, even when she was alone, she felt shy looking at the girl. When he saw the short tops clinging to her body over the kind of trousers men wore, she felt like spreading an arnai over her body. She always held hands with the tall fair young man who lived with her.

'Hi!' the girl's effervescent voice greeted her and Mainao had to look up. She got a shock, not from seeing her clothes but from seeing the boy holding her waist; he was not the man who lived with her. This one was shorter and dark. Even as Mainao looked on, both of them entered the flat. Even though she tried she could not help noticing that the boy's hands were getting more restless on the girl's body. She felt her cheeks and ears aflame. She looked at Alfred; he was talking to Daokhi and laughing. Sitting in the park, she asked him about the young couple. What she heard in reply shook her. They were not married but lived together; whenever they wanted they changed partners.

'Don't people say anything to them?' Mainao asked in utter surprise.

'Who bothers about these things here?' Alfred said quite easily.

'Don't they have parents?'

'They are adults now; what will parents say? When your son grows up he too won't listen to you.'

Mainao looked at her son, who was playing with a ball. She suddenly felt the hair on her skin stand up. She got up to pick him up. He threw the ball afar and ran to catch it. She also followed him. For some reason, she felt like hugging him close. Her son went to a secluded corner to pick up the ball. As she found herself behind some big trees, she got a jolt again; couples were sitting getting intimate under the shade of trees. She looked on for sometime. One boy smiled at her; a girl threw abuses at her in a language she could not understand. She stood stock-still. Nobody paid any attention to her. By now, her son had gone further kicking the ball. She could feel flocks of cawing crows gather around her. A naked couple in a thatched cottage set on fire—*badunga zabai*, the sinning man and woman jumping into the water. She remembered the story of Asagi and Baisagi, the handsome Chandrabao who accidentally touched the young girls, the crows telling the story of the sin to the villagers. Chandrabao could not chew the aroi rice to prove his innocence in the village court; to pass judgement on this aberration, old man Moun Ching Ching descended to earth by a golden ladder. He told them to make penance by eating human waste, pig shit and cowdung and then kneel down in front of the people of the village. Mainao could feel her skin crawl with fear, she shivered as if in fever. She thought of the malevolent spirits who moved in disguise to trouble man when he went to hunt or fish.

'What are you doing here?' she jumped at Alfred's stern voice. Her face was deathly pale.

'What's happened? Do you feel ill?'

Mainao's eyes were like that of a deer chased by a hunter. Alfred held her hand and led her out of the park. The doctor had said that pollution had infected her lungs. She was already quite weak. It was not advisable to let her travel by bus. He thought of hiring a taxi. But the thought of the fare made him cringe. With his salary, he could have managed pretty well in Assam, but here in this big city, his money disappeared in no time like water in sand. The house rent itself was quite a sum. Was it a house or a pigeon nest? Just putting marble on the floor and tiles on the walls did not make a house. At times he felt quite helpless. Since coming here, all he had managed was to buy a cooler. Mainao was breathing hard, carrying her son in her arms. He made him come down from her lap. Holding him tight with one hand and Mainao with the other, he waited for the green light to cross the road. Her palm in his hand was ice-cold. He was scared. How could a living being's hand be so cold? The cars were passing by in an unending line. Money and comfort, they announced. He felt an intense urge to put Mainao in a beautiful car, like one of those with the music on, and take her on a long drive. He looked at the handsome buildings around. Today his secret desire for a flat in one of those buildings stoked him even more. He wanted to leave his crowded locality and stay in a posh one. He found it quite stressful changing three buses while going to office because he lived so far away. He could not admit Daokhi in a good English medium school either; he had to be put in a Hindi medium government school which cost less. When he got this job in the big city, people were envious. He felt like laughing at the irony.

Mainao's palm was sweating and became colder. The coldness crept to his heart too. She looked at her husband. The ever-smiling man looked grim nowadays. Perhaps she made a mistake by going to the place where all those young people were sitting intimately, and that's why he was angry. He looked irritated, his forehead was wrinkled with worry. She felt distracted. She could feel a creeping pain in her lower abdomen. For quite sometime now, she could not feel the baby move. When she was carrying Daokhi, he kicked her stomach so much in these months that she could not sleep well.

The green light came on. He crossed the road holding her hand. She wanted desperately to go to her room and lie down in bed. These days even if she went out for a while, the dark, closed room kept calling out to her. As she lay with her face hidden in the pillow, she did not feel like talking or looking at anyone, not even Daokhi and Alari. She started walking fast. Her unnaturally fast pace surprised Alfred; even her son looked at her stunned. But she did not care; she did not hear anyone, she did not see anyone. The dark room was beckoning to her.

Her feet had been swelling a lot more these days. Alfred had asked her not to take too much salt. Of late, she hardly felt hungry. Whether the food had salt or not did not matter. Her conviction that she was possessed by the *khetra* was getting stronger. Looking at her swelling feet, she thought that *moudum bugar nai*—the malevolent spirit that took possession of pregnant women—was her nemesis too. If it did not get a proper puja it would kill her baby, or she would be killed. She dared not look at her swelling feet for long.

She used to buy banana from a vendor who came to the doorstep. Everyday at 11 o'clock he rang the doorbell. She bought the fruit at whatever price he mentioned. They communicated like two friends who had been together for long and understood each other's language. Mainao waited for the smiling old vendor. Sometimes she felt as if he was like her Abou with his white hair and white eyebrows. Often she offered him tea and snacks. While selling the bananas at double the market price the man gave her three bananas free—for the baby in the womb, he said. Even if she did not have enough money, he insisted on leaving a bunch behind; she could pay the money later, he said, telling her it was good for her health at this time. Mainao melted at his kindness. She lied to her husband that it cost her less though actually it was more.

One day Mainao told the vendor that she needed a banana leaf for the puja. At first he acted as if he did not understand what she was saying; where would he find a banana leaf in this city? Mainao was also puzzled: this man brought so many bananas but he could not get hold of the plant's leaf? At last it was decided she would pay him a hundred rupees and he would bring one the next day. Next day he did as promised and also left behind a bunch of bananas for puja, refusing to take money for it.

She washed the bananas and also had a bath herself. She drew a man's image on the banana leaf with ink and also nine vermilion spots. Taking it along with the other things needed for puja she had collected already, she went down towards the neem tree. She was not scared to come here as she did not have to cross the street.

Also she had her familiar squirrels and the visiting flock of parrots here. Though the base of the tree was cemented, there was some earth just below the tree. She swabbed the earth and then placed the banana leaf on it, lighted the joss sticks and lamp; for the offering she peeled the bananas, an apple Alfred had brought for her and a bowl of milk. She bowed low and begged the *khetra* to leave her alone. Trying to remember Abou's voice she chanted: *sath gakhounao thangdoungnou yew …* 'O God! I went to seven ghats. My feet touched the untouchable, he was maya, he was kaya …' Tears streamed from her eyes as she begged, 'Please don't harm my little girl, please go away to the arang bazaar for your shopping …'

The day was drawing to a close. By the time she had everything ready it was three in the afternoon because the vendor had brought the banana leaf only at one o'clock. People returning home from work looked at her strangely. After sometime, a traffic police came to scold her that she was dirtying a public place. He asked for a bribe, openly telling her that if she did not dish out one thousand rupees, he would arrest her. She did not understand what he was saying. As she saw the policeman stamping on the banana leaf with its nine vermilion spots, she started hurling abuses at him in her own language. The policeman thought she was angry because he had asked for money. Mainao was petrified; that man had his shoes over her offering; was he stamping over her child in the womb? The people around her started laughing at her. When Alfred arrived he saw that Mainao was engaged in a battle of words with a traffic policeman. He somehow managed to pacify the policeman by giving him five hundred rupees and showing his official ID card. He picked up all the puja things and threw them into the dustbin in front of his flat. He scolded her: why was she doing these things—it was not her village. Over here one had to go by the urban rules, etc. etc. In the village, didn't people throw out a pumpkin or gourd on the road when it rotted? They did.

Didn't they throw puja ingredients on the road once the ritual was over? Of course, they did. Here if one threw a cigarette packet the police would catch you, one would have to pay a fine, it was the law. Towards the end, his voice softened. Mainao was not listening to him at all. She was only surprised that Alari was treating her like this; he had not thrown her offering to the malevolent spirit outside but brought it to the confines of the house. She was sure the *khetra* was not going to leave her now; her baby would be killed, she might be killed too. Her own husband had brought home offerings meant for the angry spirit, which was taboo. He should have known. From her bed she looked at the dustbin—the banana leaf, the joss sticks, the red threads. And the bunch of bananas which the vendor had assured her was of the best quality lay on the table. Her whole body was wrecked with shivering. What would happen now? It meant this was the end—her baby would die, she would die. Oh, what was Alari doing? He was peeling a banana and was offering her one, too. So he really wanted that she should not be rid of the *khetra*; he wanted her to die, he wanted her baby to die. He not only brought home the bananas offered to the angry spirit, he was also urging her to eat it. Tears blinded her eyes. He was caressing her face, forcing her to take the fruit saying, 'Come, eat this! You don't take anything I bring, at least eat this which you love and buy.' His voice was full of tenderness. He decided that somehow he would buy a colour TV this month; she would be able to watch it when alone. If he could get a loan he would buy a car too. She was unable to travel in a bus; he would take her around and show her the attractions of this big city. When she recovered, he would take her to Kashmir or Manali for a holiday. She had laboured all her life and needed a break.

Suddenly Mainao became aggressive. She snatched the banana from his hand and threw it out of the window. Then she started throwing the bunch of bananas and the things in the dustbin out of the window. Her eyes became red, her hair flew around and she started trembling uncontrollably. Something like a demon overtook her and she continued throwing out the things she had collected for the puja now lying in the waste bin. He heard some people abusing them. Perhaps someone was hit by all these things down below? Worried, he ran to the lift. Yes, he was right, quite a few women had gathered and abused them calling them *junglees*, uncivilized people. He folded his hands asking for forgiveness and tried to clear the things lying around.

Mainao was mortally scared; she was sure he intended her baby to die. She ran to the bedroom and shut the door. She could hear her husband's voice, her son calling out, but she did not respond to the urgent knocking on the door. She was sinking—sinking into a world of darkness.

She gave birth to a stillborn baby. The doctor had warned that a baby that had undergone so much stress was not likely to survive; even if it did, it could be retarded. Alfred could not bear to look at Mainao's face as she stared at the nurse taking away the bluish chunk of flesh. It was a girl. Mainao looked at him without blinking, with eyes like stones. Her own skin too seemed to take on a bluish tinge. He tried to run his fingers tenderly through her hair. She had asked him once for a baby girl; she had offered him her peacock-like body. She pushed away his hand with intense hatred.

Mainao became a different person now. She liked to hide herself in the dark room. When she ate, she ate ravenously. If she did not want to eat she did not and kept to herself. Alfred had bought a red car on loan. The car had belonged to a lady officer in his workplace, so he got it at a small price. The woman belonged to a very rich family; this car was bought when she was a student so she wanted to change the model now. She even taught Alfred how to drive. She had come to their flat quite a few times in connection with this transaction. Alfred learnt driving quite fast. This was his habit, whatever he took on he did it with complete concentration. He had a reputation in office for his sincerity and capability. His soft nature also endeared him to everybody in the office.

When the woman from his office came Mainao looked at her and went inside, not even bothering to greet her. She lay in the dark, thinking about the girl. She was sure Alari wanted to kill her because he wanted to be with this girl. She remembered the couples in the park and also recalled what he had said—that different places had different norms. She thought she noticed the woman had held his hand when she came into the house, and also while going out. He had made tea for her. If he came late from office her imagination took her to the corner in the park. When he was asleep she thought that he was dreaming of her. On holidays when he went to the bazaar she wondered if the girl was waiting for him. The more she thought of the woman the more she wanted to withdraw into the dark room.

These days Alfred returned only at 8 or 9 o'clock in the evening from office; sometimes even later. Mainao never asked him anything, but in her mind she could see the girl walking alongside him. One day the girl came to meet her. She spoken in a foreign language. Alfred had translated it into her own language. She was talking about Alfred, that one could not find people like him any more; in the office he helped everybody if possible, including her; that people in the office appreciated his quiet nature and the boss liked him a lot; and that she was lucky to have a husband like him. Mainao just stood there, her head bowed. On her way out, the woman shook his hand and also did the same to Daokhi.

Mainao's son was always busy with his studies and play; her husband went out in the morning and returned late. The little work she had was finished soon and after that she just lay in the bed in the dark room. She found the image of the girl floating in and out of her mind. She felt the woman was demoness Than-Thin who tried to smother and choke her. Then her body would become cold, she would talk to herself. She took a stick from the broom and tried to cut her neck with it and chanted mantras. She wanted to pull Daokhi away from the study table and keep him inside a mosquito net so that the demoness would not reach her or her son. But there was not a single net in the house. Alfred had not bought any. He said that people did not use mosquito net here; he only switched on a light that drove away the mosquitoes. If she insisted on a net he showed her the mesh in the windows and doors. This was not her village full of jungles, he reminded her. Since there were no mosquitoes he was not going to sweat it out under a net, he protested. But she knew it was an excuse; he wanted her to die at the hands of Than-Thin demoness. This same man once scolded her when she did not want to put up the mosquito net in the village; even during the day if he or his son rested, it was always under a mosquito net. And now he… she felt her chest contract with sorrow. She knew very well what was going on in his mind. She did not see him as he was—his face tired and pulled down at the end of the day. She did not notice his body shrinking under the strain of too much work. She only saw in her mind the comet-like head of the Than Thin demoness.

It was a holiday. Alfred washed the clothes, cleaned the dirt that had gathered in the corners of the rooms, gave a bath to his son, even cooked. Mainao looked on from her bed as he did all this. Looking at his bizarre dressing, she often tried to find the boy she once knew always wearing a gamocha. When she closed her eyes she saw that boy running to her. Sometimes he had a white chain in his hand, sometimes he was empty-handed, sometimes he lifted her up and they sat together on the hillock, they ran in the paddy fields to the tune of the *nara* flute, had bath in the river—him looking at her all the time. Her chest rang with a tune, a tune that was like a whistle going through the tora shrubs, trembling on her lips. 'O, take this peacock… touch the tail of the peacock.' But the tune never came out; a whirlwind took it far away.

The doctor said she was absolutely okay now. There was no physical problem. But he advised consultation with a psychiatrist. Alfred was also thinking about it. Looking at her lying in bed, he often thought desperately how he could get his Phulmuthi maiden back.

After lunch, he went to her. How many days had it been since he had sought her out? He tried to feel her body's warmth. Long back when he was a student in the town, he would go back running for her body's perfume mixed with the smell of ripe paddy, of tekeli pitha spread on a banana leaf, and of sweet-smelling zumai. Like the touch of her fingers clinging to a warm shawl she had just cut from her loom, these smells wrapped themselves around her body. Sometimes his Phulmuthi maiden was a mustard field, sometimes the sweet-smelling joha rice, or the earthen lamp lit at the pedestal of Bathou, or the shrubs Abou planted in the backyard. Her body, mixed with all these smells, became like a whistling wind in the tora shrubs. A pea-hen blinded his eyes and he also became a peacock dancing around her.

He put his nose in her breasts and took a long breath. But he cringed at the unfamiliar odour, a sour unwashed smell that made him want to retch, an odd charcoal-like whiff clung to her body. He moved away and went to sleep with his son. Mainao's eyes filled with tears. She remembered how she scolded Alari when he would come running to her on every holiday. He did not want to leave for the town, he did not want to study or work in the city; he only wanted to stay near her. Her heart rang with a desire to find that lost boy. She kept on looking at him. After a long time, he had had some rest and now he was snoring next to his son in the bed. He was saying something in his sleep; he did this often these days. Again she saw in her mind's eye a headless woman's body flying in the air, like the fire of a shooting star on a dark night. She shivered and covered her head with a wrap.

In the afternoon, Alfred told his son to dress up and also told her to change. He wanted to take them out for a drive. He was whistling after a long time. He made her wear a churidar and kameez suit. He was whistling the tune of that song: '*My dear, untie the knot of my gamocha ...*' Stone-faced, she got ready. He had gone to much trouble to buy this car only for her. He had been waiting for this day for a long time. But looking at her grumpy face, all his enthusiasm drained out. At one place, the traffic light turned red. He looked at the crowd of people running to cross the road as if it was something new. Just a few days ago, he had done the same. He was pleased that he had been promoted in office and wanted to share the news with Mainao. But turning to her, he saw that Mainao was looking outside with wide eyes. Then suddenly she was shouting and trying to get down from the car.

'What's wrong, Mainao?' he asked.

She seemed ready to cry. He followed her gaze. A little boy was trying to cross the road. Despite the red light, two or three motorcycles rushed forward and one of them hit the little boy. The boy screamed and dropped on the street. The light changed and the cars passed on without stopping to help the boy, his face bloodied. Mainao saw that Alfred started the car without looking at the boy. She was stunned. They had a car; they could take the boy to the hospital. If the boy died, wouldn't they be cursed? She also had a son; if something like this happened to him ...? She felt himself getting angry and asked him to pick up the boy, but he did not listen. He also reminded her about what had happened when she went to give water to the old man and the police had taken her away. Her anger subsided. But a cold hatred took its place—a hatred towards her husband that she had never felt before. She could not believe he was the same Alari. How could he ignore the little boy and his bloodied face? For this man, the woman from Sivasagar came to help her with threads for the loom so that he could continue his studies. She had bought her woven clothes at the correct price and she had given him that money. The professor from town had come to the village to seek him out. And the Father, what hadn't he done so that he could study? His friend helped him so much too ... And now he could leave behind that little boy to die without caring?

He took her to a beautiful park. Everywhere were beautiful flowers and people wearing pretty clothes. She looked at him; he was frowning. They did not talk much and came out from there. Then he took her to a restaurant in an open space which had stalls from every state of India; every stall had its own ethnic food and also dance and singing performances. They went to the Bengal food stall and father and son gorged on luchi-aalur dom and sweets. She did not feel like eating anything, the food seemed to get stuck in her throat and she felt like throwing up. But Alfred did not seem to notice.

She sat in back seat on their return home. She was desperate to go back to her dark room. They reached but she kept on sitting in the car. He parked the car and got down. She sat without talking to anyone. After sometime, father and son found that she was still sitting in the car. Alfred was extremely irritated; her son laughed. But she did not hear nor did she see anything; she only wanted the dark room now and a wrap to cover herself with.

She was waiting for the banana vendor at the door. That was the only thing she could do freely on her own, buying bananas from the white-haired man. If her husband did not go to the vegetable market she had to live on an empty stomach. If he did not take her out she could not step out on her own. She could not come out of the car; he shut the doors with something that made a *pi-pi* sound, and only he could open the doors. At first she was very surprised to see a key that could open the car from a distance. She also found that if anyone touched the car it came alive with a sound. When he showed off all these things that a key could do she thought him to be a magician. Yes, her Alari had really become a magician after coming to this city. With a key he imprisoned her, released her—from far, from near.

The fruit vendor did not come. The one who came was a young wife, her body ablaze. The saree she was wearing was burning; the smell of kerosene assailed Mainao's nose. She started pouring water on the woman as she came in. The fire went out. It could not do much damage to the girl's body; only the saree was burnt. She peeled the half-burnt saree off the girl's body and made her put on a housecoat. She ground some potatoes and with great care put the paste on her burnt flesh. Oh, if only she could get some juice from saal-kuwaori plant! Abou had some in his kitchen garden. She led the woman to her own bed, forced her to drink some milk and eat two slices of buttered bread. The girl slept placing her head on Mainao's lap. As she ran her fingers through her hair, Mainao felt a great tenderness. If her daughter lived how old would she have been? This girl was very young, her parents must have brought her up with love and tenderness; now see, she had come to the in-laws' house and while trying to cook, she had burnt herself. How did the kerosene get to her body? Perhaps she had tried to pour the oil from a bottle, or was she trying to pour oil in the stove? Didn't they have gas? Poor girl! Wasn't there anyone to look after her at home? Streams of tears were flowing out of the girl's closed eyes. When she woke up she hugged Mainao tightly and cried inconsolably. Mainao hugged her back lovingly.

With the little bit of the local language she had learnt, thanks to the banana vendor, Mainao could understand some of what the girl was saying. She had brought with her in dowry almost everything demanded: TV, fridge, gold; there was also a promise of two lakh rupees in cash out of which fifty thousand had been given. The rest her father was unable to deliver because he fell seriously ill just after the wedding. That's why she got a beating everyday from her in-laws. Yesterday her father had sent five thousand rupees. In anger, her husband, her sister-in-law and mother-in-law tried to burn her with kerosene. Her husband was an engineer. He said he had had offers of more dowry from other parties, but he had reduced the amount for her parents because she was beautiful. The girl started crying again, hiding her face in Mainao's lap. She wanted to know from Mainao that since her husband was a big officer he must have got lots of things and money as dowry. They must have left them back home because in the flat there was hardly anything.

Mainao was shocked. What was she hearing? That a girl when getting married had to pay money, otherwise they burnt her? She made a cup of tea for the girl and gave it to her with biscuits and a banana. She tried to explain to the girl how weddings happened in her community. The groom's family went to the bride's house and hung two pitchers of zumai and embedded two silver bangles in the thatched roof. If those were not returned within a week the groom's family understood that the proposal was accepted. The groom's family had to learn the norms and customs of the girl's *khel*, fraternity. The groom had to visit the bride's house from time to time. His family had to bring food to give a feast to the bride's family and other people in the village. The father of the bride demanded the cost of this feast. The groom's family begged to let the cost come down. In Abou's days, if the groom's family did not give *ga-dhan*, bride price, weddings did not happen at all.

The bell was ringing again and again; somebody was also banging on the door. Through the keyhole, Mainao saw that the girl's in-laws were crowding against her door. They came, went back and returned. The girl held her tightly, pleading with her not to open the door; she was mortally scared. Letting her go to sleep on her lap, Mainao sang to her the songs that the groom's side sang begging the girl's side to reduce the burden of the cost of the feast:

Theb thepharia
The tep-tepari insect talks tep-tep
The grasshopper gets married

The girl looked in astonishment. She was a city girl. Where would she see a grasshopper? Mainao explained when the male tepari insect flew it made a sound like *tep-tep*. So the groom's side sang that tep-tepari insect got married by beating his own drum. Then why should humans have to spend so much for a wedding? If the bride's family demanded a good amount of money for the feast, the groom's side playfully sang:

Mu itha gang
Mesta and sengeri greens
With a curry with broken rice
Won't it be enough?

The girl did not understand much of what Mainao was saying but understood this much that in their land there was no dowry; in fact the groom's side had to give money to the bride's side. And she also understood that she was safe with this woman. If she could somehow spend the night here she would go home the next day. She was a graduate, she could do something on her own to earn. Mainao cooked and ate lunch with the girl. After a long time, she had a full meal.

In the afternoon the bell stopped ringing. In the evening her husband returned, her son returned too. As soon as Alfred came, the girl's in-laws came to their flat. Mainao did not want to open the door, but Alfred insisted. The girl fell at Mainao's feet, begging her to let her stay the night. Her in-laws argued with Alfred vehemently. Mainao understood that they wanted the girl to return to their flat. The husband had also brought in the police. The girl clung to Mainao. At last in front of everybody Alfred slapped her; she had to let the girl go. The mother-in-law took away the girl pulling her by the hair.

The next day Mainao saw the burnt dead body of the girl being taken away by the police in a van.

The last full meal Mainao had was with the girl. After that she hardly ate anything in the last one month; she confined herself to the dark bedroom. The doctor said it was a clear case of depression; actually she had been suffering from it for sometime. The doctor prescribed both mood elevator medicine and a tranquilizer. She was getting thinner and thinner, her skin began to hang from the bones, the eyes had sunk into the sockets. He forced her to take the medicine before he left for office but on her own she never took it. He could not force her to go for a drive; the car lay idle in the garage. The doctor said that she was not responding to the medicine, it was important how to find the cause of her depression. He advised Alfred to take her home for a change of air.

Alfred decided to take her to the village. Perhaps she would be happier there. When he thought of Assam or of his village, he found himself depressed and felt like lying down in a dark room like Mainao. The news from home was of rampage and killings. He did not feel like going home. To whom would he return anyway? He had a father but never felt that he had one, his stepmother was never fond of him. He could not forge a bond with his step brothers and sisters, and Abou had passed away too. The only person he could go back to was his dear professor. He was one person with whom he could discuss everything; he could unburden himself. Such a good man and a good teacher, but he chose to stay in the small town; he also had trouble with the terrorists. Once in reply to his letter the professor had written that he had bought life and peace with money. Asim was teaching in a higher secondary school in the same town; he got married in the meantime. He had an intense desire to meet his professor and tell him about Mainao's health.

After a long time, Alfred returned to Guwahati. He saw hordes of policemen and soldiers on the platform. He had read in the newspaper while crossing Bengal that the family of an ULFA member were brutally killed the night before—from a ninety-year-old father to a four–year-old child. He heard from some people that this morning two members of SULFA, from the surrendered faction of the militant group, were found murdered near the station. He thought of staying one night in Guwahati to do some shopping on his way home, but it did not happen. He decided to take the bus to his village. His professor had told him to take the bus as Mainao was weak and travelling in a car was more strenuous. On the way home, she did not refuse the medicines. Perhaps that's why she was not lying supine in the train; she was looking at the scenery outside and was also eating this and that. She even bought a few things on the train for people back home. After a long time, he found himself feeling lighter.

His 'Sir' was right; the new big bus was more comfortable to travel in on the broken road. If the roads were better earlier the jerking would not have made the baby in her womb suffer. It was her second pregnancy; he should have been more careful and let her stay in the village until the baby was born. But where would he have left her? Everyone had advised him to take her away. Now he noticed that her cough was subsiding, she was happier even without the medicine today. She kept an eye on the luggage and spoke with the conductor. She was talking animatedly with a woman traveller in her own language, discussing the dokhana she was wearing and telling her about Delhi.

Alfred decided he would leave her in the village for sometime. Let her revive her mood and then he would take her back to Delhi. If she wanted he would build a cement house for her; he would sell the car if necessary. If she did not want the car of what use was it for him? Just let her be happy! He would send the money from there. And someday perhaps a baby girl would arrive.

They reached the small town during the day itself. The train had reached Guwahati early in the morning, so they could catch the first bus from there. As soon as she got down, Mainao said they should have something to eat; Daokhi was hungry too. Alfred was surprised to see that the Mainao who refused to eat anything now asked for puri and bhaji. She even did a bit of shopping. He gave her more money and told her, 'You also buy something for yourself.' She went to a shop and bought good quality threads in yellow, orange and green colours; she was going to weave a dokhana. She wondered what condition her loom was in. However, before leaving he had tied it well and hung it from the ceiling so it would remain intact. She was sure her step mother-in-law was looking after the chickens, pig and the goats. Whatever be her nature, she looked after the animals very well; she did not even throw a stone at the cat, which often stole food from the kitchen. Mainao held the packet of thread close to her chest. When he wanted to take it she smiled and said, 'You are a man; you don't have to carry threads for the loom.' He felt his chest contract. This was the Mainao who never allowed him to do anything when he was studying. She would become the Phulmuthi maiden again, he was sure. He would let her stay in the village as long as she wanted. He had taken leave for fifteen days. He wondered about the house they had left behind. What state was it in? If necessary he would repair it and take some more leave. He hardly took leave anyway.

She was the one who suggested they hire a car as they had a lot of luggage. She remembered their own car and said, 'If you drove your own red car to the village people would have looked at us admiringly.' It was the first time he had heard her mention the car.

'It's okay. I'll drive this car.'

'How can you? Is this your city? Over there you drive on smooth roads, how can you drive here? Will your car go through the stream?'

'I don't think so; it's a small car.'

'Will you be able to drive over the water?'

'No.'

She was laughing; she took the initiative to call a driver to hire a car and also negotiated the price. He thought of visiting his professor before going to the village, but observing her eagerness to go to the village, he did not mention the matter.

Daokhi jumped up in fear every time the car plunged into a stream and careened this side and that side. Whenever the car crossed over a broken patch he would howl. Mainao held him close. She looked out to the paddy fields outside and sang to her son a cowherd song:

Our poor cottage is broken
Rain, please do not come
Look, there comes the sun
Come sunlight, come

The rain is coming step by step
Drive it away
Give us warmth
The water will dry up, the road will get dry
And we will have a dry road

Alfred slept, his worries gone, Daokhi too fell asleep. He knew from now on Mainao would show the road to the driver, would even give the right hiring charge. She always thought that the whole world cheated him. Now she was instructing the driver on the road.

As soon as she alighted from the car, Mainao ran towards the house. Alfred noticed that her thin body was trembling. He followed her. Her sick body must have endured a lot in the last few days travelling by train, bus and car. Seeing them, his father, stepmother and the children, even some villagers came.

But where was the house? The house she had made, the best kept one in the village? In its place was a mound of debris. The villagers stood around, their faces expressing guilt.

'What happened?' Alfred asked.

In reply they said that after they had left a 'jungle-party' started living there. At first they finished off the chickens, goats and pigs; then they finished off whatever was in the house. They brought abducted people there and extorted money; sometimes the people in the village heard men screaming at night as if they were being tortured, and sometimes even gunshots. In fear people stopped coming to this side. On many occasions, soldiers came and there were shootings. The military drove them out. Even then, sometimes at night people saw faint lights in the house, the light of cigarettes mixing with the fireflies. They heard the sound of heavy boots and whisperings. Sometimes the strong smell of foreign liquor filled the air.

Alfred stood with his head bowed. The sun was setting. A black snake emerged very slowly from under the ruined house. Suddenly there was a sharp scream; the people jumped up in fear. They saw that Mainao broke a branch of a tree and in great anger started beating the snake. The snake lifted its hood in defence. In the gathering dusk, it was difficult to make out its shape. Nobody dared to go near Mainao. They called out, 'Come away, come away, please!' Her mouth was frothing. Alfred rushed to her and held her tight. Somebody else killed the hooded snake. She was foaming at the mouth; the sides of her lip were white. Daokhi was howling. Alfred lifted her frail body and took her to his father's house and put her down on a bamboo cot. Like a half-dead bird, she thrashed about in agony. Alfred and the women tried their best but could not calm her down; he somehow pushed two sleeping tablets through her mouth. At last, she gave in to sleep and lay there like a dead woman.

The villagers sat guiltily in the courtyard. Alfred felt rather bad for them. All of them asked him to leave the place as soon as possible. Because he was a big officer, the devils had troubled his family no end. If they knew he was here they might swoop down on him and his family. Even the single woman who somehow managed to live by selling wild vegetables like dhekia and arum had to shell out money to them on a monthly basis.

Mainao slept till mid-day. She did not speak to anyone, nor did she eat anything. She ran her fingers through the coloured skeins of thread she had bought. Suddenly she wrapped them around her neck and tried to strangle herself. Alfred saw it and loosened the skeins. He gave her medicines and she drifted into sleep again. People said the evil spirit inside the house had come out in the form of the black snake. Somebody said it was a *khetra*, somebody said it was the demoness Than-Thin, somebody said it was the red-coloured demon K, while somebody else said Mainao was possessed by the spirit of the tigress. All of them performed puja the way they thought right. A red chicken was killed and offered to Kubir. Somebody thought that the more benevolent white Kubir had overtaken Mainao and sacrificed a white pig. Mainao meanwhile lay like a dead woman.

In the evening, people got really scared because the real *khetra* entered the village. They came wearing their heavy boots and demanded one lakh rupees from Alfred. They threatened him that he could not continue to enjoy the comfort of city life while they sacrificed so much for their own land and people.

The red kubir was an angry god, so a red rooster had to be sacrificed.

The white kubir was benevolent; if an egg was ensconced in the stomach of the patient he went away.

Demoness Than Thin was greedy, but if a net was spread over the ill person, she became scared and went away.

If a *khetra* troubled a person, one had to sacrifice a big pig and rooster. Even though *khetra* was a more fearful spirit, if puja was given to him it went shopping to arang bazaar, people believed.

But how could one appease the *khetra*s who were visible to the eyes? What were the ways to get rid of them? The whole village congregated in their house. From where could the young man dole out so much money? His wife was in such a state too. So they discussed and decided that early next morning they would escort them to the town catching the first bus to the city. Once he was in the city, they could not harm them. From there he would take the train; two young boys would escort him there too. That night the villagers stood guard around them, in case the gang came back, or took him or Daokhi away, or used their guns. They were scared but stood by them anyway, sitting around a fire they lit in the courtyard.

In the morning, the people put them on the bus and five men accompanied them.

Mainao was heavily drugged and Alfred had to carry her to the bus. A woman asked, 'Is Mainao dead?'

Another woman scolded her, 'What rubbish are you talking? She is not dead, she has been possessed by an evil spirit.' Another remembered, 'If Abou were here he would have shooed away the spirit with his mantra.'

Soon the bus swayed over the potholed road and disappeared from sight. The women who had come to bid farewell waited at the crossing uncertainly. They were very sad. What a time they were passing through, they mulled. The family had come to spend some time in their own village after ages, yet could not even spend two nights. They had helped Mainao set up home. Those evil men had destroyed it within one year. Only a woman understood how much effort it took to set up a home, and now in front of their eyes the beautiful house had disappeared. Standing mutely, they wondered if Mainao ever thought about them. Maybe she thought there were so many people in the village, but look what happened to her house! Her stepmother-in-law sat down and started weeping. The eyes of the other women filled with tears too as she described how Mainao had lain there like an injured bird. Her heart ached for the orphan girl who was an expert at the loom, who sang beautifully, her pretty face, her habit of melting at others' sorrow. The women sat around her in a circle, lamenting.

One of them spoke of Abou and his magic potions; she remembered how someone wanted to spoil a wedding by planting a root and ushering in the magic of *mayadhop* and *chayadhop* to make people fall ill, but Abou got rid of the magic at one go; and that woman who came back from the town possessed by *baghnisar*; would she have survived without Abou's help? Bhaben's mother was possessed by *khetra* and her feet had swelled up like an elephant's, but Abou saved her and she had given birth to sons. Yes, if Abou were there, Mainao would not have suffered from the evil touch of spirits … Ah, if Abou were here with his medicine bottles, each smelling different, if his voice like kharga, sang,

Koroti koroti nag-nagini kira kota katu
Demoness of the sky, of hell, of malevolence
Human demoness
Bad knowledge, bad mantra, reversing them all
I have cut them all

Yes, if Abou were there to destroy the evils from the sky, from deep earth, the evil in men too!

Thinking of one such Abou who was not there, they felt their hearts get heavy and, unable to keep standing with the burden of unmitigated sorrow, they sat at the crossing of the street in a circle, mourning.

Face in the Mirror

You call me a misbeliever, cut-throat dog,
And spit upon my Jewish gabardine

How like fawning publican he looks
I hate him…

The Merchant of Venice, Act I, Scene III

The year: 1967.

I was in the seventh standard. I remember it clearly because my class and the last digit of the year were the same. I studied in a missionary school for twelve years. Why my father sent me away to a Christian missionary school in the hills in the face of much objection from the family, even though there were many other schools near my hometown, was a mystery then. Today, though, I understand that he had a dream for me.

At school, I was the only Assamese girl and the only Hindu as well. Many girls from the hills of Assam were students in the school. Many girls from NEFA—now Arunachal Pradesh, Manipur, Nagaland and Mizoram—came there to study as well. I had to travel for two days to reach the school from my hometown in upper Assam. The girls from the hills took even longer. I noticed that all the girls from these areas came from rich families. There were other girls too, besides the tribal girls. Both our principal and vice-principal were Americans and there were quite a few British 'sisters' and then there were the Anglo-Indian nuns.

When I first arrived at the hostel, pushed out of the loving arms of my mother and grandmother, I cried a lot. I was used to sleeping with my grandmother. Until she told me a story, I could not go to sleep at night. Often at night, I went to the veranda of our dormitory and, cupping my face in my hands, looked up at the sky above. Next to our hostel was the bungalow of the headmistress, Dr Ivy Wolfe. The house seemed like a mini zoo to me. Two dogs, four cats, a cage of lovebirds, two pairs of white doves who danced like peacocks and a parrot lived there. After classes, I often stood in the veranda and observed the animals and birds in the bungalow. Like the other girls, I was also very scared of Dr Ivy. She was tall and her complexion was light brown. She often wore a white saree with a border. She wore her hair in a bun covered in an old-fashioned net. She never wore any jewellery except for a gold ring with a diamond. She was a strict disciplinarian and never tolerated any breach of rules set by the school. Whether it was the school or the hostel, Dr Ivy's strict personality left its stamp. Secretly the girls called her a 'she-wolf' or a tigress.

Once I had to face the wrath of this she-wolf. I was in the sixth standard. I was on holiday at home when I attained puberty. As per custom, I was presented with gold ornaments on my promotion to womanhood. However, I did not take along any of the jewellery. The only thing I carried was the lizard-shaped ring my grandmother had given me. While presenting it to me, she told me that her mother-in-law had given it to her when she came to choose her as a bride for her son. Somehow I felt that by wearing the ring I could be closer to my grandmother. In our school or hostel, we were not allowed to wear any jewellery. When Dr Ivy saw the ring on my finger she was very angry and scolded me severely. Later my school mates came to sympathize with me at my misfortune.

We had heard that Ivy Miss was brought up by the principal Irene Wolfe. She was an American missionary. She was probably the third principal in the school. We also heard that Irene Wolfe had brought Ivy Wolfe from a hospital. Somebody had abandoned her at its doorstep. She was the one who educated her and sent her to the Cambridge University to do her doctorate degree. I heard from the older girls in the school that when she was a student, maybe in the college, she was involved with the elder brother of one of her classmates. She had even visited the boy's house to get acquainted with the family. But the family refused to accept an orphan girl with unknown family roots as a daughter-in-law. After that Irene Wolfe sent away her adopted daughter to Cambridge. On her return, she took a job in the school. After her retirement, Irene Wolfe lived in the wooden bungalow with her adopted daughter who looked after her with great care until her death. It was afterwards that Ivy Miss started collecting the animals and birds. Gradually she rose in rank to become the headmistress.

In fact, it was my lizard-shaped ring, encrusted with pomegranate-like rubies, that established a relationship with Ivy Miss. That day she had accosted me like a tigress asking why I was wearing it in the school even though it was forbidden. In broken English—I was yet to be proficient in the language, I had explained to her why. That I felt close to my grandmother when I wore it—she was the one with whom I slept at home; that she gave it to me for my shanti-biya, the small wedding that happens when a girl attains puberty. Tears mixed with snot from my nose streamed when I said all this trembling in fear. Ivy Miss returned the ring to me and then gave me a pretty wooden box with lock and key. She had placed her hand on my head and said, 'Be careful!' I had thanked her and fled, relieved. But I was careful to shut the swing door softly because I knew Ivy Miss lost her temper if anyone made a banging noise while opening or shutting the swing door.

While leaving, I looked back to check that the door did not bang and then saw that she was turning the diamond ring in her finger again and again. Sparkling rays from the stone painted abstract designs on the wall of the semi-dark room.

Ivy Miss went around the school and hostel like a sleepless guard. She came to know even if a needle fell on the floor somewhere, they said. One day a small incident happened in our class room. We were in our early teens. We were yet to learn to take care of ourselves on the particular days of the month. On that day, a used sanitary napkin was found on the floor of the classroom in one corner. Nobody confessed. Ivy Miss had just entered the class. The next class was about to begin. We were standing in the corner of the room. Some girls were crying. Seeing Ivy Miss made my throat turn dry like a piece of wood. What would happen now? But to our astonishment, we saw her pick up the napkin. Suddenly from our midst, Zungmila dashed out and, taking the napkin, ran to the toilet. Yes, the very presence of Ivy Miss was enough to make girls retract their mistakes.

For the next few days, Zungmila did not speak to anyone. In any case, she was a very quiet girl. We hardly ever heard her voice. We often saw her sitting in the class, her head bowed, the face expressionless. By that time I had started enjoying school. I painted, took part in plays, did well in studies and also wrote stories that were published in the school magazine. It was a smooth life without any hassles. I felt pleased with myself and the surroundings for no particular reason. I was preoccupied with the endless possibilities of the future. My class teacher Miss Melina had given me a nickname: Little Sparrow. I also got a scolding from her for my habit of jumping around whether there was work to be done or not. I loved to talk with the girls too; everybody had tales to tell—of their lives, of their dreams.

Take Hannah, the tall girl with crinkly hair and thick lips. Her mother was from the tea garden labourer community. She had been a student in our school and later worked in a missionary hospital. She had married a Black American during the Second World War. I was very curious about her father who had come from a land so far away. She said he used to draw beautiful pictures. She even showed me some of his sketches. They were of her young mother with a baby in her lap. Hannah kept the sketches with utmost care in a jewellery box with velvet lining. Hannah also painted well. She related to her father only through the sketches. He left the country after the war.

Then there was Dorothy Mcpherlin with her red hair and white skin. Her father was manager in a tea garden. Her mother was Indian. Dorothy used to talk about her white grandmother, how she played the piano, and the yummy chocolate cakes she baked. Dorothy had been to England twice.

Basanti was from Manipur. She talked about Manipuri dance. She used to dance beautifully in our school functions. She taught me how to make the paper garlands that she wore during the performances.

Ilena was a Mizo girl. She taught me how to dance with the help of four bamboo sticks. Dorothy and Basanti made the staccato beat for the dance on a tin box. Quite a few times, I danced with Ilena wearing a Mizo sarong.

Indeed there were many stories to share. I talked about my grandmother, my great-grandmother, of my grandfather, my 'little wedding' at puberty, and Bihu dance.

One day Miss Melina asked me to sit next to Zungmila. I was very unhappy. Who wanted to sit with a grumpy girl who never talked? I felt like shaking her up at times. It was torture to sit like that, without talking. Basanti, Dorothy, Ilena, Hannah and all looked at me with sympathy. If I tried to draw Zungmila into a conversation she showed her displeasure. Melina Miss paid unwavering attention to the class. She particularly kept an eye on the Little Sparrow. There was no way I could change my seat. If I did, in all probability I would be sent to face Dr Ivy. That would be disastrous to say the least. So I had no choice but to sit quietly next to mute Zungmila.

One day I thought for a long time what would interest her and asked if she had a boyfriend back home. In answer she pushed me away with her elbow. That was enough to draw Miss Melina's attention to me. She dashed down from her desk and, taking hold of my hair, shook it forcefully for disturbing a 'good girl' like Zungmila. And there was a warning too. If I disturbed Zungmila in the class again I would be marched to Dr Ivy's chamber.

At that time I was reading the novel *Yaruingam* set in Nagaland. Of Khutingla, Charengla, Videshelli, Rishang, rivers and hills of the land. I remember the date and day clearly. It was a Friday. On this day, I had sewing class in the afternoon that stretched over three periods. We were taken to a hall for this class where we had to sit on the floor. I was bored with the darning and patch-work taught in the class. I hated it and so my work always suffered. The sewing teacher often scolded me. Zungmila was very good at it. She would even do my work. That day Zungmila finished both her own and my work fast and as usual was sitting with her head bowed. There were two long periods still left to finish. Miss Melina kept vigil with her hawk-eyes in case the Little Sparrow got up from Zungmila's side. What a punishment! In its place if she had asked me to kneel down on the veranda outside at least I could look at the flowers and birds. Despite myself, I started speaking to Zungmila and talked about *Yaruingam* and how good the book was. I wanted to tell her about Charengla and the wild orchid she held in her hand. I wanted to talk about her anger and sympathy towards Videshelli. The mute Zungmila looked up abruptly in such a way that I could distinctly hear a cracking noise from her neck. I also told Zungmila about old Nazek and how he made Thila-Kapu with Videshelli thereby making him his heir. The old man was very fond of Videshelli; he wanted to fight for an independent land in their hills. I told her about Charengla's sorrow at being left behind by Japanese soldiers. I also told her the love story of Khutingla and Rishang. Zungmila looked at me steadily with her small eyes. The boring two-hour class passed as if in two minutes.

It was as if mute Zungmila had a dammed-up hilly river inside her and now somebody had opened it. The overflowing water submerged me. She asked me again and again about the things I had already talked about. About Abei the dog, Charengla hiding behind the rocks to save herself from the soldiers, the fight between the Indian army and the fighters under Videshelli, the rebels coming in with their firearms looking for chickens and pigs in the villages.

She started talking.

Her father owned a big shop. In1942 when the Japanese soldiers arrived at the border, the Marwari businessmen from the plains left. It was then that Zungmila's father and grandfather started their own business. One of Zungmila's uncles had left home and joined the rebels. Zungmila came to know a lot of things about their land mainly from her aunt. The rebel group which her uncle had joined went to Delhi. Zungmila's memory was very sharp, so she remembered the dates and years she had heard about clearly. In the capital, the rebel group had said that on 14 August 1947, they would declare their hills as an independent country. They were also said to have met Gandhi in the Bhangi colony in Delhi. True to their word, they announced independence on 15 August 1947. In 1952 the rebels tried to boycott the election conducted by the Indian government. None from the hills stood as a candidate and no one went to the voting booth. Zungmila repeated again and again while telling all this that their hills had always been an independent land. She wrote in her palm to show me the number: 1876. This was the year when the British entered their hills. They had taken over Assam fifty years before that. I was absolutely mesmerized as Zungmila talked about her history. One of her aunts, her father's sister, also believed in the ideals of the uncle who had joined the rebels. People respected them a lot. She told me about the visit of Prime Minister Nehru to their hills. With him came the prime minister of Burma. Nehru had come to negotiate with the people. But no one went to listen to Nehru. It surprised me as I listened. Nehru was saddened. He also lost face in front of his counterpart from the neighbouring country. I had an argument with Zungmila now.

'Why did your people insult Nehru? He was such a wise man…' I wanted to tell her about the letters he wrote to his daughter Indira Gandhi which I had read in a book.

But Zungmila was angry and said: 'Our people wanted to let our opinion known to Nehru. Why didn't he listen?'

As we argued, our English was interspersed with words from our respective mother tongues. But we could understand each other without any difficulty.

Later I became the listener, mute Zungmila the speaker. Even within the strict schedule of the school, we found time to talk. The girls often found me in the wing where Zungmila stayed. The seniors used to call out to her whenever I went that side, 'Hey! Your friend, the Little Sparrow, has come.' By that time, everybody knew the nickname given to me by Melina Miss.

Zungmila told me about the terrible times that their hills had suffered. Sometimes she cried, sometimes her face became scarlet with anger.

After Nehru's tour, the police started attacking the hills. There were skirmishes between the people of the hills and representatives of the Indian government. The rebels ordered the village chiefs not to pay taxes or accept the shawls bestowed by the Indian government to honour them. Towards the end of 1955, the Indian army arrived in the hills. The people destroyed bridges and attacked the military camps. The army in turn declared an all-out war against the hill people. They burnt village after village. The paddy fields were set on fire so that the rebels would not have access to food supply.

I remember that day very well. It was before the Christmas holidays. The annual exam was two weeks away. It was getting very cold in our hill station. That particular afternoon it became quite dark suddenly. Our sewing class was on. Because the exam was round the corner, the rules and regulations in the sewing class had relaxed. If someone did Maths or went through study material during the sewing class Melina Miss did not say anything. Zungmila and I sat behind an almirah. We had in our hands the task of making holes for buttons. Melina Miss had made the holes with her scissors. We started to work on them, a new skill we had just been taught.

Zungmila told me about her aunt that day. Listening to her, my mind became like the cloth Melina Miss had given us, with lots of perforations. It was as if I were that piece of cloth where the scissors had run through.

It was 1964. At that time Zungmila was studying in a school in her home land. The villagers were getting ready to go to the field in the morning with cane horas on their heads and other tools necessary for the work. Suddenly, the army entered the village. Then they herded everyone to the big field in front of their church as if they were cows and goats. They beat them with the butts of their guns and like selecting betel-leaves to make bunches, they segregated the people into groups. The people were shivering in the cold. It was drizzling. The red earth stuck to their heels like gum. The surface of the winding road near the church had become soggy. Through this road, a jeep thundered into their gathering. An army Major alighted from the jeep. Seeing him Zungmila had hidden behind her mother. The Major told them about his colleague who was found murdered near the village and asked them to make the killer surrender. He also told them not to give rice to the men who had gone underground. Zungmila had heard this since her childhood—not giving rice to those underground. The hill people said they were '*basti laga manuh*'—their people. The army said they were enemies of the land—'*desh laga dushman*'. The army set fire to their ripe paddy fields. Zungmila also saw some people from other hills coming to their village in early mornings to collect rice.

For three days and two nights, the people of the village were kept surrounded in the church field. Zungmila shed tears when she told me about the little babies who had died from cold and hunger. She herself had fainted towards dawn. Waking up from her stupor she had looked for her aunt. When the army had visited their village and took them to the field her aunt was not in the house she had gone to collect water from the stream. After three days when the people were allowed to return home, they found that the whole village had been burnt to cinders. Zungmila desperately looked for her aunt.

By this time, Melina Miss had warned us quite a few times. But the sewing remained in our hands without any progress. Zungmila seemed like another person. She did not pay any attention to Melina Miss as she talked about her aunt. Her naked body was found in a mound of ash. Her body looked as if dogs had attacked it. I saw Melina Miss standing behind Zungmila as she described all this. I pinched her to warn her but she was oblivious. Melina Miss pulled my hair scolding, 'You Little Sparrow… You've spoiled this nice girl.' We were taken to Dr Ivy's chamber and made to stand in front of the room. Tears flowed down my cheeks. At that time, I did not think of Dr Ivy or Melina Miss. I was only thinking of Zungmila's aunt lying in a heap of ash. Dr Ivy sent us back to the class after twenty minutes.

That year when I was promoted from the seventh standard to the eighth standard the report card's 'conduct' section bore the word 'talkative.' Though I had got good marks, I was apprehensive of showing the report card at home. Later, my parents looked at the card and admonished me mildly: 'Why do you talk so much?' I did not say anything and bowed my head.

I was in the tenth standard when the incident happened in the month of May. It was getting a little warm though it was not uncomfortable as we were in a hill station. We wore long-sleeved tunics even in May. The Super reminded us to keep a light sheet at night in the bed because some girls got sick with the change of season. That night too she did the same at night and retired bidding us 'good night.' Getting ready to sleep, we heard lots of high-pitched voices and music from the wing where Zungmila stayed. We also heard shouts of 'Happy Birthday!' But we wondered why they had to make so much noise even though it was somebody's birthday. Behind that wing were the quarters of the principal and 'foreign Sisters'. Usually we were very quiet when we went that side. Weren't they scared? Suddenly I remembered that the foreign Sisters had gone somewhere for a conference. But Dr Ivy was there. Weren't Zungmila and others scared of punishment? From the bed I heard the door of Dr Ivy's door open. What was going to happen now, we shivered in fear. We heard the sound of arguments and counter-arguments. All the girls in the hostel were awake now. Our teachers got up too. We were not allowed to come out of the dormitory. We peeped through the glass window because all the rooms were locked from outside. We saw that Zungmila and the girls from the hills were ready to go somewhere with their suitcases. It was almost 12 o'clock in the night. I could feel my hands and feet shake.

Did Dr Ivy throw these girls out for celebrating the birthday party? I ground my teeth and hissed, 'You she-wolf!' Why did she have to punish these girls so harshly? I would bring Zungmila to my room and make her sleep in my bed. I didn't care who said what. I was not going to listen to the tigress. I stepped out through the back door and then I stopped in astonishment. Dr Ivy, that tigress whom we feared so much, was kneeling on the veranda and begging the girls not to leave the hostel. She was uttering Lord Jesus' name repeatedly and how he forgave Judas. Dr Ivy's pitiful eyes were unrecognizable to me. I couldn't look at those eyes for long and bowed my head. The gang of girls, including Zungmila, walked out towards the lounge without listening. One of the girls was abusing Dr Ivy, the others also followed her and said repeatedly that if necessary they would listen to the White teachers, not the 'bloody Indian'. They were not going to obey the dark-skinned woman. They had come here to study under the Whites, not these despicable Indians. Zungmila was the one who cursed Dr Ivy most. She looked very aggressive indeed.

Somebody pulled me away from the veranda and brought me back to the room. That night, not a single girl in the room could sleep. Later we heard the sound of police jeeps and heavy boots going up and down on the veranda. All of us gathered on one bed as we were very scared by the turn of events. The next day we heard that the rebellious girls had reached the station that night itself. Dr Ivy had called the police to bring them back. Zungmila and the other girls were not allowed to come out of their rooms, not even to the dining room. After one week, the girls came back into the normal life of the hostel. Except Zungmila. By then the foreign Sisters returned too. We heard that Zungmila could be rusticated from the school.

Zungmila was sent to the room meant for girls in quarantine when they were afflicted with infectious diseases. I had seen girls with pox staying here. Once a girl who had contracted diphtheria was kept there too. No one was allowed to meet Zungmila. I heard from some sources that Zungmila was not well; she foamed at the mouth a couple of times and fainted. She also talked to herself. I just couldn't bear it. One night I sneaked out to meet her. The door of the isolated room was ajar. I went in. Zungmila had just come out of one of her fits; two Sisters were holding her from both sides. Dr Ivy was standing next to her. Seeing her I felt my throat go dry in apprehension. Dr Ivy was running her hands tenderly on Zungmila's head and was saying repeatedly, 'My child … my child …' Seeing me she came towards me. I felt my heart jump up in fear. Suddenly Zungmila opened her eyes and seeing Dr Ivy shouted, 'You bloody Indian!' She was mumbling something. Dr Ivy said, 'Yes, I am Indian; why do you hate Indians? Aren't you an Indian yourself?'

'No I am not an Indian, I hate Indians,' Zungmila was mumbling. I understood what she was saying; she was talking about her aunt. When her aunt's body was dug out from the heap of ash one of her breasts was hanging, distended. She was saying that now. Dr Ivy did not understand her language, I did. Dr Ivy allowed me to sit near Zungmila. Slowly Zungmila gave in to sleep under the influence of the injection Sister had given her a little earlier.

Both Dr Ivy and I came out together from the room. When I was going to the room I was scared to walk in the lonely corridor fearing even my own footsteps. But now I was without fear as Dr Ivy held my hand. The tigress as we secretly called her was no more a fearsome character for me. I felt as if I could confide everything in this woman. So on the corridor where light and shadows played hide and seek, I told her all about Zungmila. She listened without making any comment. When we reached my dormitory she placed her hand on my head and prayed for me. I uttered, 'Amen.' After the prayer, I told Dr Ivy that Zungmila was a very good girl, she should not be sent away from the school. She told me she would come back after she recovered from her illness.

Zungmila never came back. The last time I saw her face, it was full of hatred. She kept mumbling about her aunt and her distended breast.

It was a Sunday. The month, April; Year; 1997. How can I forget those days? The air was full of the smell of blood. Fear and nervousness were floating in the air. Everything was covered by a film of hatred that stuck like the hateful jelly of a snail. One could not place the hand anywhere; immediately it felt the hatred like a snail's cold mucus. The cold hatred then spread to the veins and travelled to the heart; the breathing stopped.

It was a time when money was counted only in lakhs and the number of deaths escalated every day. The group that wanted a separate state was becoming like the bharando bird; with its two mouths, it was devouring its own body. In this unnatural time, the game of money was heating up. People did not understand what was happening. They were asked to pay lakhs with a gun to their heads. The odour of blood pervaded the air more and more as the days passed. Sometimes on a single day, ten bodies were cremated together in the burning ghat. People got letters in large numbers bearing the demand for money. It was not known who had to sell fruit-bearing trees, land or ornaments to meet the demands. Everything was done secretly. There was an overwhelming sense of fear. On the other side of the coin was hatred. A hared that was sticky and difficult to wash away.

I am talking about a Sunday during that period. The place where we worked was often shut down under an unannounced curfew. The *bandh*, a kind of closure, was called at the drop of a hat stretching to hundreds of hours, throttling the people. That Sunday was a part of a thousand-hour *bandh*. I was reading a book lying in bed. The book was by Black American writer Toni Morrison. When the man came in I was not reading the book; I was actually looking at the writer's face in the dust jacket. I was wondering what pain one has to go through in order to create such characters. The writer's pen expressed pain and hatred piling up for centuries. I was asking myself, can the colour of skin create such hatred?

He came straight to my bedroom. He entered through the backdoor opening out to the veranda. My husband and son were watching a cricket match on the TV in the next room. He shut the door immediately after entering the room. I jumped up from the bed. The room was filled with the musty odour of a thick pair of jeans, unwashed and half-wet by a drizzle. I could see a gun peeping from his loose jacket. I understood immediately who he was. I had been getting the hateful letters for the last one month. I tried to wet my suddenly dry tongue.

'What do you want? Who are you?'

Perhaps I spoke rather loudly. My husband and son came running from the other room.

He ordered, 'I want the money.'

We forgot fear and argued: 'Just because you want it, where can we get so much money from?'

'You'll have to give.'

'If we can't what will you do?'

'Haven't you seen what we can do?'

'We can't pay so much.'

'Sell your house and land.'

'Who are you to tell us to sell our house and land?' I was getting angry.

'You are asking who we are?' he took out the gun and warned, 'Hey woman! Keep quiet! Otherwise I'll blow your skull off.'

'Okay, do it! You've killed many anyway.'

The phone rang. When my son tried to take the call the assailant jumped up and held his hand. 'Be careful! Don't try to move.'

'You will have to give us some time,' my husband said. He was trying to shield me and my son as if a goat was going to be attacked by a dog.

'Okay, I give you one week.'

'No, we'll need at least a month.'

'Fifteen days. After that our people will come.'

The boy was not standing still; he was looking this side and that, as if anticipating trouble.

'But we can't shell out so much money,' my husband said firmly.

'You'll have to. All these years you have cheated us.'

'Whom have we cheated? We are working here and trying to develop this region.'

'Before you came, we had only our people here. You are the people who cheated and drove away our people. What has your government given us? What do we have?'

We could hear a car stopping outside. The boy was ready to leave. Before going, he threw the words in the air, 'If you want to live in our land you'll have to stay under us.'

I sat there on the same chair, covered by the sticky jelly of hatred, from evening until night, in the same position, my hands and legs folded.

I could not sleep. The book had fallen from my hand when I jumped up as the boy made his appearance. I picked it up now and opened it. Toni Morrison's *The Bluest Eye*. I started reading from the page where it opened:

> *...They were out of breath and sank down in the green-and-purple grass on the edge of the pine woods.*
>
> *Cholly lay on his back panting. His mouth full of the taste*

of muscadine, listening to the pine needles rustling loudly in their anticipation of rain. The smell of promised rain, pine, and muscadine made him giddy. The sun had gone and pulled away its shreds of light. Turning his head to see where the moon was, Cholly caught sight of Darlene in the moonlight behind him. She was huddled into a D—arms encircling drawn-up knees on which she rested her head. Cholly could see her bloomers and the muscles of her young thighs.

'We better get on back,' he said.

'Yeah.' She stretched her legs flat on the ground and began to retie her hair ribbon. 'Mama gonna whip me.'

'Naw she ain't.'

'Uh-huh. She told me she would if I get dirty.'

'You ain't dirty.'

'I am too. Look at that.' She dropped her hands from the ribbon and smoothed out a place: n her dress where the grape stains were heaviest.

Cholly felt sorry for her; it was just as much his fault. Suddenly he realized that Aunt Jimmy was dead, for he missed the fear of being whipped. There was nobody to do it except Uncle O.V., and he was bereaved too.

'Let me,' he said. He rose to his knees facing her and tried to tie her ribbon. Darlene put her hands under his open shirt and rubbed the damp tight skin. When he looked at her in surprise, she stopped and laughed. He smiled and continued knotting the bow. She put her hands back under his shirt.

'Hold still,' he said. 'How am I gonna get this?'

She tickled his ribs with fingertips. He giggled and grabbed his ribcage. They were on top of each other in a moment. She corkscrew her hands into his clothes. He returned the play digging into the neck of her dress, and then under her dress. When he got his hand in her bloomers, she suddenly stopped laughing and looked serious. Cholly, frightened, was about to take his hand away, but she held his wrist so he couldn't move it. He examined her then with his fingers, and she kissed his face and mouth. Cholly found her muscadine-lipped mouth distracting. Darlene released his head, lifted her body, and pulled down her pants. After some trouble with the buttons, Cholly dropped his pants down to his knees. Their bodies began to make sense to him, and it was not as difficult as he had thought it would be. She moaned a little, but the excitement collecting inside him made him close his eyes and regard her moans as no more than pine sighs over his head. Just as he felt an explosion threaten, Darlene froze and cried out. He thought he had hurt her but when he looked at her face, she was staring wildly at something over her shoulder. He jerked around.

There stood two White men. One with a spirit lamp, the other with a flashlight. There was no mistake about their being White; he could smell it. Cholly jumped, trying to kneel, stand, and get his pants up all in one motion. The men had long guns.

'Hee hee hee heeeee.' The snicker was a long asthmatic cough.

The other raced the flashlight all over Cholly and Darlene.

'Get on with it, nigger,' said the flashlight one.

'Sir?' said Cholly, trying to find a buttonhole.

'I said, get on with it. An' make it good, nigger, make it good.'

There was no place for Cholly's eyes to go. They slid furtively, searching for shelter, while his body remained paralysed. The flashlight man lifted his gun down from his shoulder, and Cholly heard the clop of metal. He dropped back to his knees. Darlene had her head averted, her eyes staring out of the lamplight into the surrounding darkness and looking almost unconcerned, as though they had no part in the drama taking place around them. With a violence born of total helplessness, he pulled her dress up, lowered his trousers and underwear.

'Hee hee hee heeeee.'

Darlene put her hands over her face as Cholly began to simulate what had gone on before. He could do no more than make-believe. The flashlight made a moon on his behind.

'Hee hee hee heeeee.'

'Come on, coon. Faster. You ain't doing anything for her.'

'Hee hee hee heeeee.'

Cholly, moving faster looked at Darlene. He hated her. He almost wished he could do it—hard, long, and painfully, he hated her so much. The flashlight wormed its way into his guts and turned the sweet taste of muscadine into rotten fetid bile. They looked like baby claws.

'Hee hee hee heeeee.'

Black Cholly could not hate the White men. He did not have the capacity to hate White men; it was beyond his experience. So he hated the girl. She was witness to his impotence, his inability to protest, his failure. He could not save her from the glaring light of the torches. Under the flashlight who enjoyed the pleasure of invading her flowerlike virgin body? He or the White men? He was confused. But he hated her nonetheless. He wanted to torture her by using her body brutally for a long time. The image of her face, the ribbon blown over it by the wind, carved itself in his mind as a symbol of hatred. He hated the black-skinned girl, his compatriot, and the White men. Morrison herself said he was impotent. If he hated the White men that hatred would burn him, like a soft piece of coal in fire. There would remain only a question mark written with smoke and ash. Morrison hoped that one day he would overcome his failure '… when his hatred could find sweet expression'. I closed the book and, like before, slunk into the chair like a tortoise under its shell.

I was thinking of the boy who had abused me saying 'Hey woman, keep quiet!' I seemed to have seen him somewhere. He had the same spiky hair, beady eyes and wiry body. Then I remembered where I had seen him. He had fainted at the gate of our compound. That day our small town had become unrecognizable. The army had organized an interview and medical test for thirty reserved posts. Though they were by no means high posts, ten thousand young men had congregated for the test. It was quite a situation; nothing seemed to work that day in our small town, not even drinking water was available. The boy who fell down at our gate had a chance to run for the test only towards the fag end of the day. His eyes had seen sparks of yellow and violet fly as he ran. Even then he managed to finish his run. He had not eaten anything during the day. He did not have dinner either the previous night. He passed by our house on trembling feet which then gave way. We made him stay in our house for the night. He polished off all the rice cooked for the family. The young man was really very hungry. He had talked about his family; his mother was at home, his father had gone to Gujarat to work as a labourer. He said lots of men from his village had gone there looking for work. An agent had started recruiting men some years ago. From then on the chain had continued—younger brother after the elder brother, then an uncle, and then a nephew, and so on. There was no choice. The people who wanted to work did not have any job at home. He had six more siblings after him. His mother worked in the field if somebody hired her. After passing the Matric exam, he could not afford to study any more. He hoped fervently to get into the army. Yes, he was the same boy. Even if he wasn't, what difference did it make? The one who was among the ten thousand boys who came to participate in the test, or the rough mannered youth who visited us? There was not much difference. All of them had the same complaint—of others taking away their livelihood. The boy who abused me, calling me 'a woman!' had left defiantly. The unbearable stench of his clothes, which had not seen water for a long time, left behind a trail in the room.

That night, three well-known businessmen were murdered in our small town. Three healthy men—their mouths spurting blood, died. One was a Bengali, one Assamese and the other Marwari. Three pyres were lit together in the cremation ground. Sparks of hatred flew from the fire.

His eyes! When he talked he became excited. The hair-like veins in the corners of his eyes became blood red, as if they were two threads in a cloth. The veins spread across his eyes immediately.

He came to me one December afternoon. It was a Sunday too. He entered the house as if he were a regular visitor. There was no one in the house. I had finished the household chores and was sitting at the study table, trying to write a story. The boy who had just blown up a bazaar was sinking in the whirlpool of the river along with his arms and ammunition. He had left behind a hell. In August, a young girl took many bullets in her body, her body was perforated by gaping holes. She had come from outside the state, looking for the body of her husband, crying and beating her breasts in sorrow. In March, a talented professor had committed suicide. 1991. The killings that defied counting. In my story, a bazaar had been destroyed by bombs. On the boy's boots clung the white matter of a dead man's brain. On the way back he had seen a snake. A dead snake and a dead cat. The river was full of whirlpools. His back ached with heavy firearms. The road was slippery with rain water; his heavy boots, red with blood, were getting stuck in the mud.

'What are you doing?'

I jumped up.

'I've come to fetch you. Let's go.'

'Where do I have to go?'

I knew but asked nonetheless. I had been contacted by his organization. I had to go and teach the girls in the camp. They had even chosen the subjects for me: 'Historical materialism', 'The role of women in the Chinese revolution,' 'Lenin's view on women's freedom,' etc. I had received quite a few letters but didn't foresee that I would have to go abruptly like this.

He pulled down the curtain of the window. When he did it the pistol on his waist showed up from inside his jacket.

'I can't go just like this. There's no one at home. To whom do I leave this house? My son, husband ...'

'We have a women cadre. We'll inform them. They will come and look after your house.'

I was almost about to blurt out the differences between my and their ideologies. I wanted to tell him about the story I was writing. The boy would not be able to come out of the whirlpool. He would die, I had decided.

'I can't wait for long. You'll go with me on the motor cycle. A car is waiting on the embankment of the river. You don't have to pack anything. The girls at the camp will give you whatever you need,' he said.

He picked up the bunch of keys from my table and asked 'Is this bunch your house-key? Lock it up. Sir must be having a duplicate key.'

I drank water from the bottle on the table and stood up. I knew one day or the other I would have to face it.

'I can't go,' I said.

'Why?' the two red veins in his eyes were getting redder.

'I don't quite agree with your ideology.'

The veins in his eyes spread out across his eyes. He was angry. I said, 'I think your main demand is impossible to come through and ...:'

I was getting excited as I spoke. 'Why did you kill 164 people in the last two months even though the hostages were under your control?' I wanted to ask him why he and his fellow rebels had turned the bazaar with innocent people into a killing field.

The boy's voice became sterner as he said, 'Why don't you talk about that girl? She was dragged away by the army from the arms of her mother and elder sister. She was found among the water hyacinths, her mouth still tied with a cloth. I don't want to stay in this state.'

'You have the freedom to express your views; so do I.'

'So you are not going?'

'No.'

'What else can one expect from the opportunist middle class?' he said and went away, his eyes bloodshot.

In his eyes, I saw a bottomless pool of hatred.

I stayed in the same town as my pehi, my paternal aunt and peha, her husband. My father's family was well known in the place. Various members of it were working as responsible officers in different corners of the world. Moreover, they were very handsome people; my uncles or aunts would stand out in the crowd wherever they went. My youngest aunt, pehi, was no exception. She could also have continued the family tradition of high achievers but that did not happen. When she was a student in college she eloped with peha. My father's family could never accept this liaison with a man who was unsuccessful and just barely managed to go along. They were never invited to family get-togethers or festivals. As to why my family was so cruel to my youngest aunt, I could never understand. Despite having so many well-to-do brothers and cousins, pehi had to live in genteel poverty. After I came out of the family's roof as an independent person after getting married, the first thing I did was to visit her. I remember that my aunt got flustered and didn't know how to receive my husband, the new son-in-law in the family. I had heard about pehi's restive youthfulness and her fiery beauty. My grandmother, I had heard, kept her under wraps; she did not allow her to wear bright colours. Pehi had begged for a red mekhela chador, but my grandmother never indulged her. Instead she said, 'You don't have to walk around in a red dress; wear it when you go to your husband's house.' My grandmother apparently always finished her speech with the same sentence, 'If we don't get her married soon, she'll bring down the family's name.'

I had heard another thing from my mother. Pehi was known to have broken many a negotiation of marriage in the neighbourhood or relatives' families. When the groom's side came to 'see' the prospective bride, pehi would go to the house to help out, making tea and snacks, cut betel nut and leaf to serve the guests. Once the groom's side saw my beautiful aunt, was there any chance that they would choose another girl? My grandmother discovered that her youngest daughter did it deliberately. One day, a family was coming to see her younger sister's daughter Tora. In no way Tora could match up to my aunt. My grandmother asked pehi not to go in front of the prospective groom's side. But she did anyway. Her long hair fanning to her hips, she was sweeping the courtyard with a bamboo broom when the people came. After that, Tora Baidew's wedding proposal failed to come through. My grandmother did not say a word to pehi. After two years of that incident, my aunt walked out holding peha's hands.

The woman my father's family had abandoned as if she were a dead person, and the one I had imagined from all these stories did not seem to match up when I met her at last. It seemed she was on the verge of breaking down at the smallest provocation. Her eyes seemed to hold many unshed tears. She bent slightly as if tired of carrying a huge burden. When she tried to smile, it seemed like she was weeping.

As I was trying to find the girl who even kept off food in anger because she was not allowed to wear a red dress in this woman, her daughter Pomi came in. I looked at the beautiful girl in the churidar-kameez suit. Well, this was how I had imagined my aunt;

as restive, as pretty. Everything about Pomi seemed to match my imagined person—except for the greediness I saw in her eyes. Her envious eyes went over the new mekhela chador and gold ornaments I wore as a new bride.

Pomi soon got married to a leader of Assam's *andolon*, agitation. She was now quite rich. But her husband had a questionable past. The past was not so far away that people would forget that under his direction all the living things in a char, river island, were annihilated. Amidst the paddy fields were found bodies of men, women and children—killed like birds by shooters. The killers had left behind smelly rotten bodies, flocks of crows and eagles and poisoned water in the green island. They cut down every tree in the island.

Since Pomi's wedding with the leader was finalized pehi's house changed perceptibly. Peha's sad-looking grocery shop transformed into a well-lit, two-salesmen-flaunting shop. There was a small house that uncle had managed to build. The bathroom-toilet had remained the same, but now two additional rooms came up next to the kitchen. I noticed that pehi's weepy face brightened a bit. She came to visit me from time to time. Like my grandmother who took along something or the other while visiting houses, she also brought along something when she came. One day, she said sadly that no one from my family's side had invited the son-in-law of the house to lunch or dinner, as was the custom. He had one day teased Pomi in front of her parents: 'I heard that you have many high-profile relatives, but no one's invited me even for cup of tea.' I registered my aunt's broad hint.

But how could I invite this man who had spearheaded a massacre? I had tried to distance myself from Pomi and her husband as much as possible. One day my aunt cried in front of me and complained, 'They haven't been accepted by the family because they are my daughter and son-in-law. Our family has not only invited Sorumai's daughter and son-in-law but also sent them back with gifts and food.' Sorumai was a housemaid in our family. I looked at my aunt's face in astonishment. Our family looked down on her husband as if he were a street dog, they left her abandoned as if dead, but I had never heard her complaining. But today she was doing it, sad that her daughter and son-in-law were not welcomed by her family. Perhaps this was how she had felt when she wanted to wear a red mekhela-chador set.

I blurted out, 'Well, I was planning to invite Pomi and her husband anyway. Somehow our timing hasn't matched. I have even bought clothes to welcome them into my house.' I showed an *eri-muga* mixed warm scarf my husband had actually bought for his niece as a wedding gift and set of shirt and trouser piece. My aunt hugged me and said gratefully, 'My son-in-law has done a lot for us. How can I forget that despite her beauty many rejected her because she belongs to a poor family?' She ran her fingers tenderly on the clothes I showed her.

When my husband heard that I was going to invite Pomi and her husband to dinner he passed quite a few sarcastic comments: 'Yes, these days connection is very important to be upwardly mobile.' I got angry and there was quite a fight. At last it was decided he would do the shopping for the dinner but he would not eat with this new leader who was by now getting more powerful in the state's political arena.

Pomi and her husband promptly arrived on the date of invitation. I had also invited peha and pehi, but they politely declined the invite. Pomi had brought along lots of fruits and sweets, even clothes for us. I made them sit and accepted the gifts saying humorously, 'Now, I'll have to ring the bell with my elbow.'

Pomi and her husband did not understand the joke. I told them: Two friends had met after a long time. The local friend showed the visitor around and at last said, 'When you reach house no 107 ring the red bell with your elbow.' The friend was surprised. Why ring with the elbow? Was it something special? The local friend clarified, why, both your hands would be full of sweets and fruits, how would you ring the bell except with your elbow?

Pomi and her husband laughed. I did too. I was more talkative than necessary. When I offered him the cup of tea in his hands I saw a Sten gun. *Thak-thak-thak*... a group of people killed like birds at the hands of shooters. When he asked me something I seemed to hear an order—'Don't leave anyone alive.' To cover my hesitation I laughed more. The man was examining my house, the garden at the backyard, his hands clasped at that back as if he was a victor of some sort. A river island destroyed and full of dead bodies. I was showing off every flowering plant in the earthen pots. He washed his hands before coming to the dining table. The white basin seemed to fill up with blood. The gamocha for wiping hands—was that blood or the design in red on its border? I ladled out the rice. Husband and wife looked astonished at the number of dishes I had prepared. I could not look at the man for long. Instead I asked Pomi, 'You're going to stay back at pehi's place tonight, aren't you?' Pomi waved off the question, her five fingers gleaming with eight rings, and a bunch of gold bangles reaching from her wrist to the elbow jingling, 'No.'

'Why not?' I asked her, I putting some rice on her plate.

'Ma has asked me, though.'

'Why don't you stay for the night? Pehi will be very happy.'

'Frankly I also wanted to, but he has a problem.'

'What's the problem? Is it work?'

'Not really. He finds it difficult using the bathroom-toilet and hand pump.'

'I told you I'll build them this year,' he said.

The leader began to talk about building a nice little house according to an architect's plan. At this moment, Zamila entered with a plate of two roasted and cleaned eggplants, roasted potatoes, chopped coriander leaves and chopped onion. She had been my help since I came to this house as a bride.

'Baidew, here's the roasted eggplants,' Zamila said as she gave me the plate. I had asked her to roast the vegetables to make mashed pitika. She had come very early in the morning because guests were coming. I saw that she looked a little tired. Perhaps she was hungry too. Pomi decided to change her richly embroidered chador before sitting down to eat.

'Wait please, don't serve the rice yet; let her come,' the man said.

I was alone with him. I didn't know what to talk about and, to break the awkward silence, I started talking about Zamila. 'We were lucky she was there when my mother-in-law was so ill,' I said.

'What was wrong with her?'

'She was sick for a long time. One side of her body was paralysed due to a stroke. The way Zamila took care of her, even cleaning up the body wastes, was hard to believe unless one saw it.'

'So your mother-in-law died here.'

'Yes, her last rites were performed here.'

Pomi was taking longer than I thought. Perhaps she had gone to the bathroom. I could hear the tap water running in the bathroom. I could see that Pomi's husband was looking angry. To break the uneasiness, I continued, 'You know, on the *shraddha* day, one of the priests didn't want to place the offerings on the sarai because it was cleaned and washed by Zamila.'

As the man listened, his forehead wrinkled in disapproval.

'I protested vehemently. This was the woman who had looked after the old woman until her death and now the chickpeas were impure because she had washed them, I argued. Luckily they accepted it eventually.'

Pomi returned.

'Pomi, I now know why your sister is so fond of Bangladeshis,' he said. Then he addressed me in a tone reserved for people who came to him for help, 'You know Baidew, don't indulge these people. You were talking about cleaning the bedpan etc. If you allow them to enter the house, they will even lick your feet.' He thumped on the table forcefully. The crockery on the table jumped up. 'Keep an eye, if nothing can be done about them we'll kill them all.'

I could not help smiling a little ironically as I said, 'We've heard that people of Assam should forget about humanity. This is the time to forget humanity.'

The phone rang. I ran to take the call. It was pehi. She asked me if Pomi was going to stay back at her house that night. Pomi smiled when I told her and said, 'No, we'll be on our way. It's only a two hours' drive and he likes driving fast.'

'This car is very good for long drives. Please come along one day. We can go to your parents' home too. A few days ago, your soru mama, younger uncle, called me.'

'Soru mama wants to open a nursing home in Guwahati,' Pomi said.

I remembered pehi's words: 'She's not accepted because she's my daughter.' She would realize soon that there was a difference between her husband and her son-in-law who was capable of largesse.

I didn't say anything and dished out the pulao. With pure ghee, cashew nuts and raisins added to the good quality joha rice, it gave out an enticing fragrance. Zamila had cooked the pulao.

'Is that so?' I asked mildly. That my soru mama was going to open a nursing home in Guwahati was news to me. And I came to know about it from the daughter of his sister who was given up as dead by the family. My mother had informed me, of course, that mama had retired as the chief medical officer of OIL India company.

'So what have you decided? I have to inform pehi.' I wanted to change the subject.

'He doesn't want to stay. After the bathroom is renovated and water…' Pomi laughed looking at her husband, 'He is also worried that my skin will get ruined using the water from the handpump.'

I didn't know what happened to me. My grandmother's teaching that a guest was like a god even if he was an enemy, my niece and husband whom I had invited myself, my pehi's face—I forgot everything.

'What did you say?' I almost screamed, 'The house of your parents, the house you grew up in, the clothes she had woven for you, the sweaters she knitted…' I lost control. 'Don't you feel ashamed saying in front of me that your skin will lose its sheen using the handpump water that you always used? How dare you say that?' My voice grew sterner as I said these things.

The dining table with its savoury dishes, the golden pulao on the ice-white plate, the eri-muga warm scarf, the trouser and shirt material—all were looking at me in astonishment.

I did not know why, but after a long time I remembered Zungmila.

The Half-burnt Bus at Midnight

Right in front of the police station at the four-lane junction, a road forks away from the national highway. Further down this road, the traffic thins down. Instead of shops and bazaars, you see paddy fields on both sides of the road. After a while, you can spot a river which runs alongside the road all the way through. Sometimes you can see the river right next to the road, sometimes it looks on from a little distance, then it disappears altogether, as if in hiding, then reappears and flows coolly along. Beyond the stretch of green fields, the hills take on the hue of peacock feathers. The paddy fields, the sky and the hills, all dazzle the eye. Occasionally, a rainbow arches right across the sky. The river borrows a bit of the rainbow and mixes the colours on its own liquid palette. When the river flows through leafy banks of trees, it turns green; the sky adds a tinge of orange in the afternoon; amid the sand banks, it seems brown and sombre. From time to time, it turns sharply, like a dancer bending her waist, then flows on.

Two rows of simolu trees flank the river near the bridge from where it flows straight on and disappears from the roadside. In the flowering season, when birds flit joyously from flower to flower, sipping nectar, the trees look as if they are covered with a quilt flecked with bright red patterns. When the seeds burst with cotton-wool, the trees look as if they are covered in snow.

The little town begins where the rows of simolu trees end. The little river girdles the town, flowing serenely by the backyard of a house, the window of another, even the front doors of some other homes. At the crack of dawn, when the sky awakes in a flush of pink, schools of small jaworia fish, too, wake up in the stream, only to disappear underwater as the day grows brighter. The river keeps the town well-watered and the trees a lush green. Upstream, the river starts playing hide-and-seek among the emerald carpets of tea bushes and then it gets slimmer and swifter and ducks for cover at will.

The people who live on the banks of the river are like a flock of chickens without the mother hen. Nobody has given them anything. Unused to privileges of any kind, they do not demand anything and probably believe they deserve none either. They get by, making do with whatever is within their reach, and somehow manage two meals a day. Of their own accord, they have kept the neighbourhood clean. The bridge has been waiting to be completed for the last two years without any progress and they have managed, or tried to, with the unsteady temporary bridge built by the contractor of the project. During the rainy season, the road gets speckled with potholes deep enough for a duck to swim. If people have to pass by that patch they do somehow avoiding the deep holes and cars and buses. Sometimes a few people get together to fill up the worst of the potholes. They are careful to look after themselves around the temporary bus-stand and the temporary bazaar avoiding any kind of trouble. Whichever political party declares a *bandh*, they observe it ; they are watchful to never get into an argument or strife and are ultra conscious that they do not get involved.

So life continues like this. The waves of conflict from outside invade their equanimity from time to time; after sometime like a flood that leaves behind destruction, they go away. The people keep to themselves for some time and then slowly venture out. After all, they have to fill their stomachs. Like flood sweeping away some, these conflicts also take away a few; those who are left behind reminisce about them and organize the funeral rites. After a period of time, all that is left of them are memories. And the town gets on, with its ups and downs. During the chhat puja festival, they light up the place on the bank with bright bulbs; loud film music blares from the microphone. On the morning of Bihu, they take the cattle to the river to give them a ritual bath; during the wedding season, women, accompanied by a band-party go to the river to collect water for the ritual bath of the bride; they perform shraddha for the departed soul on the bank, and immerse the idol of the devi after the puja is over.

On the days when trouble brews, the army puts up temporary camps on the bank of the river. On these days people avoid, though it is more convenient, the ghats where they usually wash clothes or have baths. Instead, they go up the river or use the tubewell in their backyard for the daily chores. Thus the people have learnt to cope with life in the town despite its rickety bridge and the road full of potholes. The schools and colleges hold exams, a few get through with high marks while some fail to get pass marks. Some die, some are born—in short, life goes on in its own way. Money allotted for the broken bridge and uneven roads goes to the big city to be spent by some on cars too big for the lanes and on luxurious multi-storeyed buildings. The people look at these buildings, discuss among themselves and then abandon the topic as useless.

However, sometimes the town with its winding river becomes impatient. One day, a boy returning from school was abducted in broad daylight in the heart of the town by a gang on motorbikers. As the drama unfolded with demand for lakhs of rupees the townspeople came out into the street. Though they might seem simple and yielding, at times they could prove to be obstinate too. However, because it is more peaceful compared to other towns and villages in the vicinity, it has been expanding quite rapidly. New houses have been coming up in the open fields and on the bank of the river. The higher part of land on the bank is already full; now even on the land level to the river, houses have been built as if in a frenzy. After all, this river, slim and calm, has never created trouble for anyone. Well, one should never take it for granted; the water level might rise some day, it is a river after all. But now at least there is no problem; if it happens one will see. With this thought in mind, little cottages have been coming up, their small kitchen gardens almost levelling with the water. The people living here treat the river as if it is their own pond in the backyard. Placing a stone slab on the water they have drawn out their own space, their very own ghat. How much garbage the poor householders would generate anyway? Theirs are not big houses or a hotel that will produce tonnes of plastic waste everyday. They are poor no doubt, but they have their own toilets. So all they use the river for is washing clothes and having a bath. The river does not mind, it takes that much grime nonchalantly on its way. With the moist touch of the water, the trees on the bank—coconut, jackfruit, betel nut, etc.—have grown rapidly creating a border of green on the bank.

Every member in the family living in the little cottages takes part in running the house. If the husband goes to stand in line for buying biscuits in the wholesale shop to be sold at a little profit back home, the wife leaves home to work in somebody's house as a part-timer or to the bazaar to sell the home-made puffed rice, moori. Most of them cannot afford to send their children, especially the boys, to college. After passing the school final or even before that, the boys take up some job around the place. Most of them work in car repairing garages or bakeries or as salesmen in shops. The people here are grateful to the town that somebody has not come out with a gun to shoot them dead and that they are still alive. In the evening, the earthen lamp lit at the base of the basil plant in the courtyard of every house reflects on the water like garlands of light.

One does not come across houses big enough to attract attention in this part of the town. The few which are to be found are in the centre of the town. The only big house in this area belongs to Ramgopal De. Ramgopal has left behind his original home under duress. Actually, all the people who have built their little houses on the bank of the river have been driven out of their own homes in different villages. Like them, Ramgopal had also left behind his home, fearing the ethnic cleansing some people indulged in while seeking their own land, and has now settled down here. Everybody calls him 'De babu'. He had sold off his paddy fields, house—everything, at a ridiculously cheap price before coming here. He opened a garage to start his life all over again. Besides repairing damaged cars, he has also started another business. He buys broken cars and buses, almost beyond repair, and makes them as good as new and sells them in the market. Often he buys passenger buses abandoned because they are too ramshackle for use, then makes a new body, repairs the engine, and sells them to an interested buyer. At times he even buys buses auctioned by the government agencies.

Most of the boys who work at De babu's garage belong to the houses on the riverbank. Ramgopal started prospering quite soon. Like his neighbours, he is also grateful to the town. Well, there are those who come from time to time to collect money from him. Wherever one lives, there will be a class of people who will squeeze money from people like him, he knows. But isn't he lucky that someone hasn't come to burn his cottage or shot and killed members of his family? His two sons have grown up here. Now the older one is studying for a medical degree and the younger one computer science. So he is grateful to the little town. In fact, most of the people in this town are new settlers coming from different parts of the region after leaving their homes for some reason or the other. In the last decade, lots of people from the interior parts have arrived fearing for their lives, have bought small plots of land and built new houses. They belong to different communities, all looking for a new beginning. The little town by the river has not turned away anyone. The elephant herds descending from the hills do not reach here, even those with their guns cannot come to kill the residents blatantly. Yes, from time to time, a body is found by the roadside, and a bit of looting and demand for money go on surreptitiously. But who considers these small incidents as dangerous?

The real danger is heralded by the ones with two legs. They could shoot down everyone in sight as if people were birds; they could put the houses on fire if they fancied. So the people remain fearful—like cattle after escaping from a burnt-down shed and are now so scared they fear even the hint of a red cloud. They prick their ears instantly even at the sound of crackers from a wedding party arriving at the bride's house. Has anything happened? Is there trouble somewhere?, they worry. But then life goes on. The rice stalks ripen in the field, the simolu trees flower, the silver fish play in the river, trees of ripe mangoes and jackfruit, orange and lychee bow with the weight of the fruits, the new moon appears, the full moon washes over the countryside, the dhol's beats welcome the Bihu, the dhak resounds with the puja, the ciphun flute is heard. Men with their farm produce congregate in the weekly haat as always. Yes, life goes on.

One day into this town entered a bus at midnight. Around 12 o' clock, the bus approached the road, which veers away from the national highway near the police checkpost at the four-lane junction. The bus could not progress on its own steam, a truck was pulling it. The silence of the night was rudely disturbed as the bus laboured through the road.

The lights from the cars on the national highway had obliterated the soft light of the full moon, but this lonely road was flooded by moonlight. The trembling leaves of the coconut trees took on a silver hue under the sky. And the river? It was as if it had plucked off the moon from the sky and gathered it in her breasts. The water sparkled with its silvery waves. At twenty minutes to 10 o' clock, the bus arrived on the bank of the river with a screeching sound. But now the moon resting on the breast of the river suddenly disappeared. The silver colour vanished too. The bus was being dragged along the riverbank. Wherever the truck-drawn bus passed by, the water of the river turned dark; the sky above the water became dark too. There was no moon, no stars; what remained was only an inky, dark, impenetrable sky. An odd putrid smell came out from the river water. Like the odour of clotted day-old blood. Under the dark sky as the bus went on, the water of the river became red—the colour of blood.

The truck stopped after some time. The driver and his assistant got down for a wash in the river. They had come a long way after all and needed to freshen up. They could not see any habitation around. When the driver braked to stop the bus, its front portion banged into something. In any case, the bus was in a shambles. Now a burnt splinter of wood from the bus fell into the river. Immediately the silver fish came floating up on the surface, all dead. Why did the fish die suddenly? Was it because the river got filled with blood and so they could not breathe? Or was it because the moon disappeared and darkness covered the earth? Once again, the burnt bus pulled by the truck was on its slow journey along the river where it played hide and seek with the road. Wherever the shadow of the bus fell on the river, the water became blood-red in colour and the fish died. As the bus tore through the midnight silence with its screeching *ghetleng, ghetleng* sound, the fireflies in flight above burnt into ashes and vanished into the jungle.

The truck took a turn. It was difficult to manoeuvre the bus tied to its rear. But the road was empty so it could somehow be managed. At that point, the river also took a turn. At that junction, one could see a sizeable sandbank. The land here remained fertile all through the year. Even today it was so. Newly appearing green seedlings of wheat had carpeted the soil. As the bus followed the truck at this turning, its shadow fell on the sandbank. Instantly a fire seemed to burn everything. The little wheat plants were in cinders as if a jungle fire had scorched them. The leaves became black and crumpled. Their young stalks sank to the earth. Within a minute, the green stretch ensconced lovingly in the midst of the river lost its lush cover and took on an ugly black hue.

Now the bus was travelling underneath a huge banyan tree. The ancient tree's branches had sprouted roots that penetrated the earth. It was really a huge tree. From here the wide paddy fields stretched for miles. After a tiring day in the field, the farmers took rest under the shade of the tree. They shared lunch and exchange news of the day before returning to the fields again. The trunk and branches had many hollows where different kinds of birds made their nests. Next to the tree were paddy fields, the tree provided shelter, so it was natural that birds built nests here. But now something happened to the old tree. It could not give protection to the myriad birds it had sustained for so long. As the half-burnt bus wound its way underneath the banyan tree, the birds fell down one by one like seeds. They looked shell-shocked and lay spreadeagled on the ground. A big family of salika fell on top of each other in a pile. Flocks of parrot, sparrow, bulbuli, mou-pia—lay dead in clusters on the grass below. Like the kopou birds of north India, which drop off one by one in the peak of summer, these birds of the ancient tree also fell off one by one from the branches. It looked as if life had been sucked away from them by an unbearable heat.

Darkening the sky and the water of the river, killing the fish, burning the fireflies, impaling the birds, the half-burnt bus went on towards the little town. At the edge of the town is an old pond. A thick cluster of lotus flowers has been there for ages. The leaves entangle with each other, the flowers pop up one after another adoring the moonlight. Tonight the white and red lotuses were in full glory under the silver moon. But as soon as the bus reached there, the lotuses started looking unnatural. It was as if a wind hot enough to melt metals wrapped itself around the blooming flowers. Before the eyes could blink, the flowers withered and came to rest on the leaves. But how could the leaves hold on to the flowers. They themselves crumpled up in the heat. By the time the bus left the spot, the beautiful lotus garden on the pond was gone.

The truck was speeding up a little now. The driver must have been tired after the long journey and wanted to reach home as soon as possible. The screeching sound was getting louder—*ghetleng, ghetleng*, it went. Now one could hear its approach from the rows of the simolu tree. But these trees were sturdy. Not like the delicate lotus or the tiny birds, nor like the little fish in the river, which could be killed with one slight of the palm. They had sturdy trunks and strong branches. But were they strong enough to save themselves from the poisonous gas emitting from the burnt vehicle? Now as the bus passed by the road, their leaves wilted as if singed by fire. The strong gas poisoned the trees to their roots. In a moment, the branches which were playing with the moonlight and breeze bowed down in anguish. The row of trees died instantly. The burnt leaves gathered into knee-high dumps beneath.

At last the bus arrived in the little town. It was almost dawn now. People were slowly waking up. On the right side, from where the road led to the town, there was a small, neat house. Even a cursory glance could tell that the family had moved in recently. The coconut plant was young, the banana plant had just one flower and the pomegranate tree was yet to come up to a proper height. Like the young plants the family had a little baby; two new teeth had just appeared in his otherwise empty gums. He slept by early evening, so now he was awake and playing in the bed. He got tired and started crying. His mother was still sleepy and wanted to hush him by putting her nipple in his mouth. Just then the bus crossed by their house. Suddenly the milk froze in her breast, depriving the baby of his only food. The baby started yelling and the mother looked on helplessly.

The bus rambled on in the half darkness of dawn. Through the unsteady bridge, through the broken road, it passed on.

There is a very old paddy field around here. People live on its other side. The river goes through the open field in a straight line from this corner. The field had already been ploughed. On some patches rice saplings have been planted, but most of the parts were still muddy after the ploughing. The sun from the east had just touched the field when the bus arrived there. The freshly ploughed field filled with ashes. The black earth looked grim and ugly. The bright light of the morning looked like plumes of smoke. The newly dug field ready for planting should have smelt of moist earthy smell; instead it now smelt of ashes from burnt houses and smoke.

But the bus went on, that half-burnt bus.

The black ash made the mud sticky. The frogs living in the field perished, their white bellies lay upturned to the sky. They started giving out a putrid smell that filled the air making it unbearable to breathe.

The bus was now skirting the field. A few minutes ago, a flock of white cranes had landed in the field. Now their white wings too were spattered with black soot. Then one by one they dropped on the black earth, their necks twisted at an odd angle. The white flock of cranes was now dead.

As the paddy field got left behind, the houses appeared. Most of the people were still sleepy. The bus had gone over some horrendous patches of road while passing the villages and got a drubbing. Now while coming across a big crater on this road where after a rain a duck could swim, the bus jumped at the impact. A loose glass scattered into smithereens with a loud noise. A few people who were feeling lazy to get up though they were awake found their chest pierced by shards of glass. They could feel the sharp pieces lodged in their hearts and doubled over in their beds with intense pain.

The bus left the main road unable to go ahead; the bridge in front was half-complete. The people somehow crossed over the temporary bamboo bridge, but was it possible for a bus to do so? So it took the road on the side of the reserve forest. It is a government reserve forest. The jungle is full of saal and segun trees. There are other trees too and underneath are bushes of dhekia ferns. As the half-burnt bus progressed through the forest, the thick leaves of saal trees got burnt and soon an acrid smell like burning tobacco leaves spread in the air. The bark of the trees became black and the fern leaves turned into cinders.

Destroying the forest thus, the bus went on. Bypassing the broken bridge, the bus emerged on the other side of the main road. The river too emerged at this point.

The air was heavy with moisture; perhaps it was going to rain. The dancing dragonflies indicated it. The soft light of the morning fell on their transparent wings and reflected the hues of sunlight. They went up flying into the air, waited for sometime and then started flying again horizontally. But as the sound of the bus heralded its arrival, the dragonflies died, burnt. Within a second, their thin wings crumbled and put an end to their dancing frenzy.

So it went on, this terrible bus, destroying everything on its way.

The crows started cawing from their nests. The street dogs woke up from their slumber and started barking. 'What's happened this early in the morning?' some people wondered and opened their windows to check. If someone caught sight of the bus he or she could not open their eyes any more for they started smarting. They splashed water. In agony, some wondered whether to blindfold themselves or put some cream in their eyes, but soon they realized they were losing vision.

The bus was still moving. Its destination was the garage of De babu.

The boys were coming out from the houses on the edge of the river, houses where the earthen lamps lit in the evening at the base of basil plants reflected as garlands on water. It was early morning, too early, in fact, for them to start work. But today their boss had asked them to start earlier than usual. A new job was coming up. The malik had already bought the material for seat covers, bundles of rexine and leather, steel sheets and other knick-knacks needed to convert a broken down bus into a new one. In fact, De babu had arranged to bring some more half-burnt buses for repair work. After all, these kinds of buses were not found at all times. He was expecting some good profit. The young men were approaching from the opposite direction of the oncoming half-burnt bus. They seemed very enthusiastic. This job meant some extra money for them. Which meant they could fulfill some secret desire. They gave their regular earning for keeping the home fire burning, but this money could buy a pair of jeans, a cell phone, a pair of shoes perhaps. So those boys at the cusp of adolescence and youth were coming early without complaining and chatting happily.

The bus had by that time reached De babu's garage. The young boys saw the bus from a distance. A half burnt bus with a long body black with soot. Even in this state, it was easy to see that it was a luxury bus meant for long distance travel, comfortable and smart. They were sure that with their experienced hands they could make it as good as new.

The young men approached the bus with hammers and other tools. Two of them slid down under the bus, two went to the front, two stood by the side of the bus. They were ready to start. But as soon as they touched the bus they were turned into stone. Yes, those fresh young men standing between adolescence and youth turned into statues.

That bus, which had entered the town at midnight aiming at De babu's garage, had come from a place that had reverted to an uncivilized age. The community that wanted its own state wanted to establish its right over others and had called for a bandh. The bus had entered the area early in the morning. It was full of passengers. The morning was bright and sunny. Under that bright sun, the bus was burning furiously. Not a single passenger could escape from the bus. The windows and door of the bus were shut tight and a can of petrol was emptied on the vehicle. Even before the fire caught properly, the poisonous gas asphyxiated the little children in the lap of their parents. On the lonely road, the bus burnt unattended. Before fleeing the scene, the attackers had aimed their rifles at the bus, the bullets came in torrents. Of course, not a single passenger survived. By the time the police, military, administrators and fire brigade vans arrived, the people inside the bus were dead, their bodies only clumps of burnt flesh.

Yes, the half-burnt bus entered the town at midnight.

Kunu's Mother

Do you see that thin brown woman, walking fast, basket on head?

That's Kunu's mother. Neither too tall nor too short. Must be about thirty. Perhaps less, perhaps more. Who keeps a tab on age anyway? Her skin is chapped, her teeth dark, and her hair all coarse and coppery from too much sun and wind.

There is a strong whiff of spices trailing Kunu's mother now—a pungent bouquet of cumin, peppercorn and garam masala made from cardamom, cinnamon and cloves. That's because she has just finished grinding spices at the roadside eatery. There are different smells trailing Kunu's mother at different times of the day: early in the morning, it's goat dung and the droppings of ducks and chickens; later in the day, it's the aroma of puffed rice or boiled rice, the sharp tang of bamboo shoots and kolmou, dhekia or dhania greens. Post-lunch, it's sweat mingled with the dust and stench of the bazaar. When the sun moves westwards, Kunu's mother walks up to that small bridge over there, the smell of spices trailing her, to take a quick dip in the stream. Finally rid of all the smells of her long working day, she walks back home to her little cottage built on two kotha of land. As darkness descends outside, Kunu's mother stretches her aching feet at last. A soft sweet smell perfumes the air when Kunu brings her mother a glass of tea with salt.

Kunu, her only daughter. Curly-haired, wide-eyed, soft-skinned young Kunu, student of Class Nine at the local school, proud possessor of two sets of school uniform and lavish user of soap, shampoo, talcum powder and Fair and Lovely and Vaseline creams. When Kunu leaves for school wearing the mekhela and starched blue-bordered chador, how her mother's chest puffs up in pride!

These days, Kunu even makes dinner by the time her mother is back. Look at her—she doesn't even need a ladle to stir the simmering fish curry; instead, she holds both sides of the wok with wads of cloth and flips the fish expertly, a skill she learnt from her mother. Today Kunu had also prepared a dish with green papaya, charred banana stem and raw fish, and chopped up a sprig of coriander for the garnish.

When Kunu's mother came back home that evening, she found the bed sprinkled with red flowers, faintly fragrant with soap. Kunu had spread that white-and-red floral print bedcover that she had bought after much pleading and bargaining. Lulled by the inviting freshly washed smells (Kunu took great care to wash the bedclothes ever so often in the stream behind their home), Kunu's mother lay down on the bed and slipped into a snooze in spite of herself.

'Mai! Why have you…?'

She woke up with a start, hearing the reproach in Kunu's voice.

'Oh, I forgot, sorry!'

Kunu put down the wok and rushed over to snatch the bedcover. Folding it up carefully, she muttered, 'How many times have I told you not to lie on this? What if it is torn? Can we afford another one?'

'Why would it tear if I sleep on it?' smiled Kunu's mother. 'Do I have thorns on my body?'

The girl began to weep. Kunu's mother got up from the bed and promised hastily, 'Okay, okay, I won't do it again.'

Wiping her tears, Kunu busied herself, trying to arrange the folded clothes evenly on the clothesline that hung across the little room. But try as she might, the rope continued to sag under the weight of clothes sliding down from either side. In a bid to placate her, her mother said, 'Kunu dear, this time I'll get Roma carpenter to make a wooden clotheshorse for you.'

'Really?' Kunu's face brightened instantly.

'Well, I have a bit of money… but won't you need some for school this time?'

Kunu was silent. True, it was time to pay her school fees. In fact, she needed a new chador as well; her old one had torn after a stiff dose of starching the other day. But how could she possibly ask for a new set of clothes? Especially when it was only too painfully evident how the old woman toiled day and night to make ends meet.

With an aching heart, she went up to her mother and put an arm around her. 'Come Mai ei, let's have dinner.'

They sat down to their frugal meal of parimol rice from the ration shop, fish with mustard and onion and papaya curry. After dinner, as mother and daughter lay down to sleep, holding on to each other, the scent of jasmine wafted in from the garden, playing a game of hide-and-seek as it enveloped them like a comforting coverlet.

Kunu had brought home the jasmine sapling from a friend's house sometime ago. She always brought along a cutting of some variety of plant. Her young hands fashioned a garden round the little house. Her mother regarded these as useless plants and sometimes they argued over it. Kunu's mother pointed out that the shrubs reached upto their small veranda and filled half the plot of land too. Frogs and a pair of muchuragom snakes which liked to devour frogs hid there. In winter, if she wanted to grow some vegetables, she did not find enough space. But Kunu wailed when her mother said all this. So she had stopped saying anything. Let her be happy, she thought. On the morning of Saraswati puja and other such occasions, she kept awake through the night guarding her beloved garden. Once, before the puja, a gang of children invaded her marigold flower patch. Kunu had kept awake all night but had dozed off towards the wee hours. Hearing a sound, she woke up and saw that her marigolds were gone. She cried her heart out. This was Kunu. How could she ask her to do away with her 'unnecessary' plants? Instead, she planted fat black chillies in the free space. Selling them in the market would at least take care of the salt and oil for the house.

Taking advantage of her mother's indulgence, Kunu enthusiastically planted flowers of various kinds while her mother tried her best to plant those she thought useful. Near Kunu's hibiscus flower tree was a cage for the goats; near her rose bushes she planted a row of sanchi trees, ten of them, which she had bought for rupees five each. The plants were already tall enough. At times Kunu's mother looked mesmerized at the growing trees. If she could get the amount of money selling them at the price people said she would! Even if she got half the money, it would be enough to finance Kunu's wedding. At this point, she stopped thinking for sometime. Well, one day she would have to marry Kunu off. What kind of bridegroom would she get? She was trying her best to give her daughter an education. She was hoping that after passing the school Kunu would go to college. She was hoping to marry her off to a graduate boy, a nice, quiet one. And why shouldn't he like Kunu, anyway? A girl like her was rare in the community. In looks, work, manners, she could not find anyone matching up to her daughter, because frankly, there was none. In her imagination, she was often absorbed thinking of her graduate pair of daughter and son-in-law.

'Mai ei, what are you doing staring at the trees? Come, have tea!'

Her reverie was broken by her daughter's call.

She looked at Kunu and said, 'Study well. Don't busy yourself with housework alone.'

Kunu's mother had also maintained a coop for ducks and chickens. Kunu loved a mash of boiled egg and potatos tempered with salt and mustard oil with her rice. By selling the extra eggs, she managed to buy Kunu's pen-pencil, her exercise books, eraser etc.

She had also planted a bamboo stem in one corner; from it a few slim bamboos were coming up now. Under it was a cage for a pig. Kunu did not like it at all; she hated it because it was such a dirty animal. She often told her mother, 'Bring a calf instead. I'll look after it; you can sell the milk and use the cowdung for the garden too.'

Her mother laughed and teased her saying, 'Well you can use the pig shit too.' Kunu got very angry when she said that; her fair skin turned pink with indignation.

However, Kunu's mother had been thinking of it for quite sometime and thought of selling the pig and bringing in a calf; she had even made enquiries. Kunu kept pestering her to buy the calf with a white spot on its forehead from their neighbour Shanti's house.

The only thing Kunu approved of were the three honeycombs her mother kept. She often kept staring at the bees jumping from one flower to another in her garden to collect honey for the combs. She learnt from her mother how to clean the combs and also squeeze out the honey. With the money from selling the honey, she bought a cane table and chair. She had also embroidered a table cloth to cover the table and showed off her work when her friends visited. She had already told her mother that this time when they sold the honey she would buy a small radio set.

Kunu's mother had also planted near the bamboo cluster three sturdy gomari saplings. Now they were flourishing too. The vendor in the market had told her she would be able to sell them after ten years. The price of one would be enough to buy Kunu's jewellery. A bejewelled, graduate bride and ... she would again be lost in thought when Kunu would call 'Mai ei, why do you look at the trees all the time, come have tea.'

Gomari and Sanchi trees, the new bamboo trees, ready-to-sell pig, the egg-laying chickens and ducks, plans to buy a calf, honey combs paying for the cane chair and table, the flower garden around the thatched house, the red embroidered bed cover—this was the world of the mother and daughter living happily in the little house. In the moonlight, the house was flooded with a white light; in the setting sun, it took on an orange hue and in rainy days it turned silver.

Inside, the woman and her daughter chatted about this and that, absorbed with each other.

'Mai ei, with the money from selling the honey please buy a clotheshorse.'

'You know Kunu, each of those trees sells for how much?'

'Oh, you are lying.'

'When I sell the pig I'll make a pair of gold bangles for you.'

'No, I don't want it. Please buy me a radio. It has programmes on our studies too.' Then Kunu hugged her mother and said, 'No Mai ei, I don't want anything. You don't even have a warm shawl.'

'Oh, this one will do for the time being. Or I'll buy one from Mainao's mother; she's weaving quite a few. I don't have to pay in cash as long as we can supply the eggs. Do it from now so that by winter the cost will have been paid.'

She touched the curly hair on her daughter's forehead and said, 'So it also talks about your study material?'

'Where?'

'Why, on the radio!'

'Oh, say that then!'

'Once I sell the pig, I'll buy you a radio.'

Their budget, their plans would go topsy-turvy with plans for selling this and buying that for the house as they talked.

Soon Kunu's eyes would become heavy with sleep. Her mother would lovingly run her fingers through her daughter's hair, many thoughts running through her mind. She would buy her a radio. Kunu would listen to the radio talk about her studies. She would learn new things; then she would pass out from the college and she would marry her off, bejewelled with necklace and earrings, to a boy passing out from college… Who knows Kunu could even become a teacher and the boy would be… He would call her like Kunu 'Mai ei!' No she did not want anything more. She did not need anything; she had her own house. And she would live here until her death. She was on her own. Her mind roamed around her small piece of land with the coconut trees, bamboo grove, honeycombs, the ducks and chickens….

Kunu's mother was always alert though. Even the sound of a falling leaf made her jump up. The bitch at Babli's place had given birth to six puppies. She must bring a black and white puppy for herself. It could sleep on the veranda. They were two lone women in the house without a male member. If there was a dog she would feel a little more secure. From the time Kunu started wearing mekhela chador, she felt restless and fearful from time to time. At these moments, she remembered her man, and her tired eyes welled up with unshed tears.

Then she felt a surge of anger that shook her whole being with its force. From her childhood, she had had to manage on her own. Her mother died when she was very young. Her father married again. Before bringing the second wife, he took her to the town to stay with a family as a housemaid. When she thought of her father she felt her heart getting heavy with sorrow. He spent his life being ill-treated and neglected by his second wife. He did not enjoy a good meal nor could he afford a presentable dress. He roamed from bazaar to bazaar selling ice in the summer and fried chickpeas in winter. His earning was not enough to feed his wife and children. He died without treatment because he did not have enough money to buy medicines. Yet he never touched his daughter's earnings. The lady of the house where she worked had opened a bank account in her name and kept her salary there. Where were her step brothers and sisters now, she wondered sometimes. Their house in the village was gone perhaps. Her stepmother was dead. The children went away to lead their own lives at different places. Sometimes when she faintly remembered the house, she felt like going there. And when Kunu's mother remembered her man, she remembered her jethai, her elder maternal aunt, too. She lived in the town where she stayed for a long time. She had introduced her to a house to work as a housemaid afterwards. She was the one who kept in touch with her. Her jethai brought up her two sons with great difficulty. She worked as a part-timer in four houses and at home made *thonga*, paper packets, from old newspapers. Every month she came to the house where Kunu's mother worked to collect the newspapers. Sometimes she took her to a house in the slums at a distance from her house. Next morning she brought her back to the house. Kunu's mother called her cousins 'Dada'. Both of them worked as electrical mechanics. They took their mother along with them to Arunachal Pradesh where they found enough work. In the town there were many like them, but in the hills they were in great demand due to paucity of skilled mechanics. So they could open their own repairing shop there, build their own houses and settled down after getting married. At the time of the wedding of the younger son, her aunt had taken her to Arunachal. Her mistress had given her new clothes and jewellery to attend the function.

She looked very attractive then, brought up in the town and

with two good meals at the kind household. She, in fact, looked like a 'town girl'. She shone like a princess in the interior town amidst Arunachal hills. The man saw her at the bride's place and proposed to her then and there. He was a carpenter and had his own shop. She also liked the handsome man instantly. After one month, she got married from her aunt's place. Her employer back in the town cried when she heard of the news. After that, she moved to another town with the man.

When she came to the new place she found that instead of a furniture shop, he owned just a ramshackle shed. The house was a small room squeezed between a row of rented houses. More than working at his carpentry, her husband spent time playing cards with his cronies under the peepul tree. When she discovered that she was pregnant she took a part-timer's job in a household. Rambha who was her neighbour in the slum had organized it. The employer liked her work very much. At least she did not have to worry about two meals and clothes now. She began to accept her life with the man who was busier gambling than working. Let him play, she thought. At least he did not drink like the others; he never beat her like many other men in the locality. When he did not indulge in gambling he made chairs and tables and went to sell them in the bazaar carrying them tied to his bicycle. She was hopeful things would improve one day. She was capable of looking after herself. She was planning to buy a goat with her salary. Though she often felt tired when morning sickness overtook her and vomited copiously, she bore it silently. She must not rest; she must not lose her job.

One day her husband went to the bazaar with four stools to sell but never returned. Later she came to know from other people that not only did he sell the stools but he also sold the cycle that day. She also learnt that he was a married man; his family and children lived in a village somewhere in Coochbehar. He had quarrelled with his father and come here. His family had come to know of his new wife and descended on the bazaar to take him away. He had sent half the money from selling the stools and the cycle through Ramu of their basti. That whole night, she sat holding the money tightly in her palms. She threw up repeatedly and lay down like someone dead, alone, in her one-room tenement.

By the time Kunu's mother came back to the household in the town where she had spent years, she did not look like the girl who had invited admiring looks at her cousin's wedding in Arunachal. The clothes hung on to her body somehow, her face was pale, hair uncombed, and her eyes were red with constant crying. The people at the house were astonished looking at her. How could people change like that within a short time? They were nice people; they took out the money from the bank which was in her name, arranged a job at the house of the mistress's sister in another town and sent her away. And so she reentered her old world of fridge, pressure cooker, running water, piles of clothes and utensils to be washed, cooking fish and chicken curry, and so on. Unfortunately when she was just settling down, the family had to leave the town as the master got transferred. They did not want to take her along. Seven months pregnant, she stayed back in a rented room on the fringe of the town. At first she started by making paper thongas. She did not have to go anywhere to sell them; the vendors in the basti came home to collect from her. Often she remembered the man who had abandoned her. If he were there now! She cried at first but later, an uncontrollable anger overtook her. At those times, she was like a mad woman.

It happened today too. Her eyes welled up thinking of him. Had he been there, would she have to worry about her daughter like this? Or would she have had to labour from dawn to dusk? A man in the house made all the difference. Why did he do this to her? He was soft-spoken, neat and handsome, the man she loved—and he left her like this? She remembered that terrible night. Holding a few notes in her hand she was crying through the night, vomiting and half conscious. Her head was spinning. She could not sit, she could not lie down. There was only a bamboo cot in the room where a half conscious woman was spinning, spinning. The world would end now, everything would be dark, she thought. What had she done to get this punishment? Why did he marry her almost forcefully, knowing everything? He had a house, he had a wife and children, then why did he come to her? For her body? Was it enough to leave her, throwing a few rupees? Why didn't he think of the new life growing inside her, of his young wife and how she would fend for herself? He did not bother, he just left, the brute! Well, maybe he left under duress. Okay, he did not want to take her to his native village. But at least he could have enquired after her later on, and whether the baby was a girl or a boy. Or, if she was dead or alive. Was he a man? But even if he was here what solace could he have brought her? Anger and resentment washed over her body like a tide. She had loved and revered him like a god. She waited for him to come from his gambling den to have food together. With her weak body she worked in others' houses and even bought shirts and vests for him. How many stools and chairs did he sell anyway? Who actually provided for the meals at home? She. But she never said a word. Yet he cheated her like this?

Kunu's mother found herself raging with anger. No, she did not need a man like him as a figurehead. She was fine; he did not have to enquire about her. Even a bird wailed in desolation when a partner went missing or died. He, as a human being, was not even comparable to one in the animal world.

She got up, unable to rest. She drank some water and with her wet hand rubbed the back of her neck. She looked at the bed. Kunu was trying to find her even when half asleep. She would wake up soon. When she did not find her mother in the bed she would be worried and cry, 'Mai ei, what has happened? Are you feeling unwell?' She would not sleep after that. She would run her hands through her hair to comfort her, pull the fingers, massage her legs and forehead, enquiring again and again, 'Mai ei! Are you feeling better?' Kunu usually got up even before the crows and dogs. Then she sat at her study table. Soon she got ready to leave for school. The work at home was also there to take care of. She did not allow her mother to do anything at home. If she could not sleep well her face would show the strain. As a mother how could she inflict such pain?

So she went back to lie in the bed. Kunu tried to massage her head even though half asleep. Her hand slipped off in slumber. All the words, all the worries would leave Kunu's mother at these moments. Tenderly holding the hand which had unsuccessfully tried to comfort her, she also gave in to sleep. The hard labour of the day pushed her to drowsiness even though she wanted to think more about her future more, and about her daughter.

Yet, even with this hard labour lately Kunu's mother was unable to sleep. She could not bring her eyelids together. She was not the only one; the whole basti lost its sleep. Was it possible? So much money! Where would they get so much money just because it had been demanded? They were in a tizzy. People had thought that those terrible days were over. They were just recovering from the memory of those days. They never thought that the same things would come back in another format. But it happened anyway. The insurgents emerged from the hills. The whole town was interspersed with welcoming gates to take them back into the fold. Kunu's mother went to the bazaar walking under the gates, Kunu and friends went to the school crossing them too. The men with garlands on their necks travelled in a convoy of cars. People did not get worried at all, things were getting normal. But soon the letters arrived to make them worry again. They remembered in horror the terrible days which they had thought were over.

Kunu's mother sold the pig on a haat day. Kunu did not ask her anything, her mother also did not say anything. Both of them knew, though unspoken, that some danger was lurking in the background. Kunu's mother delivered the money after the sale to the man of the basti who was collecting the money on everybody's behalf to be given to the letter-writers. When she gave the money she could feel her heart heave. But then she reasoned: let the money go; at least they were safe.

But the sense of safety eluded them.

One day a 'surrendari' arrived at their house after parking his dazzling new motorcycle. He was plump and fair. He was wearing an expensive pair of jeans and matching jacket. He sat unceremoniously on Kunu's cane chair. Kunu's mother saw the gun hanging from the holster on his waist. She had seen enough of this kind of men in the past, and enough of these guns too, so she was not that surprised. She was also not unduly worried that he entered the house like that, without invitation. Men like them entered houses to leave behind letters demanding money. She was ready with her answer. She had already given money to a particular man in the basti. She did not have anything to fear. Even so she felt her throat go dry.

When she saw someone like him for the first time she had trembled like a leaf. It was in this town when she came to work at the house of her mistress's sister. She was pregnant then. She was recovering her health as she was able to have two meals a day and could sleep well. Both her employers were doctors at the hospital in the town. They gave her vitamins and other medicines too. The day when she had the encounter, she was alone in the house. There were six men; they had different weapons hanging from their waists. They had left a letter with her. It was the time when none of the two parties of insurgents were overground; they stayed hidden in the jungle. Some days after the incident, her employers left the town. So with the money given by her former employer and the doctor couple, she immediately bought the two kattha of land at the outskirt of the town. The milkman Basanta Mandal who supplied milk at her mistress's house also got a letter like this. He sold his land at half price and left for Coochbehar in great hurry. When people of her community were running away from the town, Kunu's mother decided to use all her savings to buy this plot. Around her were people from the community to whom the extortionists belonged. Many of them were well-wishers and told her not to invest in the land. But she did not listen. After a few days, her baby would arrive. If she were alone she would not have minded even living on the veranda of a house, cleaning leftovers from utensils. But where would she keep the baby? So she did not listen to anyone, did not fear anyone. She entered the house left behind by Basanta the milkman with its two kattha of land. She found that though the families around her were from the community of the men exhorting money they were all not that bad. In fact, they were also apprehensive of the boys. The men took money from them too, killed their ducks and chickens to eat.

Sometime later, Kunu arrived. She forgot everything after that. She tied the baby to her breast and went around the whole day working here, working there—in the bazaar, selling puffed rice, selling cane baskets, looking after ducks and chickens to sell eggs, searching for dhekia and greens to sell in the market. So where was the time to think of anything else? Her whole life revolved around earning money for the little niceties for the baby girl—a little dress, some milk, a bit of soap, a rattle, and of course, food to fill the stomach. Managing everything on her own, she had become like a cat. When even a little sound came from somewhere, she stopped and waited to see if she should run or give a fight.

Today also Kunu's mother was waiting silently in front of the uninvited guest. Looking at him, the hair on her skin stood up. Yes, he was the man who had been after Kunu for some time. As he sat he did not mention money. She could feel herself going rigid. This kind of men did not come to sit down in somebody's house, did not ask for water to drink. They came, delivered the letter of demand and left; at best they would warn 'not a single paisa will be reduced; if you don't deliver by that date your head will roll' etc. But today this man's behaviour was different. He was looking this side and that, as if searching for something. At that moment, Kunu came in with a pitcher of water. Women collected drinking water from the water tap provided by the government at this time. Her mother looked at Kunu as if she were a stranger. The water splashing from the pitcher had wet a part of her dress near her chest. The cotton cloth clung there. Her fair face was pink with the strain of carrying the pitcher. A few strands of her curly hair stuck to her cheeks wet with perspiration. The dress near the thigh where she carried the pitcher, had lifted up slightly revealing her white skin. Perspiration and water made her skin look like a smooth banana leaf with water drops. The man was looking at her without blinking. Kunu went inside and called her mother. She followed her daughter inside. Well, what was inside anyway? The kitchen shed adjacent to the main room.

'Mai ei, this man follows me when I go to school.'

'And he said he would give you something?'

'He sent me some gifts through Ila. I didn't even touch the packets.' Kunu was trembling with fear. 'Mai ei, why has he come here?'

'Go to Shanti's house through the backdoor. Go!' she ordered her daughter and came back to face the man.

He stood up and declared, 'I'm going to marry Kunu.' He was looking at her threateningly. That look seemed to her like the warning 'otherwise we'll blow off your head'.

She could feel her legs shaking. Things around her seemed to spin out of control. A coldness travelled up her body.

'Your daughter will live well, don't worry. The government will give us a lot of money. I'll soon buy a car. Bolero.' Naming the car he laughed, his teeth showing. He left abruptly. The sound of his motorcycle seemed like a thunderclap. Whichever way he drove it seemed to burn everything on the way.

Within a day, Kunu's mother sold a few ducks and chickens, three goats and a few bottles of honey. She felt sad that she had to sell these things in a hurry though she wanted to retain them until she got a better price. Her sadness touched Kunu too.

'Mai, Mai ei, you've got very little money for the goats, the ones you sold earlier… I thought I'd buy a clotheshorse with the money from the honey… and the hens were just laying eggs… the ducks.' She could not finish a single sentence. Her voice became smaller and smaller in fear.

Her mother tried to reassure her: 'My aunt's sons have their own electrical repair shop. They have their own house, not like ours. They are concrete houses. You won't have any problem. My aunt will take care of you.'

'Will their wives like to having a stranger live with… Kunu could not speak; something constricted her voice.'

'Are we going to have them spend money on you? I'll regularly send money from here. You'll study in a school over there; your brothers will arrange a good groom for you too.'

'But I don't want to get married. I want to stay with you. Mai ei, how can I stay away from you?' Kunu cried her heart out.

Mother and daughter held each other and cried. The garden around their small shed of a house was filled with the aroma of jasmine flowers. It entered their small room through the cracks and washed over them.

There was nothing to do but cry. As dawn broke, mother and

daughter got into a train going towards Arunachal Pradesh asking neighbour Shanti's household to look after the house. Mother and daughter sat in the compartment, their eyes red with all the crying. They trembled in fear. What if that thundering sound of the motorbike followed them and the stern eyes came chasing them?

The train started. Odours of different kinds overtook them, not of fresh flowers but odd ones. The exhaustion of the sleepless night caught up with Kunu's mother. Different images faded in and out of her dreams. The honeycombs, the goats, the garden with flowers, the bedspread with red flowers, the sanchi trees, a row of mist-covered hills, a cement house, an old woman, two young men, two daughters-in-law of the house—everything got jumbled up. A motorcycle ran forcefully over these pictures, its booming sound trailing it. A man with a gun came on like a destructive wind. Mother and daughter clung to each other in fear, sleeping, waking up and again sleeping. They were going to the house in the hills, to the well-to-do household of Kunu's uncles. They would keep her, won't they, Kunu's mother thought to herself. She would send money every month to cover Kunu's meals, clothes and study material. The most important thing was that she should stay there. Let her be hidden by the hills, let her be far away from the sound of the motorbike which burnt everything on its way.

After leaving Kunu behind in the hills, when her mother returned she found that even Shanti's house was locked. Apparently they had also left for some time. The story was that Shanti had gone to attend a wedding at her uncle's place in Barpeta. Some in the neighbourhood wondered why they had packed so many household things to go for a wedding. Shanti's family had an office-going person in the house; they heard that the demand for money from them was beyond their capacity to pay. Kunu's mother walked towards her house. Since she had left everything in Shanti's care who would have looked after the house now? She was sure everything was gone. Who would have tied the goats to the post? Who would have shut the door of the coop of ducks and chickens? And the new calf she had bought recently? Who would have given it water to drink? She was sure that the fast growing gomari trees, the young bamboos, Kunu's beloved garden had all been destroyed by goats and cows. The honeybees must have flown away. Was the cottage still there at least for her to sleep in? Or the windows and doors were gone? She would have to start all over again. She had promised to send money for Kunu every month. She walked apprehensively towards her compound. The stone chips on the path flew helter skelter at her fast pace.

As she opened the gate to her little cottage, her heart skipped. Who was that woman? She belonged to the community of the motorbike man she wanted to avoid. So not finding Kunu, in anger, he had taken over the plot…? As she came nearer, she saw that it was Mainao's mother. She came towards her with a rope in her hand.

'Kunu's mother, I have just tied the calf,' she said. She did not say anything but looked around. She was astounded. The calf had been given fodder, the ducks and chickens had broken rice grain to peck at. Mainao's mother had even cleared the weeds from the patch where she had planted some radish seeds before leaving. The woman now took out the key from under her clothes and said, 'Shanti and her mother had to leave. They left behind your key with us. Take it. There are few eggs from the ducks and chickens. Mainao will bring them for you now.'

Kunu's mother looked at the woman. Then she said suddenly, 'Send Mainao to eat with me. I have left behind my daughter…' she could not finish her words. Her eyes streaming, she leaned against Mainao's mother.

'Well, well, something will work out. Don't worry too much,' the woman said rather abruptly as if embarrassed and left.

Mainao came and cleaned the house and swabbed the floor. She washed some rice and brought the drinking water. She boiled eggs in lentil and both of them sat down to eat. Their shadows played on the wall. She was sitting where Kunu used to sit. Kunu's mother looked at her round face with small eyes. When she smiled her eyes closed into slits.

'Mahi ei!' Mainao jumped up as if she had seen a snake.

'What happened, Mainao?' she asked and stopped eating.

'Look, they are coming.'

Kunu's mother could hear the thundering bikes coming their way.

'You run away by the backdoor. Go!' she ordered.

Mainao ran towards her house in the darkness. Kunu's mother took the chopping *boti* in her hand. There was no one else in the house, she was alone. Like a cornered cat she stood. The men entered. The plump, fair one shouted 'Where did you send your daughter?" She held on tightly to the *boti*.

'Tell me, where did you leave your daughter?'

'How does it matter to you?'

'What, you ask why we are interested? Old woman, be careful what you say.'

'You want money, I have given it. Why do you want to know about my daughter?'

'So you are not going to let your daughter marry me?'

The plump man stamped on the ground.

Kunu's mother went out into the courtyard like one possessed. She shouted, 'Hey you all! Do you hear me? These men want to feast on my daughter's flesh!'

The man took out his gun and threatened, 'If you don't marry your daughter off to me, you won't be able to live in this house.'

'What did you say? I won't be able to live in this house? Is it your father's or mother's house? Or your party's house?'

'It doesn't matter. If you want to live here you will have to obey us.'

'Your daughter will have to marry this man,' one of the group said.

'We can drive you away in one day.'

'Go bring your daughter, we won't harm you.'

'This is our land. If we want we can throw you away.'

'Hello! Please, please you all out there! Drive away these vultures from my house!' Kunu's mother shouted at the top of her voice.

'Tell us when you'll bring your daughter here.'

'Otherwise pack your bags.'

'Hey you! Bring a few chickens from the coop.' somebody ordered. She was thinking of her promise. She said she would send money every month.

'You don't have any right to touch my chickens,' Kunu's mother uttered defiantly.

'You won't be allowed to stay here a day longer.'

'Who are you to drive me away?' Kunu's mother challenged like a cornered cat.

Meanwhile, there was a great hullabaloo in the basti. Somebody said the old woman was about to be killed; somebody else said her legs and hands would be tied and taken away in a car; somebody said the house would be burnt down. As the word spread from mouth to mouth, more people gathered. And then in the evening light the people surged towards the house of Kunu's mother. She saw that among them was Mainao's mother too.

The people came in and stood silently. Kunu's mother saw that her small courtyard was now full of people.

The Girl with Long Hair

Mainao stands on her toes at the threshold of youth. She is a cheerful, attractive girl with small, twinkling eyes and rounded limbs taut with the touch of sun and rain. Her complexion is a sunburnt brown, with tints of copper. When she laughs, her small eyes crinkle and look even smaller.

The firstborn in her family, Mainao has three younger siblings. Her father teaches in a primary school about three kilometres away; her mother takes care of the household. They are not too badly off; there is enough rice in the granary, cattle in the shed and arecanut trees and betel-leaf creepers aplenty in the kitchen garden.

This is the year of Mainao's all-important matriculation exam. She works hard at her lessons morning and evening, although she's not very bright at studies and would much rather do the household chores instead. And how well she does them! When she swabs the courtyard, it looks so neat that you could eat off the floor! When she cuts loose the warm shawl woven with a *farou-megan* motif from the loom, even the pigeons on the roof seem to coo their approval: 'Why Mainao, you've worked our eyes and feathers into the loom so deftly!' When she weaves an arnai chador in the dhekia pattern, the ferns underneath the arecanut tree bow shyly, wondering, 'Are we that pretty? O Mainao, you've made us look so good with your weaving!'

Mainao has long lovely hair that reaches down to her hips, black and silky and well-oiled. When she gathers it all up into a bun at the nape of her neck, it looks only a little smaller than her head. She is rather proud of her hair. She washes it with jetuka, henna leaves and hibiscus flower petals. She begs her mother for money to go trim it in the beauty parlour in the town about a kilometre away. Her parents scold her sometimes because of the preoccupation with her hair. But who can be angry with Mainao for long? She will be crestfallen for some time and then grin. Nowadays, she likes to imitate a Hindi film heroine with long hair. Like her she embellishes her hair with colourful clips. However, her mother and others who see her busy with the household chores—swabbing, weaving, cooking—are not aware what goes on in the girl's mind. When she returns from the parlour in the town, she washes her hair with hibiscus or jetuka leaves and then with the colourful clips adorning her hair stands near the gate in front of the house. At these moments, can anyone peep into her mind? No. Secretly she plays and laughs with a young man. The image of the young man is vague; he is somewhat similar to the handsome young man who courts with his songs full of yearning and running on the sea beach with the heroine whom Mainao adores. Sometimes he seems to look like the son of the headmaster of her father's school, who is now studying somewhere in a distant city outside Assam. When she thinks of him, she seems to be assailed by the citrus scent of a lemon flower.

The headmaster's son had visited their house once. His father had sent some papers to her father through him. He was home on summer holiday. Mainao had served him tea and steamed tekeli pitha filled with ground sesame seed and jaggery. After he finished off three at a go, her mother had asked if he would like to have some more. He had asked for two more. Mainao's parents had praised him a lot. After he left, the house was filled with an aroma like that of lemon flowers. He perhaps had bought the bottle of perfume in the city where he was studying, she thought. She wanted to ask him if he could bring a bottle for her as well the next time he came home. She would pay, of course! She had some money stashed away from selling three pigs, chickens and pigeons.

One day as she went to the town with her friends she tried to inhale the perfume bottles in the shop that sold cosmetics. She was disappointed; not a single bottle had that lemonish aroma. So she bought another, quite nice though, in a beautiful bottle. They had reached home late that day. Her mother was waiting anxiously at the front gate, her father cycled to the four-lane junction searching for her. Reaching home, she faced a barrage of admonishment from her parents. Wasn't she aware of what was happening all around? The andolon was at its zenith. How many boys were like the son of the headmaster, anyway? Most of the young men had left their studies or work and joined the agitation. The boys had learnt lots of new things, even how to use the gun and ammunition. They had a lot of power now. Even the elderly in the society were scared of them. The demand for their own state had changed a lot of things. Wasn't Mainao aware of it?

Mainao does not bother much about these things. Sometimes people come out in processions, sometimes there is a call for a bandh, sometimes the boys get into skirmishes with the police and the army personnel, but those things had been happening elsewhere, not in her village. She has heard from others that there were even shootings between the rival parties sometimes. But these meetings, processions, people piling into buses and trucks to hold public demonstrations, or shutting down roads and train lines, have been happening since long—what's the big deal? She has grown up seeing all this. Her ears are tired of listening to the same old instructions from her parents—don't go there, don't do this, and so on. These things have happened and will continue happening is her philosophy. For these mundane things, why should she stop going to the bazaar if she needs threads for the loom, or when she wants to buy a pair of earrings, clips for her hair or a chain? So she gets very angry when her parents go on and on with these warnings about trouble. Isn't there anything else to talk about except this?

Mainao is basically a happy-go-lucky girl. She hardly finds anything to be unhappy about. And especially at this time of the season, how can she remain morose? After all, Durga puja is round the corner. There is a small shrine dedicated to God Bathow in a corner of the courtyard which she swabs to a perfect red; next to it is a sewali flower tree. Now she can see its base covered with the white flowers in the morning giving out a heady smell thus heralding the autumn festival; the shops are full of colourful balloons and garlands. As in other years, in a corrugated tin shade in front of the house on the railway line, they have started making the idol of the devi. By now, Mainao has finished weaving the red dokhana. It is of the brightest red, and on it she has woven designs as in Assamese mekhela chador. The flowers in the design are yellow in colour; spattered in between the lines are butas in black and white. She already went with Binuma, Champa and Reema to the town to thread her eyebrows and trim her hair. They are her friends studying in the same class in the high school. Their group of ten to twelve girls have all grown up together and are inseparable. Binuma has bought a beautiful paat silk mekhela chador for the festival. Mainao has copied the design in her dokhana. When her friends saw it they praised Mainao to high heaven for her skill. Champa has bought a blue churidar-kameez suit with white flowers. Reema has bought a saree with bright chumki work—then there is Biju… and Konika… and Nilima. All of them have bought new clothes for the festival. Each new dress bought by one of the group called for a celebration. Mainao had wanted to buy a churidar set too. But the boys involved in the agitation had given strict instructions that girls of their community could wear only dokhanas. A pehi of Mainao, her father's sister, who was a college student had to use a bicycle to reach the college in the town; finding the dokhana cumbersome, she had stitched a salwar-kameez set to wear to the college. In the institute the salwar suit has now become almost like a uniform for the girls. But the boys had only warned the girls of their community about wearing it. Taking a pair of scissors, a few boys had cut her aunt's dress almost to tatters. Weeping all the way, she returned home. Her friends had used a copious number of safety pins to hold up the dress somehow. That day a high fever afflicted her aunt. It took three days for her to recover. Mainao sat next to her, regularly changing the wet handkerchief on her forehead to help keep the temperature down. Her heart went out to her aunt; such a bright student and now lying like this, she thought. Her *pehi* was mortally insulted at the treatment meted out to her in broad daylight and in front of so many people. These days when Mainao thinks of wearing something else other than her usual traditional dress, she instantly remembers the face of her aunt, burning with fever.

There were only three days left for the puja. Mainao had finished her puja shopping. She had gone with her friends to the town to buy a pair of earrings with red stones. The parlour was getting crowded so she had gone early to finish her beauty regimen. Then suddenly they heard that the people of their community were not allowed to participate in the Hindu puja celebration. The boys engaged in the andolon announced the ban and warned that those who defied their order would be punished. Their word was law. People these days bowed to their diktat, not unwillingly too.

They reasoned that the boys were trying to offer something to the people—a dream. It would come true, won't it?

So, what Mainao regarded as something distant and not affecting her became a reality. She would not be able to visit the pandal of the puja. Binuma, Reema and her other friends would go and she would stay back—washing, sweeping, cleaning the cattle shed. She would not be able to wear the new dress she had just woven. What was this? How could it be possible? What would she do? The devi's idol had been put on the pedestal, the dhak drum was making a pulsating sound, the air smelt of jalebis and savoury bhujia, the colour of the balloons dazzled the eyes.

Her friends, Binuma, Reema, Champa and the gang went in a group to visit the puja venue. On their way they called her asking if she would go. She shook her head sadly. On the way back, they brought small little mementoes for her. As she took those things from her friends, her chest seemed to contract with sorrow. Seeing her like this, the eyes of her friends too filled with tears. They gave her a suggestion. After the next day, the puja would be almost over and the idol would be immersed in the river. So she could go the next day with them; who would notice her among so many girls? They would put her in the middle, hiding her and drop her back home. It was going to be a secret among themselves. Even Mainao's parents did not get a hint of the plan.

In the afternoon, Mainao was ready and on her way to Binuma's place. When she found her mother looking at her suspiciously, she said defensively, 'What are you looking at? I couldn't wear this for the puja, I might as well wear it to Binuma's place. Her mother has just started the loom to weave a new set of clothes, she has asked me to come over to see it.' By the time she finished saying all this, she had already reached the gate. As a precaution she told her mother that she should not worry if she got a bit late.

The girls did not wait for sunset. As soon as Mainao arrived they took her under their wings and were on the way to the pandal. A few of her friends told her to change her prominent dokhana. But Mainao remembered her aunt's feverish face and refused to change. Someone, probably Champa said, 'Oh, from a distance it looks like mekhela-chador. Nobody will notice.'

Mainao was drowned in the sight and sound of the balloons, smell of jalebi, the beat of the dhak and lights. Her apprehension vanished. She put a new kind of hair-band in her beautiful hair. Her hair caught the breeze and swayed in waves; she looked as if a dragonfly was jumping around.

When she returned home it never occurred to anyone that she had already been stamped a criminal. Within the span of day, Mainao became an enemy of her own people; she stood like a hillock in front of a river of revolution. Yes, she was an enemy of the people. That night itself a meeting was called by the protesters. They congregated in the courtyard of Mainao's house; a few leaders of the movement came too. The accused Mainao was yet to change out of her red and yellow dress, the new hair-band was still adorning her hair and the generous splash of perfume stuck to her clothes. She was crying with her head between her knees and for the first time she felt the things happening around her were consuming her skin like burning charcoal.

One of the leaders passed the verdict that her hair should be snipped off. A girl who defied the diktat should be taught a lesson. Somebody brought a pair of scissors. Mainao's weeping increased. No she would not allow it; she would not cut her precious hair. The arrogant boy who had brought the scissors was ordered to cut her hair nonetheless. The stocky man, perhaps about five years older to her, dragged Mainao to the centre of the courtyard. Her soft wrist showed the marks of his rough fingers. Mainao was not a weak girl; she tried to push against the young man. But he was stronger and held her firmly. It was not very easy to trim Mainao's hair. The woman in the beauty parlour always brought a special pair of scissors when she visited; first she would spray water from a sprinkler and then carefully trim her silky hair. The man's scissors were not very sharp and he had to use all his force to cut Mainao's hair. She cried as if her heart was breaking. Binuma and her friends were watching from a distance. Now they too started weeping. Look what had happened because of their innocent fun.

Mainao's parents watched without protesting. Their daughter was in the wrong. There were so many girls in the community, but she was the only one to go against the diktat of the leaders without informing anyone. They prayed that the matter would end with the snipping of their daughter's hair and not go beyond to guns and shootings. People watched the man and Mainao. From a distance the pair looked as if they were lovers entangled with each other's body. The man could cut her hair only by grabbing her close to his chest. And she was jumping like a kawoi fish rubbed with salt to smother it. With each bunch of hair snipped off, Mainao would curl like a kawoi fish on death throes. Her heartrending cry rent the air. In the tug of war between the two, the red dokhana slipped off, the beads of her red and yellow necklace tumbled down on the courtyard. Now she was only in her blouse and petticoat. The lower portion of the red blouse came off in the struggle. Her breasts in the new bloom of youth showed from beneath the torn blouse, her lovingly woven red and yellow dokhana lay crumpled on the ground and on it were scattered tufts of hair cut unevenly. An elderly man from the audience put up his hand and ordered that it was enough. He was the priest. Even the young men could not defy the stern tone of his voice. Mainao somehow held on to her blouse with its hooks coming off and ran into the house.

Now another crime had been added to Mainao's original sin. Her virgin body had been touched by a man in public view. Nobody could deny it; all of them saw it. The young man could hold onto her only by grabbing her close to him. Her clothes were also coming off. She was seen touching his body. So another meeting was called at the temple courtyard. Mainao was summoned along with her parents. A court was held and judgment given. Mainao must marry the man who had cut her hair. Why? Because of the age-old story of Asagi and Baisagi that had been told for generations.

The sisters Asagi and Baisagi often stole from the fruit garden of handsome Chandrabao. One day he set a trap and caught both of them. He held their soft hands and freed them from the trap. But the matter did not end there. The next day darkness descended at daytime, crows cawed unnaturally; in fact everything looked abnormal. People understood that somewhere a young man and woman had committed a sin. In the meeting Chandrabao and Asagi-Baisagi confessed to the sin. What was the sin? When Chandrabao freed the young women he must have had to touch their bodies. So the judgment was given. Chandrabao must marry both the sisters. Otherwise who would marry young women who had been defiled by the touch of a stranger?

The tradition of this judgment regarding Asagi-Baisagi was followed by people of Mainao's community. Like Chandrabao that man who had cut Mainao's hair had to concede to the rule too. Who dared to defy a social diktat going on for hundreds of years? After all, oral history like this held their people together.

And what about Mainao? What was she thinking all this time? Her mind was absolutely blank. All she was looking for was the smell of a lemon flower. When she tried to breathe in that refreshing smell, something else, a stinking odour of sweat mixed with the moldy smell of a pair of thick jeans that hadn't touched water for a long time, assailed her nostrils. And slowly, that awful smell travelled from her nose to her young breasts.

The man was asked to stand up. Someone with a deep voice asked Mainao to kneel down and seek the blessings of the people.

But Mainao kept standing as if turned to stone; the ability to speak, walk or move the limbs seemed to abandon her.

Streams of tears flowed down her cheeks. She wiped them, but they flowed again; she wiped them again, but they flowed nevertheless.

Surabhi Barua and the Rhythm of Hooves

'Once upon a time,' began Grandfather. 'There was an old woman who slept inside her *pera*.'

'A wooden box? Why did she sleep in a box?' the little girl wanted to know. 'Wasn't there a cot?'

'Yes, there was a bamboo cot.'

'Didn't she have a bed like ours?'

'Those days, they didn't have beds like these.'

'But why did she sleep inside a box?'

Grandfather's voice dropped to a whisper. 'The old woman had a basket of silver coins, three seven-strand necklaces, one Jonbiri necklace with a crescent-moon locket, two heavy gamkharu bangles…'

'Ah! So she was scared that a thief would steal them all?'

'Right! And so one night a gang of thieves raided her house. They carried off the box after breaking open into the house.'

'And the old woman was inside the box?'

'Yes, the thieves carried her along too without knowing it. On the way, they had to cross a small stream. The thieves folded their clothes to cross the stream, but water entered the box. The old woman shouted, "Lift up, lift me up, thief! My hip is wet."'

The little girl listened. Then she said, 'Kaka, will you allow me to enter your box?'

'What will you do inside the box?' the old man did not seem to like the idea.

'No, I want to see how the old woman crossed the stream while still inside the box.'

The old man was indeed very fond of his granddaughter. He allowed her to sit inside his old wooden box and the girl sang with gusto, 'Lift up, lift me up, thief! My hip is wet.'

That little girl, Surabhi Barua, was now twenty-six years old and a professor in a college. She liked to go deep into things using her own judgement and experience everything before getting convinced. And now even before the sun was up and the mist was thick, she was ready to leave home to go somewhere. Over her sweater, she wrapped a red Naga shawl with which she had also covered her ears and head. If one did not look intently, it would be difficult to recognize her face. Why had Professor Barua covered herself like this? After all, it is not that cold yet. Was she trying to hide herself from public gaze? Perhaps.

Surabhi Barua organized her luggage in the cycle rickshaw. While ready to get into the rickshaw she looked back at her house. Her mother was standing at the gate leading to the compound. She was wiping her eyes with the end of her chador. She opened the gate and approached her daughter and said, 'You didn't eat anything.' She was wiping her eyes again. Surabhi did not say anything. She touched her mother's feet and got up to sit on the rickshaw. Then she told the rickshaw-walla,

'Please hurry up! I have to catch the first bus.'

The first bus from this small town left for Guwahati city at 5 o' clock in the morning; today it was leaving a bit late because of the mist. She closed her eyes and tried to calculate the time. The bus would reach Guwahati around 3 o' clock in the afternoon. She would have to spend one night there. The next day at 6 o' clock in the morning the train would leave for Delhi; from Delhi she would have to take a connecting train to the small hilly town. She would reach there the next morning. Everything had been arranged; someone was going to receive her at the station. Her room at the hostel had also been arranged. She had gone there once before to appear for an interview at the study centre. Surabhi Barua's curriculum vitae was exceptional. The interview went off very well. So it was easy to obtain the research scholarship for the span of three years.

As the rickshaw progressed through the screen of mist, suddenly Surabhi Barua felt very restless. She felt like flying to the peaceful institute in the hill station and getting immersed in the books. Then she would forget everything. It was too early for the shops to open. An orange sun was trying to peep through the mist now lifting a little. The road was becoming visible now. Torn sandals, strips of clothes were scattered all over. A few street dogs were eating something by the roadside. Surabhi Barua felt her skin prick. Last night, this place had witnessed a huge incident. All these days the andolon for self-assertion was on, but there was never any confrontation with the police and military. They had taken out processions with flaming torches, organized meetings, sat in protest in front of the oil refinery; sometimes they beat drums and cymbals to express their protest. The young men also shouted slogans of self-sufficiency and sold vegetables from carts on the street. Surabhi Barua observed that when these young men came along with their carts and announced their arrival by blowing a horn, the women from the houses emerged and with great respect bought their ware. They did not protest if the vegetables cost more, or were not fresh, but took them to the kitchen as if they were nirmali, flowers blessed at the temple.

The first clash Surabhi Barua had with the protestors was

through the boys who glibly talked about self-sufficiency. By this time, all knew about her opposition to the agitation. She was a woman who liked to judge things coolly and so she could not flow with the tide of sentiment. She became one of the few who stood against the Assam agitation. She wrote a few articles, saying again and again that this overwhelming sentimental outlook would stand in the way of constructing a strong Assamese national character. These articles came out in a Leftist magazine. Though with a small circulation, people came to know about them and whenever the articles appeared there was some trouble in the town. Once the young men got together at the main tri-junction of the town and burnt the magazine in public view along with her effigy. She was almost excommunicated. Now these things had stopped. Surabhi Barua had now been relegated to the fringe of the society.

Perhaps it was the sight of the dogs trying to slurp at the dried blood, the torn sandals and torn clothes on the road or thinking of these things that Surabhi Barua could feel her heart pounding fast. She felt as if she would faint. The back of her head felt unusually hot. She started sweating. It had been like this for the past one year since she started opposing the movement. She realized that she would feel like this for some time now. She opened the water bottle and took a gulp. Thankfully, the bus stand was not very far away. A white car passed by. Did it bear a Red Cross sign? And who was driving the car? Surabhi Barua looked on till the car disappeared into the mist. Into her mind floated the image of a man she had met six months ago. He was a handsome man but that was not why she had found him attractive. Somehow when she first saw the man she felt that this man was uncomplicated and open. Dr Alok Kalita had come straight to the point after meeting her and proposed to her. Even without knowing him, she had become excited by the prospect of spending her life with this man.

There was a secret fountain bubbling inside her heart. She took some time to think before accepting the proposal.

Both the things happened on the same day. That day as usual she had entered the class room. Which class was it? Oh yes, the first year of the higher secondary class. She always felt excited about this batch. As she looked at the young, fresh faces of the students who had just passed out of schools, she immediately became fond of them. Soon these young faces, ready to burst into laughter at the slightest opportunity, would mature into faces of students of the degree class, quieter and more experienced. She waited eagerly for the new batch every academic year. From the time she joined the college she had taught three batches of them until now.

That day she was supposed to discuss a poem. Its theme was a gentle love story between a dacoit and a pretty girl. The previous day she had read out the lines to her students. The poet had written the poem with great skill in a rhythm echoing the sound of horses' hooves. Surabhi Barua was explaining to the students how sound could transform into notes of music through lyrics. A student who was good in studies and looked younger than his years had commented, 'Madam, it seems as if the poem has the pace of a galloping horse.' When the students heard the story in the poem, their young faces seemed to fill with sadness. When his ladylove died the dacoit did not care for his safety any more and came out from his hideout with a sword in broad daylight. He was shot dead like a street dog. Surabhi Barua was yet to elaborate on the story of the lovers' transformation into ghosts and the scene when the dacoit's body lay on the street. In fact, today she planned to elucidate those parts of the poem. But as soon as she opened the register book of attendance the students left the class room en masse. A few shouted loudly while going out, 'Get rid of the Badans of the land,' probably referring to the historical figure of Badan Borphukan who had betrayed the country during the

Ahom rule. A few shouted, 'Jai Ai Asom!', glory to the motherland of Assam. The register book remained open in her hands. She was stunned. She met the eyes of the young student who had done so well in the exam. He also walked out slowly. When she came out of the classroom she saw that even Professor Bijoy Bordoloi's classroom of degree students was emptying out. He was a veteran in the institute and had only three years left before retirement, but they were openly criticizing his Leftist ideology and were shouting in unison with a slogan, 'We won't allow, we won't allow this CPM*giri*.'

Bordoloi did not belong to any party; he was a well-known intellectual and historian on Leftist ideology. Surabhi Barua had heard that these days he was hooted with shouts of 'The Badans of this land, be warned!' The college premises seemed like a crows' nest put on fire. The teachers in the staff room sat silently. The principal advised Surabhi Barua to take a few days' leave.

Two of her students came and requested her, 'Baidew, please go home. We'll accompany you.' A young girl whispered, 'Lots of these boys are outsiders; they're not from here.' The principal had offered police escort to Bordoloi and Surabhi. She had refused. Even the rickshaw puller turned his face away from her. As she stepped out on the road to go home, a few students quietly walked on too at a little distance as if spreading an invisible protective net around her. That boy who had found the rhythm a galloping horse in the poem was one of them.

The rickshaw puller was taking a short cut now. The main road was much longer and took more time. The pebbled road did not have the torn sandals, tattered clothes and stray dogs. The neat little houses with small gardens in front were still asleep. Who could tell from this peaceful scene that there was a fire of conflict burning all around?

That day too Surabhi Barua had taken the dirt road from the

college rather than the main road as she was asked to avoid it by her few loyal students. There was some incident on the chariali four road junction, she was told. It was only yesterday, or was it long ago? How much time ago? Twelve hours? Ten hours? Maybe even less, but within that span so many things had happened.

She had just changed her dress after coming back from the college when she found that Alok's mother had come. To tell them that she was unable to welcome Surabhi as a daughter-in-law into her house. The people were on one side and she on another, she had said. They did not have any problem with her as a bride-to-be but now she had become a dangerous association. That afternoon some people had thrown stones at Alok's chamber. He was a doctor after all, he had to deal with the people every day. How could he go against them?

Surabhi Barua understood that this excuse had come from the doctor himself. His mother did not even take a glass of water at their place. She did not even show the courtesy of meeting her at least once either. She hurried out as soon as possible. That evening she heard, someone—perhaps her elder brother on his way back from college said it, that some boys had severely beaten up Professor Bordoloi and the cornea of one of his eyes had been damaged. He had been taken to the city for treatment.

The day had arrived like a devastating storm. Like people who try to assess the losses the next day after a storm, Surabhi Barua looked back on that terrible day. She knew that days like this, or even worse, were waiting to happen in the future. That day itself she had sent off the application to the study centre. She had previously done a three-week course at the centre; her work had impressed the director and he had told her that the institute was eager to offer scope to scholars from the North East for research work. When she came down from the hills where the institute was located, she also brought along with her a secret fountain of hope.

As she reminisced the horrible day and its aftermath the next day, she made up her mind. At midnight, she took out the page with *The Highwayman,* the poem by Alfred Noyes she had intended to teach in the class. She read out, keeping to the beat of horses' hooves:

> *'The wind was a torrent of darkness among the gusty tree*
> *The moon was a ghostly galleon tossed upon cloudy seas*
> *The road was a ribbon of moonlight over the purple moor*
> *And the Highway man came riding,*
> *Riding—riding.'*

The wind was a stream of darkness among the trees caught in the madness of the storm. The overcast sky looked like a sea. In that sea, the moon was a ghostly galleon boat. The water took on a purplish tone. The road was like a ribbon of moonlight. On that ribbon came riding the dacoit to meet his lover. The girl with pearly lips tortured to death by the king's soldiers—her body and her lover's lying on the road—their ghosts floating in the air on moonlit nights. The story in the poem brought tears to Surabhi Barua's eyes. She felt as if the atmosphere around her was like that in the poem—the young horseman lying in a pool of blood on the street, the girl tied to the pole, her mouth gagged by the soldiers, the ghosts of them trembling in the air.

The rickshaw arrived at the bus stand at last. She bought a few newspapers and magazines. She was impatient to get into the bus. Bus, train, another train, and then into the bosom of the hills surrounded by cedar, pine and fir trees and that beautiful house filled with shelves of books. Nothing else would be there. She remembered her mother's face and how she wiped her tears. Well, her brother and sister-in-law might have regarded her as a liability, or her relatives thought of her as a sickly street dog, but why did her mother behave like this? Why didn't she utter the words that she should not leave her home, whatever further studies she wanted to do she could as well do from her own home? She would have stayed on. And what about that handsome man? Why couldn't he come personally to collect the engagement ring given to her? Wasn't he the one who proposed to her? She remembered her colleagues, their faces sullen and eyes downcast to avoid looking her in the eye. She remembered her father. Had he been alive would things have taken this turn?

Surabhi Barua was in college at the time. It was the phase when she learnt to think of the world and herself in a new way. She devoured books hungrily, joined the existing Study Circle in the college, took part in plays, and wrote articles. One day the principal of the college had sent for her father. He spoke to him about her. He talked about her thoughts, her work, her friends circle and also cautioned him to keep an eye on her. The college expected a good result from her; she should not waste time on unnecessary diversions. The principal was especially opposed to her philosophy, her idealism. What was her father's reply? Standing in the queue in front of the ticket counter at the bus stand, she remembered that her father had told the principal that he had full faith in his daughter's judgement, nobody should try to curb her way of thinking. He had no problem with the way she wrote her articles, the inherent logic behind it; it was her own opinion.

That day after her father returned, he sat in the drawing room and asked her to bring him a cup of tea. He told her about what had happened. Then he caressed her hair and said, 'My dear, whatever you do in life do it after giving it a good thought.'

After a long time, she felt the touch of his loving hand on her head. Had he been alive would he have allowed her to leave home like this, struggling with her luggage? She had bought the only car in the house. Why her mother didn't say that if her elder brother was hesitant about driving her to the bus stand they could hire a driver at least? Her mother perhaps thought of her family and the house, about the safety of her brothers. Surabhi Barua's eyes filled with tears as she thought of her dead father. Her elder brother had bought a plot of land; the night somebody put fire to the rented houses in that plot, her mother herself told her that it would be better if she kept away from the house for some time. Her brothers and sisters-in-law stood around silently. It was not difficult to understand her mother's words were coming after long discussions with others in the family. She deliberately told them that she had received a scholarship from the institute in the hills. Everybody was elated at the news, she knew, but pretended they were sad that she was leaving.

After buying the ticket, Surabhi Barua arranged her luggage in the open space, sat down on top of a box to wait until the bus was ready. An unknown young man came towards her. Instantly, Surabhi Barua was alert like a mongoose, the quills standing up. She remembered Dr Bordoloi had suffered a torn cornea; that a young painter's fingers were chopped off and after beating him up with rods, his body was thrown on the road. Surabhi Barua could feel droplets of sweat trickling down her body even in the cold. A gang of young boys would follow him any moment now and they would shout in unison, she apprehended. A damaged eye, a few chopped off fingers, a head split apart by rods and bleeding. Surabhi Barua stood up. The young boy was standing next to her now.

'Baidew, I have come from Guwahati by the overnight super bus,' he said.

'What can I do about it?' Surabhi Barua's voice was sterner than she meant it to be.

He came nearer and said, 'Sir has sent me.'

'Which sir?'

The boy uttered a name in reply. The professor was almost under house arrest now. For the last three months, he had not been able to come out of the house; it was anybody's guess how long he would have to stay like this. Some others like him who thought on the same lines were living a life like the Jews under Hitler. The person who had sent the young man to her had gone to the bazaar one day and got beaten up; he returned home with eight stitches on the forehead.

'I have bought a ticket in the same bus as yours. I'll keep an eye on you. Sir has asked you to stay the night at his place. Our duty will finish only after putting you on the train,' the boy said. He got up and boarded the bus. Surabhi got her luggage together and went towards the bus which had just entered the depot.

'Baidew, please let us help you with the luggage,' Surabhi Barua found that some of her students had come too.

One of them had a neatly packed parcel. He gave it to her and said, 'Jonali and the girls have prepared some snacks for you to take on the journey.'

The tender-faced first year student asked almost in a whisper, 'Ma'am, after you finish your studies, will you stay back and work there?'

Surabhi Barua understood that it was a question all of them wanted to ask.

'No, I'll come back.'

'Ma'am when will these things end? We've heard that this year even the exam may not be held. Is it true?'

'Sometimes these things happen, everything goes awry, there's chaos everywhere. People as a group make mistakes,' she said.

'They try to gag the mouths that speak the truth,' the face of the BA final student hardened as he spoke.

'People will learn to judge the right from the wrong. Why not? Wait till that time. I'll be waiting too,' Surabhi Barua told them.

The boys were lifting the boxes one by one. 'Baidew, we'll write to you,' they said as they put the luggage in the dickey of the bus. They handed her a pen and asked, 'Will you write back to us?'

As she took the pen, streams of tear flowed down Surabhi Barua's cheeks.

Ayengla of the Blue Hills

Ayengla lives amidst the blue hills. She is a happy woman. And why shouldn't she be? She has a loving husband, two children, paddy fields and a *chang ghar* with pigs and chickens. Her husband works as a security guard at a bank, some way off from the village. He goes out early in the morning and returns late in the afternoon. How proud she is when she sees him at the doorstep in his uniform!

Ayengla works hard and runs the household single-handedly, doing all the chores, tending the fields and caring for her daughter and son. She loves the blue hills that rise high behind her home. On most days, they are covered with cottonwool clouds and veils of mist; on sunny days, they shine like bright jewels under the sun. Her heart aches if she cannot see those hills, even for a day. No wonder she felt so lonely when she visited the town in the valley a couple of times with her husband. She was homesick for her hills.

The hills have also given them a lovely little brook. Every day, when she leaves for the fields, she can hear its gurgling from afar. The brook itself isn't visible; one has to go deeper inside, to a quiet bowl-shaped clearing surrounded by the hills, to see it. Here it tapers off at a spot flanked by two stone slabs. Perhaps there was just one big rock long ago, which was then worn down the middle by the water. Not too many people come here; sometimes animals visit at night to drink water. Ayengla often wonders about its source. They say it begins in that steep hill over there, beyond the dense jungle where nobody lives. She tells herself she'll go there some day with her husband; surely they can hack their way through the wilderness with his curved dao. Alas, for years, her plan has remained just that—a plan.

The brook has made a little pool between the stone slabs. The village women come here to wash clothes and have a bath. On the bank stands a tree as ancient as the brook, a wild orchid blooming among its boughs in vibrant yellow bunches.

Yes, this is Ayengla's own private nook. When she sits by its banks, she feels a great sense of calm. While going about her chores, she often hums a few lines from a song that her grandmother had taught her, a song she had been named her after. A song about a cheerful young woman named Ayengla who charmed the Sun God and brought him down to earth.

Yes, she is quite contented with her lot. From time to time, though, she muses: What do people want? Why do they create problems and conflicts? Recalling the incidents of the recent past, she trembles at the memory of those gun-toters who emerged from the jungle at midnight and knocked at her door during the first week of every month. She is loath to part with her husband's hard-earned money and the share of rice that they demand, but does she have a choice in the matter?

Poor Ayengla cannot make sense of all this. What do they want? If they did succeed in getting their own land, who would rule it and who would have to leave? What had become of her beloved hills? Just last month, an army truck had turned round a bend in the hills, when a landmine planted by those in the jungle had blown it to smithereens. Every single jawan in the vehicle had been killed. The villagers' description of the scene of the accident was enough to make Ayengla lose sleep for several nights running, haunted by the spectre of bloodied, dismembered hands and limbs. Sometimes, she pulled her sleeping children so close to her and held them so tight that they cried out in pain. If only she could, she would have clung to her husband too like this. Fear and apprehension take root, making endless little ripples in her pool of contentment.

Ever since the bomb blast, people barely stepped out of their houses. A funereal silence now shrouded the entire village. The weather, too, had been dark and overcast of late, with thick curtains of mist all over. Most men were already in hiding; most women had long since borne the brunt of running the households and working the fields anyway. The place was now overrun by army men who would barge into houses at will, demanding, 'Where's *deshlaga dushman,* the enemy?' and warn the inmates of dire consequences if they were to ever give rice or money to 'those men'. The jawans did not allow anyone to harvest their crop, and even burnt whole paddy fields to prevent those in the jungle from getting their share.

Those men continued to come out of the jungle at midnight all the same. They did not demand chickens or pig as in the past. Just a bit of salt, if possible. Caught between the *deshlaga dushman* and *basti laga,* their own people, the villagers became the proverbial blade of grass between two warring buffaloes.

On that fateful day, when the sun broke through the fog at long last, Ayengla had gone along with a few other women to the brook to wash clothes.

That morning Ayengla gathered in a bundle all the dirty clothes waiting to be washed. Many of the village women were already there to wash their clothes. She went to sit near the stream. Whenever she came here Ayengla felt a calmness descending over her. Often she hummed a few lines from the song her grandmother used to sing. The lyrics were actually built around a folk tale which her grandmother had learnt from her own granny. Today also as she soaped the clothes she started crooning the song softly. The story talked about a girl pretty like the stream, and always laughing happily. Her name was Ayengla. Her grandfather had named her after this character. When she was young she often listened to the story from her grandmother and loved it; so her grandmother gave the name to her. Ayengla of the story had fallen in love with the Sun God. One day when she was busy in the field she saw a handsome ethereal figure standing in front of her. Her beauty and sweet voice had brought down the god to the earth. The godlike figure told Ayengla at the outset that he would not be able to stay with her all the time, and that it was not possible for him to be bound down with family life with children and all. But he promised that he would come to her as soon as people saw the sun set every day. Ayengla built a cottage in the hills where the sun was seen last after the day's end. She took leave from all her relatives and went to live there. As soon as the evening set in beyond the hills, Ayengla's little cottage became bright with the sun's presence. She spent the whole night in the loving company of her lover. As the dawn broke, Ayengla's house became dark. But soon Ayengla found herself very restless. For the sake of the Sun God, she had left behind all her near and dear ones to live in this peak. Her days without speaking or hearing anybody's voice became unbearable. She also wanted a family with children. Her lover did not want to be a part of it. He was a god, he did not like any kind of restriction.

A year passed by like this. She saw that every day when he came to meet her, the Sun God took off his bright shining crown and then became like any other common man. He ate the dinner Ayengla cooked, slept on the bamboo cot with Ayengla. One day when he was asleep, she took the crown and threw it down the slopes of the hill. The Sun God woke up in excruciating pain, and in front of Ayengla he transformed into a bird. The bright yellow bird started flying following the way the crown rolled down the hill. Ayengla wept copiously and followed the path of the bird. What had she done? She lost something so precious to her. Wherever she ran, her tears created a stream. The crown rolled down and stopped at the place looking like the bottom of a bowl. The Sun God in the form of the bird snatched the crown and went away carrying it in its beaks. Ayengla cried so much sitting on the stone slab that it broke into two. Her tears made a puddle and the stream carrying her tears joined it to make a pond. Ayengla cried day and night and one day she too disappeared into the little pond.

She often mused over the Ayengla of the story. Even today as she was washing the clothes she was thinking of her. She was tired of all this talk, repeated again and again—army, bomb, dead soldiers, the anger of the soldiers unleashed on the village people, the fear of revenge. All this gathered into a feeling of fear that spread a sheet of apprehension on the people's heads. At these moments, Ayengla felt like crying her heart out like the folk tale's Ayengla and sweep everything away at one go. The women were talking and discussing and were on their way home with their half dried clothes already. On the way, they came across a few groups of soldiers. When they saw them they stood aside to let them pass.

The women were exchanging news about their children. Ayengla's daughter had a stomach upset. God knows what she had eaten and where and now look, she was sick. But she was getting better after taking the medicine her father had brought. In between her daughter was going through a bad period and soiled the bedsheets. Today her mother was washing these sheets, vigorously slapping them on the stone. As usual she sang softly the song of the brook's origin. She was almost finished when somebody came from behind and held her forcefully. Four to five army jawans lifted her up and took her to the jungle near the brook. She then turned into a stone. When she regained consciousness it was evening. She did not bother to find her clothes. She walked unsteadily like a drunk man. When she reached home she lost consciousness again. For one day and one night, she lay like that in the hospital. After one week, when she returned home, the happy, ever-laughing Ayengla had disappeared, she was a stone-like person without any emotion. Wherever she was told to sit or lie down, she would do that, without any protest, without any response.

But how long could people spend time with this woman who had turned into a stone-like being? Yet, the people tried, one must say. They offered puja to the gods; her maternal and paternal aunts took turns to fetch her to spend time at their places. Her husband too tried his best. But it was of no use. Some people suggested that she would be better if she had a baby. A baby needs care and she would come out of her stupor. But it was painful to watch the pregnant Ayengla. From the stone-like woman came out a stillborn baby, a girl ahead of the due date. Dead. People thought she would die. But she was a young healthy woman; it was not easy for death to take her away so soon. After some months she sat up. By this time, her husband had brought home a new wife. Ayengla dragged her cot out of the house into the open space in front. She sat there day and night.

She still does. The new wife has given birth to three children. Her own children are busy with their own work and life. But Ayengla sits on in her stone-like stupor. Her hair reaching to her hips now has more white than black. Wrinkles have invaded her face. She never talks to anyone; neither does anyone try to talk to her. People come and give her something to eat; a woman comes and changes her dress. Sometime ago the women used to take her to the brook to give her a bath, or wash her hair. But the Ayengla who sat like a quiet child always changed into somebody else as soon as she reached that place. She ran helter skelter, tears brooking down her cheeks. Her copious tears seemed to make puddles, her tears seemed to break down even the stones. The women were unnerved by this Ayengla.

One day her husband's second wife took Ayengla to the brook to give her a bath. There the ghost of Ayengla, wife of the Sun God, possessed her. She trembled furiously as she sat on the stone slab and started crying silently, her body shaking from head to toe. The second wife got scared and ran away. She had never seen this numb, stone-like woman behave like this. She fetched other women from the village and found Ayengla sitting frozen between the two slabs where the brook had disappeared. She was trembling like a banana leaf against the wind. From time to time, she gnashed her teeth.

In Search of Peace

Ranjita Biswas

P.S.

Insights
Interviews
& More...

In Search of Peace

Ranjita Biswas

Arupa Patangia Kalita is one of the most important contemporary writers in Assamese literature today. Her body of work—short stories, novellas, novels and a translation of Toni Morrison's *The Bluest Eye,* encompasses a wide range of subjects. In fact, she has used a passage from Morrison's book in the story, 'Face in the Mirror', in this compilation to illustrate the atrocity of dominance. At the core, her novels and stories probe human suffering and predicament.

The earliest memory Arupa has of writing something came out as a reaction to encountering a will-o'-the wisp. 'I was about ten years old then. We lived in Golaghat, a small town in upper Assam. This area is famous for huge expanses of paddy fields. One night we were returning late from a wedding reception. While crossing the Hamdoi field, I saw an orange ball of fire from the car window. Suddenly I saw it breaking into smaller balls of flame. They danced across the field on that moonless night. My grandmother asked me to avoid looking at the fireballs. My mother was mumbling some kind of mantra as if to shoo away an evil, and the driver accelerated the car. But I rolled down the glass anyway and kept on looking at the mysterious fire-dance. For the next few days, its image refused to leave me. I saw it all the time in my mind's eye. I was a little afraid too: did I commit an offense by not listening to my elders and looked at the will-o'-the-wisp on that inauspicious moonless night? I was suffering from an unknown pain and restlessness. One day I pulled out a piece of paper and started writing about what I had seen that night. A calmness fell over me once I put it down on paper. The fireball left me alone at last. That was my first piece of writing.'

Arupa writes in longhand and prefers working early in the morning. She has been teaching English literature for thirty-six years in a college in Tangla, a little town at the foothills bordering Bhutan in northern Assam.

The rebelliousness that was embedded in her at a tender age even as she ignored the will-o'-the wisp, and the lightness of being that she associates with the process of writing, slowly became a part of her life. 'From that day, when I sat down to write down about the vision of the fireball I saw on that dark night, until today, writing has been my escape route. I pour out my reaction to life's many experiences—the strife I see around me, the pain I experience, on paper.'

Many of Arupa's protagonists are strong characters who defy the diktat of society, even though they have to suffer for it. She herself has faced much hostility for not going with the tide when Assam underwent a period of major conflict in the late seventies and early eighties, generally referred to as the Assam agitation. It grew out of a public protest against illegal immigration from neighbouring Bangladesh, which was seen as a threat to the demographic contour of the land, but later it deteriorated into violence, internecine killings, ethnic cleansing, even infighting for grabbing leadership.

The writer clarifies that she was in support of the core idea of the Assam agitation i.e. driving out the illegal migrants, but 'I couldn't accept the jingoism and chauvinism that accompanied the demand. I felt that such extreme intolerance would one day destroy the meaning of Assamese nationalism and would usher in terrorism. I knew the danger of standing against the wind, but still expressed my view that an agitation for self-identity could not sustain only on emotional outbursts. My point of view helped me look at these things more dispassionately,' she says.

Those unsteady times have been a recurring theme in many of her writings. 'I can never forget the plight of common people during that period. Friends became enemies; secret killings ruined many families who were innocent but suffered because a family member became an absconder to join an outlawed group. These families got caught up between the law-keepers and the law-breakers.' The novella *Arunima's Motherland* brings out the horror of such secret killings.

The story 'Surabhi Barua and the Rhythm of Hooves' reflects the plight of a section of intellectuals who had to pay a heavy price for protesting against the unreasonable diktat of the so-called separatist leaders.

As to her own trouble during the period, Arupa recalls, 'Even from my student days at Guwahati University in the seventies, my future husband (Rajendra Kalita, a well-known critic, poet, and colleague) and developed certain political beliefs. For me it was, and is, like a beacon that helps me find my way as if in a forest in the dark night. I still believe that only an equitable distribution of wealth can bring peace to this world. Not hegemony but democratic values can end this violence.'

The husband-wife duo opted to take up teaching jobs in a local college and settle down in the extremely backward town of Tangla at this time after post-graduation. 'With our qualifications, we could have taken up jobs in a better located town, but we wanted to experience life and look at the world from close quarters. True, coming to Tangla created some personal problems for me, but because of it, my writing got an extra edge,' Arupa says.

Later in Tangla, Arupa encountered another agitation spearheaded by the Bodos, a plains tribe in search of self-identity. 'For me terrorism is not something distant; I have lived in the midst of it for years. A professor from our college was shot dead in broad daylight in 1998. The image of his corpse still chases me. Then there was a grenade attack on our staff room. Many like us have faced unsavoury incidents and extortion threats from extremist groups. These things trouble me no end. What else can I do but write about them? These writings stemming from painful observations are not tools to establish myself as a writer but a weapon of protest for me.' One can detect a semi-autobiographical element in the story 'Surabhi Barua ...' in this compilation.

Arupa has seen, from close quarters, the horrific impact terror has on society and how women, in particular, suffer in such circumstances. What was Mainao's fault? Why was she punished in that extreme manner in 'The Girl with Long Hair'. A girl wanted to flourish like the golden manikimodhuri paddy field; she was displaced not once but twice in 'Cursed Fields of Golden Rice'. Arunima lost her home while Surabhi Barua had to run away almost surreptitiously from her hometown. And Ayengla was transformed into a stone of a woman. A woman is invaded not only through physical atrocity; she can be violated by other means too. A patriarchal society always writes another history alongside the mainstream one. That which ignores the women. I believe if women keep silent they, in a way, also allow the male-dominated society to continue judging them.'

Arupa admits that there is a certain empathy for women in her work. 'I have seen a lot of injustices being done to women because they are women. You can call me a feminist or a humanist, whatever, but I feel being a feminist and a humanist are not contradictory.' Despite that, Arupa once refused to accept a literary award from a prestigious Assamese organization that had chosen her as the best 'woman writer'. 'Why should I be judged separately in a common ground like literary writing?' she justifies her point.

Perhaps Arupa's strong beliefs are rooted in her childhood memories. Her first published story was based on the life of a maid in her parental house. She was the same age as her and they were friends. 'That year we were supposed to send her to her parents in the village to celebrate Rongali Bihu, our biggest festival ushering in the new year in spring. She was very excited. She used to tell me about her village, the river that flowed by it, the keteki orchids that bloomed there at that time of the year. With her, I also roamed around her village in my imagination. I had packed two of my dolls and frocks for her two sisters in her box without telling anyone. But just before the festival, a lot of guests came to stay with us. She couldn't be spared because of the extra work load. I perhaps shed more tears of disappointment than her. Why couldn't she be allowed to go? That thought pursued me relentlessly. I felt an urge to write about it.' The story was named 'Banchit' (Deprived) and was published in *Moina-chara*, the children's section of a well-known magazine. Arupa received a lot of praise from the teachers of her missionary school and her parents for the story. She was around thirteen at the time.

Arupa also recalls how she once encountered a fisherman in tattered clothes carrying a beautiful silver fish. 'His feet and hands were shrivelled from constantly working with water. In contrast to the healthy fish he was carrying, he looked frail. Perhaps he would buy a little rice after selling the fish. But he couldn't afford to eat it himself. Like the will-o'-the-wisp, like my maid-companion, he too entered deep into my heart. I had to write about him. Today when I read those stories written in my teens, I find that the lives of those disadvantaged, their happiness and their sorrows figured in most of my stories.'

Arupa's own childhood, however, was very happy. She did not lack in anything. Books were her constant companion. Although she studied in a missionary school, her stories draw an authentic picture of the Assamese life. One often finds her using folk elements to illustrate a situation or as a symbol. For instance, in the novella *Arunima's Motherland*, she writes, '... above all, she detected another smell. A smell stronger than all the condiments, the flowers and the pure ghee fire of the *hom*. She was swimming in that aroma like a kandhuli fish zig-zagging in the pond, its white back taking on the afternoon glow of the sky. Like the fish coming up and down in the water and making rings and bangles on its surface, she was swimming in that exquisite aroma.'

Arupa says she owes it to her grandmothers, from both sides of the family, who introduced her to the folktales and oral tradition of the land. On the other hand, 'Cursed Fields of Golden Rice' is replete with the lyricism of Bodo tribe's folk tradition. The story is set against the backdrop of the Bodo movement for autonomy in the nineties.

For this story, Arupa had to read extensively on the community while trying to understand their culture and also consult experts. 'Despite that, I found it hard to begin writing the story, though I thought about the subject for almost five years,' she remembers. 'How could I tell the story of this simple tribal girl caught in a conflict that she couldn't fathom but had to suffer anyway? She was illiterate but highly intelligent. She was the perfect housewife, if you will, and a mother, but she became homeless, literally and metaphorically. Her life was like a field with the delicate rice grain, manikimodhuri, which got destroyed, never to flourish again. Then I discovered their folk stories, their songs, and I found the thread and understood how to place her story in her own milieu,' Arupa says. (*'Her fair body shone under the moonlight. He could not take his eyes off her. He had remembered the story of Phulmuthi that Mainao had told him. Now she seemed like Phulmuthi's replica. Phulmuthi had become a young woman. Her face was like the wide leaf of tora grass, her waist was slim like the middle of the big red ant, her nose was like the sharp thorn of a ghorakagzi lemon tree, the calves of her legs were like the bamboo shoot stalk, the neck was like that of a deer, the eyes were like the brown eyes of a pigeon. With her voluptuous breasts, long fingers, long straight hair, she looked like the heroine of the folk tale…'*).

Arupa's stories and novels cover a varied landscape, as in 'Morubhumit Menoka' set in Rajasthan, or a common fisher woman's defiance in an Assamese village ('Doiboki'), as also a woman going against the grain in pre-Independence Assam in the novel *Ayananta*. But a strong voice against oppression always runs like a hidden stream in her stories.

From her prolific body of work, the stories in this compilation have been chosen to focus on the conflict in her homeland and its impact on the common people, particularly women. The universal reality of war affecting women, children and the old unfortunately remains, even as we have already crossed the first decade of the 21st century. The promise of 'never again' gets lost as history repeats itself. Hence whether it's Mainao or Arunima, Ayengla or Kunu, the suffering continues.

Arupa's observation of the scenario of the North-East, particularly Assam, makes a strong comment on the meaninglessness of violence and revenge.

The story 'The Half-burnt Bus at Midnight' perhaps brings out her philosophy best. 'My maid's son worked in a garage. From her, I heard about a passenger bus found burnt on the highway in one of those extremely volatile socio-political situations at the time. The thought of that bus, though I didn't see it, remained with me for days, torturing me. For me the bus in the story is a symbol of the ugliness of violence, of man killing man in a world so beautiful. It's a devastated world where flowers do not bloom, butterflies do not fly, birds die as the odour of death pervades the air. I believe in peace. Human beings in general want peace. But where is it today?'

Translator's Acknowledgements

I thank Arupa Patangia Kalita for sharing her experiences from those turbulent times in Assam, which have been the mainspring of the stories in this compilation. She has also helped me understand better the stories behind the stories.

Rajendra Kalita, Arupa's husband and a well-known critic and poet himself, helped with valuable inputs, and I thank him too.

I also thank researcher Hira Charan Narjinari who helped me fathom the meanings of many Bodo words and legends occurring in the novella *Cursed Fields of Golden Rice*.

I must thank HarperCollins, particularly Shantanu Ray Chaudhuri, for coming up with the idea of compiling literary works built around the conflicts in the North East and their effect on the society.

Though these stories have been written mainly during the peak of agitation for self-assertion expressed through political clashes and ethnic violence in the region, some of the problems still hold true as some recent incidents in the Valley demonstrate.

The North East may be one corner of India where these stories are placed, but their likeness can be found in many areas of the world today. One only has to scratch the surface to come face to face with the truth.

A special thanks to Minakshi Thakur for her sensitive and skilled editing of the stories in the compilation.

My family—husband Arup, children Rimli and Rahul, and daughter-in-law Ruchika—is the bedrock which I can always fall back on. They help me remain focused on my work, reminding me of the deadline when distractions threaten to slow me down. Thank you!

HARPER**PERENNIAL**

Harper Perennial presents special editions of its finest books in translation

Age of Frenzy
Mahabaleshwar Sail
Translated from the Konkani by Vidya Pai

A Life Incomplete
Nanak Singh
Translated from the Punjabi by Navdeep Suri

Mohanaswamy
Vasudhendra
Translated from the Kannada by Rashmi Terdal

The Music of Solitude
Krishna Sobti
Translated from the Hindi by Vasudha Dalmia

No Presents Please: Mumbai Stories
Jayant Kaikini
Translated from the Kannada by Tejaswini Niranjana

A Preface to Man
Subhash Chandran
Translated from the Malayalam by Fathima E.V.

The Secret Garland
Andal
Translated from the Tamil by Archana Venkatesan

Shala
Milind Bokil
Translated from the Marathi by Vikrant Pande

The Weary Generations
Abdullah Hussein
Translated from the Urdu by the author

Written in Tears
Arupa Patangia Kalita
Translated from the Assamese by Ranjita Biswas

HARPERPERENNIAL

Bhima: Lone Warrior
M.T. Vasudevan Nair
Translated from the Malayalam by Gita Krishnankutty

Chemmeen
Thakazhi Sivasankara Pillai
Translated from the Malayalam by Anita Nair

Ghachar Ghochar
Vivek Shanbhag
Translated from the Kannada by Srinath Perur

Hindutva or Hind Swaraj
U.R. Ananthamurthy
Translated from the Kannada by Keerti Ramachandra & Vivek Shanbhag

The Liberation of Sita
Volga
Translated from the Telugu by T. Vijay Kumar & C. Vijayasree

A Life Misspent
Suryakant Tripathi Nirala
Translated from the Hindi by Satti Khanna

The Sea Lies Ahead
Intizar Husain
Translated from the Urdu by Rakhshanda Jalil

Selected Poems
Joy Goswami
Translated from the Bengali by Sampurna Chattarji

Wild Animals Prohibited: Stories/Anti-stories
Subimal Misra
Translated from the Bengali by V. Ramaswamy

Wild Words: Four Tamil Poets
Malathi Maithri, Salma, Kutti Revathi and Sukirtharani
Translated from the Tamil by Lakshmi Holmström